D1711954

THE TRUTH ABOUT FAMILY LIFE

THE TRUTH ABOUT
FAMILY LIFE

MARK J. KITTLESON, PH.D.
Southern Illinois University
General Editor

WILLIAM KANE, PH.D.
University of New Mexico
Adviser

RICHELLE RENNEGARBE, PH.D.
McKendree College
Adviser

Renée Despres and Lynne Griffin
Principal Authors

■☑®
Facts On File, Inc.

The Truth About Family Life

Facts On File, Inc.
132 West 31st Street
New York NY 10001

Library of Congress Cataloging-in-Publication Data

Despres, Renée.
    The truth about family life / Mark J. Kittleson, general editor; William Kane, adviser; Richelle Rennegarbe, adviser; Renée Despres and Lynne Griffin, principal authors.
        p. cm
    Includes index.
    ISBN 0-8160-5305-7 (alk. paper)
    1. Family—United States. 2. Teenagers—United States—Family relationships. I. Griffin, Lynne Reeves. II. Kittleson, Mark J., 1952– III. Title.
    HQ536.D43 2005
    306.85'0973'03—dc22   20005001358

Facts On File books are available at special discounts when purchased in bulk quantities for businesses, associations, institutions, or sales promotions. Please call our Special Sales Department in New York at (212) 967-8800 or (800) 322-8755.

You can find Facts On File on the World Wide Web at http://www.factsonfile.com.

Text design by David Strelecky
Cover design by Cathy Rincon
Graphs by Jeremy Eagle

Printed in the United States of America

MP Hermitage 10 9 8 7 6 5 4 3 2 1

This book is printed on acid-free paper.

CONTENTS

List of Illustrations and Tables   vii

Preface   ix

How to Use This Book   xi

Family Life in America   1

A to Z Entries   **11**

  Adoption   13

  Arguments and the Family   24

  Day Care   29

  Death in the Family   38

  Divorce and Families   42

  Elderly Family Members   51

  Families, Blended   63

  Families, Divided   72

  Families, Racially Mixed   78

  Family, The New   83

  Family, The Traditional   87

  Family Rules   98

  Family Traditions   102

  Financial Management, Marital   107

Gay Parents   114
Marriage and Family, Changes in   121
Media and the Family   129
Pets in the Family   133
Religion and the Family   138
Single-Parent Families   142
Stepparents   154
Teenage Parents   162
Teens in Trouble   175
Violence and the Family   181

Hotlines and Help Sites   187
Glossary   195
Index   201

LIST OF
ILLUSTRATIONS
AND TABLES

Adoptive Parents Are More Likely to Have
College Degrees   13

Number of Hours Children Are in Day Care Per Week   32

Life Expectancy in the United States by Ethnicity
and Gender   52

Legal Documents for Unmarried Couples   108

Median Age at First Marriage, 1890–2002   124

Percentage of Nonfatal Dog Bite–Related
Injuries, 2001   137

Work-Life Earnings Related to Educational Attainment   152

Teen Parents in the United States and Other
Developed Countries   163

PREFACE

In developing The Truth About series, we have taken time to review some of the most pressing problems facing our youths today. Issues such as alcohol and drug abuse, depression, family problems, sexual activity, and eating disorders are at the top of a list of growing concerns. It is the intent of these books to provide vital facts while also dispelling myths about these terribly important and all-too-common situations. These are authoritative resources that kids can turn to in order to get an accurate answer to a specific question or to research the history of a problem, giving them access to the most current related data available. It is also a reference for parents, teachers, counselors, and others who work with youths and require detailed information.

Let's take a brief look at the issues associated with each of those topics. Alcohol and drug use and abuse continue to be a national concern. Today's young people often use drugs to avoid life's extraordinary pressures. In doing so they are losing their ability to learn how to cope effectively. Without the internal resources to cope with pressure, adolescents turn increasingly back to addictive behaviors. As a result, the problems and solutions are interrelated. Also, the speed with which the family structure is changing often leaves kids with no outlet for stress and no access to support mechanisms.

In addition, a world of youths faces the toughest years of their lives, dealing with the strong physiological urges that accompany sexual desire. Only when young people are presented the facts honestly, without indoctrination, are they likely to connect risk taking with certain behaviors. This reference set relies on knowledge as the most important tool in research and education.

Finally, one of the most puzzling issues of our times is that of eating disorders. Paradoxically, while our youths are obsessed with thinness and beauty, and go to extremes to try to meet perceived societal expectations, they are also increasingly plagued by obesity. Here, too, separating the facts from fiction is an important tool in research and learning.

As much as possible, The Truth About presents the facts through honest discussions and reports of the most up-to-date research. Knowing the facts associated with health-related questions and problems will help young people make informed decisions in school and throughout life.

Mark J. Kittleson, Ph.D.
General Editor

HOW TO
USE THIS BOOK

NOTE TO STUDENTS

Knowledge is power. By possessing knowledge you have the ability to make decisions, ask follow-up questions, or know where to go to obtain more information. In the world of health, that is power! That is the purpose of this book—to provide you the power you need to obtain unbiased, accurate information and *The Truth About Family Life.*

Topics in each volume of The Truth About series are arranged in alphabetical order, from A to Z. Each of these entries defines its topic and explains in detail the particular issue. At the end of most entries are cross-references to related topics. A list of all topics by letter can be found in the table of contents or at the back of the book in the index.

How have these books been compiled? First, the publisher worked with me to identify some of the country's leading authorities on key issues in health education. These individuals were asked to identify some of the major concerns that young people have about such topics. The writers read the literature, spoke with health experts, and incorporated their own life and professional experiences to pull together the most up-to-date information on health issues, particularly those of interest to adolescents and of concern in Healthy People 2010.

Throughout the alphabetical entries, the reader will find sidebars that separate Fact from Fiction. There are Question-and-Answer boxes that attempt to address the most common questions that youths ask about sensitive topics. In addition, readers will find a special feature called "Teens Speak"—case studies of teens with personal stories related to the topic in hand.

This may be one of the most important books you will ever read. Please share it with your friends, families, teachers, and classmates. Remember, you possess the power to control your future. One way to affect your course is through the acquisition of knowledge. Good luck and keep healthy.

NOTE TO LIBRARIANS

This book, along with the rest of The Truth About series, serves as a wonderful resource for young researchers. It contains a variety of facts, case studies, and further readings that the reader can use to help answer questions, formulate new questions, or determine where to go to find more information. Even though the topics may be considered delicate by some, don't be afraid to ask patrons if they have questions. Feel free to direct them to the appropriate sources, but do not press them if you encounter reluctance. The best we can do as educators is to let young people know that we are there when they need us.

Mark J. Kittleson, Ph.D.
General Editor

FAMILY LIFE IN AMERICA

Although families exist in every society, their organization, cultural role, and responsibilities can vary greatly from place to place. Despite these variations, in almost every society, the family has six basic social functions:

- Regulating sexual behavior by limiting whom people may marry, when, and under what conditions
- Assuming responsibility for reproduction
- Nurturing and protecting children and providing emotional support for adults
- Teaching children and other new members of a society what they need to know in order to participate in that society
- Producing and consuming goods. In some societies, the family is the center of economic production and its members produce most of what they consume. In other societies, including American society, families produce little of what they consume.
- Determining an individual's ascribed status in society—that is, his or her status at birth. The status of children in almost every society, and therefore their life chances, are based on their parents' race, ethnicity, wealth, and related social factors

HISTORY OF THE FAMILY IN AMERICA

In the 1950s, according to comparison data in the U.S. census report of 2001, about two-thirds of children in the United States lived in families that consisted of a mother, father, and their children. In most of these families, the father was the breadwinner and the mother cared for the home and children. By 2002, only 10 percent of families fit this portrait of the traditional family. The traditional family has become just one of many family forms.

According to family demographer Jay D. Teachman, changing economic patterns was one reason for the shift in family life. The 1950s were a time of economic affluence for many families. Government-backed programs provided inexpensive home loans, support for veterans to attend college, and other benefits. The minimum wage was high enough to support a family of three above the poverty level.

By the 1960s and 1970s, families were finding it harder and harder to survive on the income of one wage earner. To maintain their standard of living, many families needed more than one wage earner. Many wives and mothers returned to the labor force to help their family make ends meet. The women's movement of the 1960s encouraged this trend. By 2003, 70 percent of married women worked outside the home, according to the Bureau of Labor Statistics.

Teachman and other researchers observed that as women achieved greater economic independence, they were less likely to stay in unhappy marriages. The rate of divorce—the legal ending of a marriage—increased dramatically during the last 40 years of the 20th century. Data from the National Center for Health Statistics (NCHA) show that the divorce rate nearly doubled between 1960 and 1970. It continued to climb until 1978, when it reached a high of 23 per 1,000 married women. It dropped slightly to about 20 per 1,000 during the 1980s and leveled off during the 1990s. By 2000, almost half of all marriages ended in divorce, with 20 percent of those marriages ending within three years.

The increasing participation of women in the labor force also affected the way families interacted. For many couples, a more equal division of financial responsibilities led to greater equality in the division of household labor and child care responsibilities.

THE NEW FAMILY

If Americans are not living in nuclear families headed by two parents, what kind of families are they living in? More people today are choosing to marry later. Census Bureau data show that the percentage of married-couple households dropped from more than three out of every four households in 1950 (78 percent) to slightly more than one-half (52 percent) in 2000. The percentage of households occupied by one person increased from 11 percent in 1950 to almost 26 percent in 2000.

In 1959, nearly half of all women were under the age of 19 when they married. Since the mid-1950s, the median age at first marriage has been rising steadily, with the largest increases occurring since 1980. By 2003, the median age at first marriage had reached 27.1 years for men and 25.3 years for women. In 2002, more than half (54 percent) of men had not married by the time they reached their 30th birthday, while 40 percent of women were single at 30. However, most people do eventually marry. In 2003, according to Census Bureau data, only 12.7 percent of men and 9.5 percent of women had never married by the time they were 45 years old.

Because of the high divorce rate, many children are likely to be reared in a home that does not include their two biological parents. In 1972, 73 percent of children lived with their married biological parents; by 2003, less than half of all children lived in this type of family.

Between 1970 and 1998, the number of single-parent families tripled from 4 million to 12 million. Nearly 60 percent of all children will live in a one-parent household for at least a portion of one year before they are 18 years old, mostly because of divorce.

Blended and reblended families are created when a divorced or widowed parent marries a new spouse. These families are becoming more common as divorced parents remarry, half of them more than once. In 1998, the last year in which the Census Bureau collected data on remarriages, in 46 percent of new marriages, the husband, wife, or both had been previously married.

Census Bureau researchers predict that more than one-third of all children in the United States will live in a blended family before they reach the age of 18. Census 2000 data show that in 2000, an estimated 3.2 million children were living with a stepparent.

Americans are having fewer children. In 1900, married women had, on average, five children. Other data from the NCHS show wide fluctuations in the **fertility rate**—the average number of children a woman has in her lifetime. In the late 1950s, the average woman gave birth to 3.5 children during her lifetime. The fertility rate dropped to a low of 1.8 births per woman in 1972, then climbed slightly and stayed at between 2.0 and 2.1 births per woman from the early 1990s through 2003.

The declining fertility rate has led to smaller families. In 1960, the average number of persons per family was 3.67; by 1990, that number had dropped to 3.18. The proportion of married couples with children also has declined, according to the Census Bureau. In 2003, only 23 percent of households in the United States included married couples with children, a dramatic decrease from 40 percent in 1970.

The percentage of unmarried women who gave birth to children climbed from 5 percent in 1960 to 34 percent in 2002, according to data from the National Center for Health Statistics. Teens accounted for 34 percent of all births to unmarried women in 2002, a decrease from 50 percent in 1970. The decrease was due to the fact that a greater number of older unmarried women were choosing to become mothers.

Many of the women counted as unmarried mothers by the Census Bureau are living with a partner. The practice of living together without marriage is known as **cohabitation**. According to data from the census, 5.5 million couples were cohabitating in 2000. About 60 percent of those couples were between 25 and 44 years old, and more than one-third (36 percent) had children under the age of 15. According to the 2000 census, more than half of heterosexual couples who planned to marry lived together before they were wed. In 1965, that figure was 10 percent. Other couples choose cohabitation because they wish to share their lives with a partner and have children even though they do not wish to marry.

Of these cohabitating couples, 4.9 million lived with someone of the opposite sex and just under 600,000 had same-sex partners. Many of these same-sex partners have not married because they are not allowed to marry. Although same-sex couples can marry in Massachusetts, other states forbid marriages between partners of the same sex. Some cities and businesses recognize same-sex couples as domestic partners.

Of the same-sex couples who have children, these families are formed by previous heterosexual relationships, from the process of adoption, or through medical procedures such as **artificial insemination**, the injection of a man's sperm into a woman's vagina using a syringe. Researchers from the National Adoption Information Clearinghouse estimate that between 2 and 6 million same-sex couples in the United States are rearing between 6 and 14 million children.

Some of these couples are choosing to build families through adoption. About 100,000 children are adopted each year in the United States. In 2000, 1.5 million children under age 18 were living with adoptive parents. In 2002, about 20 percent of all adoptions involved children from countries outside the United States. Open adoption, in which communication occurs between the birth and adoptive parents and child, is becoming more common.

Another important influence on family life has been the increasing number of elderly people in the United States. The 2000 census revealed that 12 percent of the population—35 million people in all—were age 65 or older. These people are spending a greater percentage of their lives without young children in their households. However, as people age, they are more likely to require health care and assistance with daily living. When an elderly parent is no longer able to care for himself or herself, family members may be called upon to provide support.

As family structures evolve in response to social, economic, and technological influences, the ways in which Americans think about family life are changing. It is likely that the "new" American family will change even more during the 21st century. Learning about the diverse family structures in which families live can help you to find creative and flexible options for raising children, maintaining intimate relationships, and finding fulfillment.

RISKY BUSINESS SELF-TEST

Everyone has experienced some sort of family. So you could say that you are, indeed, an expert on families. But how much do you really know about building healthy families and relationships?

To test your knowledge about families and relationships, grab a pencil and separate piece of paper and jot down your answers to this multiple-choice quiz. Following the self-test are the answers and explanations to rate your score.

What's my family and relationship IQ?

1. If my parent hits me in anger,
   a. I deserve it. It's just normal discipline.
   b. I hit him or her back.
   c. I seek help.

2. If my partner hits me,
   a. I put up with it because he or she apologizes later.
   b. I leave and seek help.
   c. I take it as a sign of how much he or she loves me.

3. If I become a teen parent,
   a. I will probably finish high school and go on to college.
   b. I will probably marry my child's other parent.
   c. I will probably remain single, need to take a part-time job to pay for my child's expenses, and need a lot of support to finish high school.

4. The best way to handle an argument with my parents is to
   a. run to my room and lock the door.
   b. talk to my friends about it.
   c. wait until I've calmed down then talk to them about my feelings.

5. If I marry and eventually divorce,
   a. I will never be able to face my family and friends again.
   b. I will remain single for the rest of my life.
   c. I will probably have a rough time for a while, but I'll survive and learn from the experience and probably marry again.

6. If I marry while I'm in my teens,
   a. I decrease the chance that I will divorce.
   b. I increase the chance that I will divorce.
   c. I won't affect the chance that I will divorce.

7. If my parents divorce, but I get along well with each of them and they don't draw me into their arguments, it's most likely that
   a. I'll experience behavioral and emotional problems and have difficulty forming intimate relationships as an adult.
   b. I'll be just as emotionally healthy as kids whose parents aren't divorced.
   c. I'll be the only kid in my school with divorced parents.

8. Intimate relationships between two people of the same sex are
   a. markedly different from other intimate relationships.
   b. similar to relationships between heterosexual couples.
   c. unhealthy for children to grow up in.

9. Single parents
   a. provide their children with the care they need.
   b. can't provide healthy homes for their children.
   c. are always poor.

10. If my parents divorce and remarry,
   a. I'll be disloyal to my biological parent if I become close to my stepparent.
   b. it will probably be difficult, but I can handle it.
   c. I'll be angry at my parents for divorcing and remarrying.

Answer key

1. c. Any act of violence from one family member to another is cause for concern. If your parent strikes you, find a safe place, such as a friend's home, and arrange to talk to your parent with a counselor or friend. If any parent strikes you repeatedly, seek out a domestic violence shelter and get regular help from a counselor, teacher, pastor, friend's parent, or other adult.

2. b. If your partner hits, slaps, or otherwise physically assaults you, he or she is abusing you. Leave. Seek help from someone you trust, such as a teacher, pastor, parent, friend's parent, doctor, or other adult.

3. c. Even though most teen mothers believe they will marry their child's father, the reality is that less than 8 percent will do so within one year. In fact, according to the Alan Guttmacher Institute, a nonprofit organization that performs research on reproduction and health, less than 40 percent of mothers who have a child before age 18 ever complete high school, and fewer teen fathers complete high school than those who wait to become parents until they are 21 years old. Their low educational levels make it unlikely that they will ever qualify for a job that pays well.

4. c. Tightly knit families discuss important things instead of avoiding them. Often the best way to resolve a dispute, or at least to learn to live with it, is to allow each family member to clearly describe his or her position in a safe environment such as a family meeting with established rules.

5. c. Divorce is usually accompanied by emotional pain, sadness, anger, and many other difficult feelings. But when people choose to divorce, it's usually because they are not satisfied with their current relationship and they believe they can create a better one with someone else. Both children and adults experience divorce in a series of stages similar to those described by Elisabeth Kübler-Ross in her book *On Death and Dying* for terminally ill patients: denial, anger, bargaining, depression and acceptance. About two-thirds of people who divorce each year eventually remarry.

6. b. One of the most important predictors of divorce is age at first marriage. Teenage marriages are the most likely to end in divorce, probably because teens are still in the midst of developing their own value systems, identities, and choosing careers. One-third of marriages that occur before the woman is 18 end in divorce within three years. Half of those marriages end within 10 years.

7. b. Several studies have linked parental divorce to behavioral problems in children. However, the conflict that often surrounds divorce, not the divorce itself, appears to be the trigger for behavioral problems in children of divorced parents. Current research shows that parental conflict is a greater threat to children's well-being than is family structure.

8. b. Researchers have found few differences between heterosexual and homosexual couples except the sex of the partner. Same-sex couples fall in love, feel the same passions, experience the same doubts, and feel the same commitments that heterosexual couples do.

9. a. Single parents face many challenges, including reduced income, lack of family time, and the lack of another adult to share parenting and household responsibilities with. However, a single-parent family can provide a healthy environment for its members. Most single parents give their children the structure, values, and nurturance that they need. Children thrive in a warm, supportive home, regardless of whether it is headed by one or two parents. Children adjust better when they have a good relationship with a single parent than when they live with two parents who are in constant conflict.

10. b. The adjustment to a stepparent is often difficult for children of all ages, especially young teens. A stepparent is not a replacement parent, and developing a relationship with a stepparent does not mean you're abandoning your biological parent. There's no rule that says you can't love two adults who play parental roles in your life. In fact, most teens are pleased when their custodial parent remarries. One reason may be that money problems tend to decrease with remarriage. In one study, the most frequently used word used by teens to describe their reactions to their custodial parent's remarriage was *happy*; *satisfied* and *pleased* were the second and third most common terms.

See the Hotline and Help Sites section of this book for several places to contact if you want to talk with someone about a stressful family situation and what you can do to begin to feel better.

See also: Arguments and the Family; Divorce and Families; Families, Divided; Gay Parents; Marriage and Family, Changes in; Single-Parent Families; Stepparents; Teenage Parents; Teens in Trouble; Violence and the Family

A TO Z ENTRIES

▇ ADOPTION

Adoption is the legal transfer of the biological parents' rights to a child to another adult or couple. The adoptive parent or parents assume all of the parental rights and responsibilities of the biological parents, including care and supervision of the child, nurture, training, education, physical and emotional health, and financial support.

RATES IN THE UNITED STATES AND ABROAD

The 2000 U.S. census provided the first comprehensive nationwide data on adoption. It indicated that 1.5 million children under the age

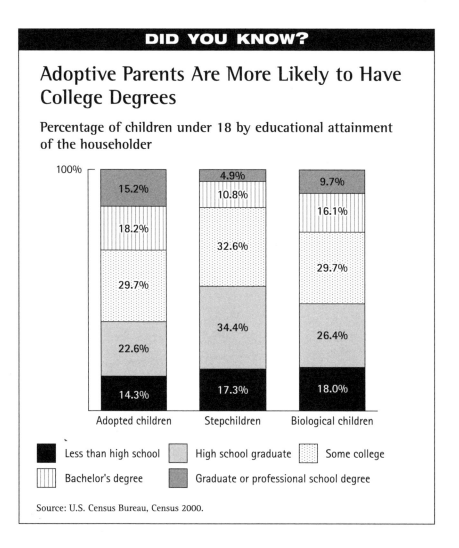

DID YOU KNOW?

Adoptive Parents Are More Likely to Have College Degrees

Percentage of children under 18 by educational attainment of the householder

Adopted children
- 14.3% Less than high school
- 22.6% High school graduate
- 29.7% Some college
- 18.2% Bachelor's degree
- 15.2% Graduate or professional school degree

Stepchildren
- 17.3% Less than high school
- 34.4% High school graduate
- 32.6% Some college
- 10.8% Bachelor's degree
- 4.9% Graduate or professional school degree

Biological children
- 18.0% Less than high school
- 26.4% High school graduate
- 29.7% Some college
- 16.1% Bachelor's degree
- 9.7% Graduate or professional school degree

Legend:
- Less than high school
- High school graduate
- Some college
- Bachelor's degree
- Graduate or professional school degree

Source: U.S. Census Bureau, Census 2000.

of 18 were living with adults who had assumed legal responsibility for them. These adults are known as the child's **adoptive parents**. About 2 percent of all children in the United States are adopted. An additional 473,000 children above the age of 18 were living with adoptive parents. These 2.1 million adopted children represent 2.5 percent of all children in U.S. households.

The 2000 census data concerning adoptions is incomplete. Census takers did not ask whether adopted children were biologically related to their adoptive parents. For example, some adults adopt nieces or nephews. Others adopt stepchildren. The census data also does not indicate whether a child was adopted through a government agency or private organization.

Information related to those issues is available from public agencies and private organizations that place children in adoptive homes. According to the National Council for Adoption (NCFA), for instance, more than 5 million adults and children in the United States have been adopted. The group estimates that more than 100,000 children are adopted each year.

Other data collected by the NCFA shows that slightly more than half (50.9 percent) of those who adopt a child are related to that child in some way. Often, these adoptions simply formalize an existing arrangement. Most related adoptions involve a stepparent (usually a stepfather) adopting his wife's children. Many states have a streamlined process for stepparent adoptions. However, in some states, parents must be married for at least one year before such an adoption will be approved.

Unrelated adoptions account for slightly less than half of all adoptions. Almost 40 percent of unrelated adoptions in the United States are handled by government agencies, usually a state social-services agency. The National Council for Adoption reports that in 1992, about one-third (29 percent) of unrelated adoptions were handled by private agencies. This rate has continued to hold steady. Some adoptions are privately arranged. A pregnant woman or her attorney may reach an agreement with an individual or couple eager to adopt her unborn child. Such adoptions make up the other 31 percent of unrelated adoptions.

State laws govern the adoption of children in the United States. While all states require that adoptive parents be at least 21 years of age, age requirements vary from state to state. Americans who wish to adopt a child from another country must be U.S. citizens and at least 25 years of age. Adoptive parents may be married or single. They may already have children or they may be childless.

Healthy, white infants are the most likely to be adopted. The Census Bureau estimates that nearly 42,000 children under one year of age were adopted in 2000. However, according to the National Adoption Information Clearinghouse (NAIC), adoption is less likely for children who are eight years or older, have siblings, belong to a racial or ethnic minority group, or have mental, emotional, or physical disabilities. In 1997, Congress passed the Adoption and Safe Families Act (ASFA). The law was designed to promote the adoption of children who face barriers in finding adoptive homes. For the purposes of adoption, the ASFA classified children who face one or more of these barriers as "children with special needs." State agencies provide financial and other support to parents who adopt children with special needs as defined by the ASFA.

Many children with special needs are in the care of public agencies. Children who have been abused, neglected, or abandoned by their birth parents are placed in state foster care. These children live with **foster parents** who care for them while their birth parents receive counseling and other services. Foster care programs are designed to help birth parents reunite with their children. However, if reuniting is not possible, the agency may take away, or terminate, the birth parents' rights to the child. The ASFA requires courts to seek termination of parental rights for children who have been in foster care for 15 out of the previous 22 months, except in special circumstances.

The National Council for Adoption estimates that the ASFA has led to 11,000 additional adoptions each year. The number of children adopted from foster care rose from 31,000 in 1997 to 50,000 in 2001, according to the Adoption and Foster Care Analysis and Reporting System (AFCARS). Of the 263,000 children in foster care, 18 percent were adopted. Most of the others who left foster care were reunited with their birth parents, living with other relatives, or were **emancipated,** meaning they were older than 16 years of age and able to live on their own as adults.

Many children in foster care are waiting to be adopted. About three-fourths (76 percent) of those children have been in foster care for three years or longer. Their average age is 10 years. Thirty-seven percent are African American, 12 percent are Hispanic, and 34 percent white. Only 25,000 children in foster care in 2001 according to AFCARS were living with foster parents who planned to adopt them.

International adoptions, often referred to as **intercountry adoptions**, are becoming more common. Census 2000 data showed that nearly 13 percent of adopted children were born in other countries. In 2002, according to data from the U.S. State Department, 21,616 children were adopted from countries outside the United States, representing about 20 percent of all adoptions. Of those children, 6,859 were from China, 5,209 were from Russia, 2,328 were from Guatemala, and 1,790 from South Korea

TRANSRACIAL ADOPTION

A transracial adoption is the adoption of children whose racial or ethnic backgrounds differ from those of their adoptive parents. In the United States, most transracial adoptions involve white parents and children of another race. Transracial adoption rates appear to be increasing. In 1987, estimates from the National Health Interview Survey (NHIS) indicate that about 8 percent of adoptions involved parents and children of different races. The data provided by the 2000 Census found that more than 17 percent of adopted children were of a different race than the head of the family.

The law that governs transracial adoption is the Howard M. Metzenbaum Multiethnic Placement Act of 1994 (MEPA). MEPA prohibits any organization involved in adoptive or foster care placement that receives federal assistance from delaying or denying the placement of a child on the basis of the race, color, or national origin of the child or the adoptive or foster parent. In 1996, MEPA was amended by the Interethnic Adoption Provisions Law, which forbids agencies from denying or delaying placement of a child for adoption solely on the basis of race or national origin. The 1978 Indian Child Welfare Act strictly limits the adoption of Native American children by adults who are not Native American. The act requires that agencies begin by trying to place the child with a member of his or her extended family. If that is not possible, agencies should try to place the child with other members of his or her tribe. If agencies are unable to do so, the child may be placed with a Native American family that is not a member of the child's tribe.

Despite the increase in the number of transracial adoptions in the United States over the last 20 years, sociologists, child development experts, and others involved with adoption continue to debate the effects of placing a child in a family with a different racial or ethnic background. The debate began in earnest in 1972, when the National Association of Black Social Workers (NABSW) published a position paper "vehemently" opposing the placement of African-American children with white families. The NABSW called for African-American children to be placed only with African-American families, whether in foster care or for adoption, and argued that "black children belong, physically, psychologically and culturally, in black families in order that they receive the total sense of themselves and develop a sound projection of their future."

The NABSW reaffirmed its opposition to transracial adoption in both 1977 and 1985. In 1985, the president of the NABSW testified before the Senate Committee on Labor and Human Resources. His testimony focused on two main points. The first was that African-American children who grow up in white families suffer severe identity problems because they are not fully accepted by white communities and do not have significant ties with other African Americans. The second was that transracially adopted African-American children do not develop coping mechanisms necessary to function in a society that is inherently racist.

A growing body of research does not support either argument. It suggests that most children who are adopted across races or cultures fare well. Rita Simon, a professor in the School of Public Affairs at the Washington College of Law at American University, and Howard Alstein, a professor in the School of Social Work at the University of Maryland, conducted one of the most comprehensive studies of transracial adoption. The longitudinal study, which began in 1972, followed 206 families with 218 children, including birth and adopted children. In 1990, the researchers contacted 98 of the children who had participated in the 1972 study. Based on their interviews with the children as adolescents and adults, Simon and Alstein concluded that the transracially adopted children were comfortable with their racial identity. However, as adults, 91 percent of the transracially adopted children said parents who adopt a child from another culture or race need to be sensitive to racial issues. Nine percent said they should reconsider their decision to adopt a child of another race.

In 1983, Arnold R. Silverman, a professor of sociology at Nassau Community College in New York, reviewed nearly a dozen studies of transracial adoption. His analysis showed that about 75 percent of transracially adopted preadolescents and younger children adjust well to their adoptive families. Ten years later, Silverman published "Outcomes of Transracial Adoption," in which he again reviewed existing research on the adjustment of transracially adopted children. Based on this second review, he concluded that transracial adoption is a viable means of providing stable homes for nonwhite children awaiting placement.

GAY PARENTS AND ADOPTION

By law, same-sex couples are allowed to adopt children in four states—Vermont, New Jersey, Massachusetts, and California. In contrast, for example, Florida prohibits gays from adopting children. In January 2004, the Florida Supreme Court upheld the state's ban on gay adoptions. Although most other states do not legally prohibit same-sex couples from adopting children, they discourage all single people (not married) from adopting children, including gays. The state of Massachusetts is the only state in which a marriage between same-sex couples is legal.

In most cases, when a child is born to or adopted by a same-sex couple, only one parent is legally recognized as the parent. For instance, if a same-sex couple chooses to have a child through **artificial insemination**, only the birth mother has parental rights. The other partner does not have any parental rights—including the right to make decisions about the child's medical care—or responsibilities—including the responsibility to pay child support if the couple separates—unless he or she formally adopts the child. The American Association of Pediatrics (AAP) argues that "children deserve to know that their relationships with both of their parents are stable and legally recognized," whether their parents are of the same or different sexes. Thus, the AAP supports the adoption of children by the second parent in families headed by a couple of the same sex. The AAP bases its recommendations on "a considerable body of professional literature" that shows that children who grow up in one- or two-parent gay or lesbian households "can have the same advantages and the same expectations for health, adjustment and development as can children whose parents are heterosexual."

In 2003, researchers from the Evan B. Donalds Adoption Institute published *Adoption by Lesbians and Gays: A National Survey of Adoption Agency Policies, Practices, and Attitudes*. The study, which was conducted between 1999 and 2000, surveyed adoption agencies as to whether they permitted adoption of children by gays and lesbians and how many children they actually placed with same-sex parents. The study also examined the attitudes of birth parents and agencies regarding the adoption of children by gays and lesbians.

Survey results show that as lesbians and gays are adopting children from both public and private agencies at a growing rate, the practice is becoming more acceptable. Adoption program directors from 277 private agencies and 30 public agencies responded to the survey. About 60 percent accepted adoption applications from gays and lesbians. About 39 percent had placed at least one child with gay and lesbian parents between 1999 and 2000. Of the 91,118 adoption placements reported by the agencies, 1,206 (1.3 percent) were with gays and lesbians. Researchers caution that this number may be considerably less than the actual placements because most agencies do not keep records of the sexual orientation of adoptive parents. Of the agencies that responded to the survey, 25 percent said prospective birth parents did not want to place their child with gays or lesbians. On the other hand, 15 percent of all agencies said birth parents had requested or chosen lesbian or gay prospective adoptive parents for their child. Researchers also asked whether agency staff would be interested in receiving training to work more effectively with prospective gay and lesbian adoptive parents. Almost half (48 percent) of agencies indicated they would be interested in receiving such training.

Fact Or Fiction?

Open adoption causes problems for adopted children.

Fact: Adoptions occur along a spectrum of openness, ranging from direct contact and communication among all parties to complete confidentiality. Open adoption, in which interactions take place between birth and adoptive parents—and often the adopted child—are becoming more common. While open adoption may not be the best situation for every adopted child, a growing body of research shows that open adoption may actually be *good* not only for the adopted child, but also for the child's adoptive and birth parents. Findings from the Minnesota/Texas Adoption Research Project, a study that compared open adoption to other types of adoption, debunk many myths about open adoption. Results from the study showed that open adoption does *not*

- Prompt birth mothers to try to "reclaim" their children
- Make it harder for birth mothers to resolve grief. In fact, birth mothers in open adoption situations show better grief resolution than those in confidential adoptions
- Make adoptive parents feel less in control. Adoptive parents have a greater sense of permanence about their relationship with their adopted child
- Cause children to feel confused about who their parents are, the roles of their birth parents versus their adoptive parents
- Appear to negatively influence children's self-esteem.

FAMILY DYNAMICS

The introduction of a new child into a family changes the way the family functions and how members interact. While related adoptions may not substantially change a child's daily routine, unrelated adoptions almost always involve a significant change in a child's life. That change usually includes the establishment of new relationships. Early results from a study at the University of Minnesota's Center for Twin and Family Research, Sibling Interaction and Behavior Study (SIBS) may shed some light on the effects of introducing an adopted child into a family. The SIBS study, which began in 1999, examines how siblings interact and influence one another and how family dynamics can affect the psychological health of teens. To determine psychological health, researchers measured negative behaviors such as delinquency, antisocial attitudes, aggression, substance abuse, and other problem behaviors. They also measured positive characteristics such as sense of well-being, a positive self-identity, and academic achievement.

Q & A

Question: How can I explain that my adopted sister is my "real" sister?

Answer: There are many ways to build a family. An adoptive family is as real a family as one in which parents and children are biologically related. You can start by encouraging your friends, parents, and teachers to use correct terminology. The language people use reflects and influences their beliefs, and the language that people use about adoption sometimes suggests that adoptive families are somehow inferior to biologically related families. Tell your friends that your sister is your real sister even though you do not share the same birth parents. She is a member of your family.

Of the 600 families in the SIBS study, 400 include an adopted child. Early findings from the study, published in 2002, showed little difference in psychological functioning between children reared in adoptive families and those reared in **birth families**. Sibling relationships appeared to be equally close and loving among adopted and biological siblings. While adopted children and parents reported more conflict, they also said they felt as attached to one another as children and parents in birth families.

Adoptive siblings in the study do not share genetically linked personality traits such as shyness or gregariousness. They do, however, show remarkable similarity in academic achievement. According to SIBS researchers, this finding suggests that parental influence plays a major role in academic success. In contrast, younger siblings were more likely to display problem behaviors such as smoking, drinking, or disobedience when older siblings engaged in such behaviors. Preliminary results from the SIBS study suggest that sibling influence may be a more important determinant of problem behavior than parental influence.

Until the 1970s, adoption was rarely discussed and often kept a secret from the children who were adopted. Few adopted children ever met their birth parents and birth parents rarely met adoptive parents. Today, these confidential adoptions, in which the adoptive family and birth parents do not communicate, fall at one end of a spectrum of adoption practices. In the middle of the spectrum is semi-open adoption, in which birth and adoptive families communicate through a third party, such as an agency caseworker or attorney. At the other end of the spectrum, and becoming more common, is open adoption. In open adoptions, the birth and adoptive parents and the child communicate directly with one another. Interactions may range from letters, e-mails, and telephone calls to visits based on the needs and interests of the members of both families.

According to the National Adoption Information Clearinghouse (NAIC), adoptive parents who choose open adoption try to minimize the child's loss of relationships and acknowledge all connections in the child's life. A growing body of research supports the view that openness in adoption can be a positive experience for both children and parents. Findings from the Minnesota/Texas Adoption Research Project, a longitudinal study that compares open adoption with other types of adoption, suggests that ongoing contact between birth parents and adopted children increases satisfaction with the adoption. Of the 190 families in the study, 46 were in direct or indirect contact with each other since the child was placed with an adoptive family. Most respondents who had ongoing contact reported that they were either satisfied or very satisfied with the level of openness shown by the child's birth mother: 83.7 percent of the adopted adolescents, 93.5 percent of the adoptive mothers, and 84.8 percent of the adoptive fathers. The teens reported that they hoped their contact with their birth mother stayed the same (55.8 percent) or increased (41.9 percent) in the future. Only one adolescent (2.3 percent) hoped for a decrease.

When the researchers compared the teens who were in contact with their birth mothers to those who were not, they found that adolescents who had contact with their birth mothers reported higher degrees of satisfaction with the level of adoption openness and with the intensity of their contact with their birth mother than did adolescents who had no contact. Teens were least satisfied with openness about adoption during middle adolescence (ages 14–16), slightly more satisfied during early or late adolescence.

In another study of openness in adoption published in April 2004, Richard Sullivan of the University of British Columbia in Vancouver asked 1,007 Canadian birth parents and adopted children who had met each other about their reunion experiences. More than 90 percent of the participants in the study said that the reunion was a positive experience. They overwhelmingly agreed that reunion services should be available to anyone who seeks that option.

In summary, about 100,000 children are adopted each year in the United States, and in 2000, 1.5 million children under age 18 were living with adoptive parents, half of which were related adoptions, usually involving a stepparent adopting a new spouse's child. The Adoption and Safe Families Act (ASFA) of 1997 was designed to increase adoption of children who are eight years or older, members of a minority group, in a group of siblings, or who have mental, emotional, or physical disabilities.

Children who have been abused, neglected, or abandoned by their birth parents are placed in a state foster care system, in which children live with foster parents who care for them while their birth parents receive counseling and other services. If the children cannot be safely reunited with their parents, they become eligible for adoption.

Controversy still surrounds the practice of transracial adoption, in which parents adopt children of different racial or ethnic backgrounds. Some researchers argue that transracial adoption is a means of providing safe, permanent homes to the many minority children who are in foster care and awaiting adoption. Others hold that minority children experience problems with racial identification when they are reared in white families. Although controversy also surrounds the rights of same-sex couples to adopt children, studies show that children who grow up in one- or two-parent gay or lesbian households do as well emotionally and socially as children with heterosexual parents. Open adoption, in which communication occurs between the birth and adoptive parents and child, is becoming more common.

See also: Divorce and Families; Families, Blended; Families, Racially Mixed; Family, The New; Gay Parents; Marriage and Family, Changes in; Stepparents

FURTHER READING

Eldridge, Sherrie. *Twenty Things Adopted Kids Wish Their Adoptive Parents Knew.* Los Alamitos, CA: Delta Publishing Company, 1999.

Gilman, Lois. *Adoption Resource Book.* New York: HarperCollins, 1998.

Gritter, James. *The Spirit of Open Adoption.* Washington, DC: Child Welfare League of America Press, 1993.

Pertman, Adam. *Adoption Nation: How the Adoption Revolution Is Transforming America.* New York: Basic Books, 2001.

Urmy, Danne, ed. *The Family of Adoption.* New York: Beacon, 1999.

■ ARGUMENTS AND THE FAMILY

A certain degree of conflict exists in all families. When conflicts are handled directly and appropriately, they cause few long-term problems. However, when left unresolved, arguments can lead to long-term disagreements and destroy relationships among family members. Families that learn to handle conflict directly can often use conflict to grow closer.

QUARRELS AMONG SIBLINGS

In the United States, most children have at least one **sibling**, a brother or sister. Siblings can be close companions who support and help each other as they grow into adulthood. Most children feel a deeper, stronger affection for their siblings than friends outside the family. Yet many also experience intense competition and resentment of their siblings. Intense sibling rivalries can span a lifetime, starting during early childhood and extending into adulthood. These dual feelings of caring and anger are common in sibling relationships. These who have such mixed or uncertain feelings are said to be ambivalent.

TEENS SPEAK

Making Peace with My Brother

I can't remember a time when my brother Mike and I didn't fight. We've always had a love-hate relationship, maybe because we're so close in age. He's 17 and I'm 16. When we were younger, we fought about things like which television show to watch or who got to sit in the front seat of the car. Those were little-kid kinds of fights. Eventually we'd make up. Mom or Dad often had to step in, which usually meant that the television got turned off or that both of us had to ride in the backseat.

These days, we fight about politics and ideas. I spend summers working at a garage to make enough money to fix my motorcycle. I barely have a C average at school, except for my art class, where I always get A's. If it weren't for art, I'd probably drop out of school. Mike, on the other hand, is Mr. Successful. He dresses neatly, cuts his hair the same way that our father does, and has a 4.0 grade point average. He'll probably be valedictorian of his class. Last summer, he did an internship at a broker's office.

We've fought for as long as I can remember. I never knew how it affected our parents until the day Mike launched into another lecture about how global warming was just a scare tactic created by environmentalists and I responded by telling him what a selfish pig he was. I didn't know it, but my mom was in the room. When I turned around and saw her crying, I knew that our arguing was hurting our family. I needed to make peace with him. I asked my parents for help. My mom called a counselor, and we went to family therapy sessions for a while. We have weekly family meetings where we've learned to discuss our differences respectfully, without calling each other names or trying to persuade each other that we're right.

Mike and I have agreed to disagree. He'll be leaving for college next year. He's planning to get a degree in business. He told me that one of his goals is to make his first million by the time he's 30. I'm thinking about spending a year or two in the Peace Corps before I go to college. We're still as different as different can be, but we've learned that our differences don't mean we have to be enemies.

A growing body of research suggests that conflict among siblings can have positive effects. Arguments with a sibling allow a child to test and develop the skills necessary to resolving conflicts. Judith Frances Dunn of the Institute of Psychiatry, King's College in the United Kingdom, has been studying sibling relationships since the early 1980s. In 1985, she and her colleagues published a study entitled "Becoming a Family Member: Family Conflict and the Development of Social Understanding in the Second Year." They noted that the children in their study, ages 18 to 21 months, developed an understanding of the feelings and intentions of others by arguing with their mothers and siblings.

In subsequent studies, including one published in 1997, Dunn and her colleagues found that young children also develop the skills to constructively resolve conflict by arguing with mothers and siblings, skills that they later apply to relationships with friends. Dunn's research suggests that sibling relationships may provide the context for children to learn to negotiate with others. Dunn's work and that of other child development specialists suggest that even when children are very young, sibling squabbles can help children learn to compromise, understand another's point of view, use logic to persuade, and control emotions.

According to psychologists Catherine C. Epkins and Angela Dedmon, the research suggests that children's interactions with siblings are affected by birth order and age, gender, and the age difference between the children involved. Older or firstborn children tend to be more aggressive than younger or second-born children. Younger siblings often learn to cajole, negotiate, and compromise; they may become practiced at sensing others' needs and feelings.

The difference in ages among the children in a family may also affect the way that siblings interact. Wyndol Furman, a professor of psychology at the University of Denver, and his colleague Duane Buhrmester, a developmental psychologist at the University of Texas at Dallas, were among the first to examine the effects of age difference on sibling relationships. Their research, published in 1990, which has been supported by several subsequent studies, suggests that siblings who are closer in age tend to experience more conflict and rivalry. Siblings who are farther apart in age tend to argue less and show more affection toward each other. According to this research, three years is the critical age difference: In most of the studies, siblings born one to three years apart were more likely to act aggressively toward each other, while siblings born three or more years apart tended to get along better.

Gender also affects sibling interactions. Although girls are as likely as boys to argue or fight with their siblings, same-sex siblings are more likely to argue than siblings of opposite genders.

As they grow older, children focus on the larger social, psychological, and emotional context of arguments. Instead of being occupied with just the facts, they argue about opinions and ideas including current events, other relationships, and preferences in music, food, or dress. They are better able to discuss their disagreements by clearly expressing their own thoughts and feelings. Older children and teens may use sarcasm, teasing, or insults to show displeasure.

In a 1999 study, Laurie Kramer, a professor of psychology at the University of Illinois at Urbana-Champaign, asked parents in 88 two-child, two-parent families how they managed sibling conflicts. Kramer found that parents were three times as likely to not intervene in their children's arguments as they were to stop fights with such methods as punishment and compromises. Most parents did not think that ignoring the conflict was the best strategy, but they tended to follow the advice of parenting books that warned against their involvement. When parents in the study did not intervene, siblings became more aggressive toward each other.

Kramer suggests that up to about age nine, children need parents to model ways to work out conflicts. As children grow older, they develop the skills necessary to resolve their own arguments. While most siblings find ways to resolve their conflicts on their own, parents need to monitor conflicts. If conflicts lead to physical aggression, an adult's help may be necessary.

Fact Or Fiction?

Teens fight with their parents about important things.

Fact: Although conflicts between parents and teens are common and often intense, the things they fight about are not likely to be important. Sociologists such as Brian K. Barber, whose 1994 study of parent-child conflict provided the basis for much current research, reveals that teens and their parents rarely fight openly about economic, religious, social, or political values, or even about sexual activity and drug or alcohol abuse. Conflicts usually focus on more mundane matters, such as helping out around the house. Most of these arguments center on how much freedom teens should have or how soon they should be able to do something (like have the keys to the family car).

In a 1993 study of parent and adolescent interactions, A. J. Fuligni, associate professor in the departments of psychology and psychiatry at the University of California–Los Angeles found that conflict between parents and teens is most frequent during early adolescence; becomes more intense, although less frequent, in mid-adolescence; and decreases in late adolescence. Fuligni and his colleagues suggest that the increased conflict in early adolescence may be related to the changes that accompany puberty and the need to assert independence. Less stormy relations during late adolescence may occur after parents and teens have successfully renegotiated their relationship.

WHAT WAS IT WE WERE FIGHTING ABOUT?

Conflicts arise in all families and between all members of a family. Some arguments—like who should take out the trash—may be easy to settle. However, when the argument is about a fundamental belief or idea such as religious values or political ideas, it can damage relationships among family members. In most cases, it is not the conflict itself but how it is handled that determines the outcome.

Tightly knit families discuss issues instead of avoiding them. In contrast, when conflict is not handled in a mature and open fashion, it can lead to long-term estrangements between family members. Often the best way to resolve a dispute, or at least to learn to live with it, is to allow each family member to clearly articulate his or her position. A family conference may provide an environment that allows all family members a chance to state their position in a safe, respectful environment. To set up a family conference, set aside a time and choose a place where everyone can discuss his or her feelings openly. Before the discussion begins, establish ground rules. These may include things such as agreeing that only one person will talk at a time, identifying a signal to indicate that someone would like to speak, agreeing not to interrupt each other, and avoiding name calling. Designate a leader to direct the discussion. Experts recommend that every family conference have a different leader, so that family members change roles. The leader should use open-ended questions like, "How do you feel about what's going on?"

A family conference is not a forum to try to convince anyone that he or she is in the wrong or for parents to educate children about their beliefs. It is a time and place where everyone in the family can express ideas and opinions in a safe environment. The goal is to leave the conference aware of each others' feelings about a difficult subject.

Q & A

Question: What can I do about my mother? We are always fighting. She has so many rules and she snoops. I found her in my bedroom reading my diary.

Answer: It's not surprising that you are fighting more with your mom. Teens often feel a tension between their need for independence and their connection with their parents. For instance, you live in your parents' house and you're probably expected to abide by their rules, but you may not agree with all of those rules. In the same way, your mother may want you to become independent yet find it difficult to let go. It may be hard for her to accept that the child who once cried if she was lost in the supermarket is now dating, driving a car, and making decisions about life.

You can help your mother accept your independence by acting responsibly. Let her know that you are able to take care of yourself by doing it and doing it well. And don't be afraid to speak. Remind her that you still love her and you need her guidance every now and then, even if you don't need her to hold your hand when you cross the street anymore. Make some time for just you and her to do things that you've never had a chance to do before, like cooking dinner or going to see a movie. You may be surprised at what you discover about your mother—and yourself.

Arguments are an inevitable part of family life. Handled well, arguments can help family members learn about each other and grow closer. Learning to resolve differences with siblings can help them to develop the skills they'll need to have successful relationships with peers, teachers, coworkers, bosses, and spouses. Respectful, open discussions of conflicts can lead to greater intimacy between family members, even if family members cannot agree on the issues.

See also: Divorce and Families; Families, Divided; Teens in Trouble; Violence and the Family

FURTHER READING
Stone, Douglas, Bruce Patton, and Sheila Heen. *Difficult Conversations: How to Discuss What Matters Most.* New York: Penguin, 2000.

◼ DAY CARE

Daycare is the provision of physical and emotional care to children while their parents or other caregivers are at work. Although the primary goal of day care is to provide for the needs of infants and young children, some providers may offer preschool education or after-school care for school-age children.

TYPES OF DAY CARE

Day care arrangements are classified by type. The three main types of day care described by the U.S. Census Bureau are care provided by relatives, family day care, and center-based care.

Day care provided by relatives involves an arrangement in which a family member other than a mother or father regularly cares for children. Parents either take the child to the relative's home, or the relative comes to the child's home for the hours the parents are away.

In family day care, the care is provided in the family residence of a provider. In some states, such a provider must attend an orientation and/or complete training to obtain a license. Regulatory requirements differ state to state. A provider might be approved, certified, registered, or licensed under state or local laws. California, for example, allows a provider to care for no more than four infants or six children without the help of an assistant. This regulation includes the provider's own children under the age of 12. With an assistant, the provider may care for 12 children; but no more than four may be infants, including their own children under the age of 12.

A third type of day care is center-based care, which involves the provision of care in a facility that is not part of a home. Centers may be in schools, churches, or company buildings and must meet specific health, safety, and other regulatory standards as outlined by specific states. The staff of day care centers are trained and credentialed in early childhood development and education.

ALTERNATIVES TO DAY CARE

The U.S. Census Bureau reports smaller numbers of parents choosing alternatives to the three main types of day care. One alternative is to form a neighborhood day care cooperative. According to Jane Filstrup in the book *Monday through Friday: Day Care Alternatives*, every parent in the cooperative provides care to a group of children for an agreed-upon number of days per month.

Another alternative is to hire a live-in nanny, governess, or au pair to tend to the children. An au pair is a young man or woman, often from another country, who lives with a family while caring for their children. This day care alternative is costly and not usually an option for mid- to low-income families.

AN EXPENSIVE SERVICE

Day care is expensive. For example, to care for an infant all day at a commercial day care center in Louisville, Kentucky, the cost was a little over $6,000 per year in 2004, according to the National Economic Development and Law Center (NEDLC), a nonprofit public-interest organization. That same care cost $9,000 in Marin County, California, according to the Marin Child Care Council.

Day care fees can take up a significant portion of a family's income. The Children's Aid Society of New York in its 2002 study, "The Human Cost of Waiting for Child Care," found that families claim to spend one-fifth to half of their earnings on day care. In the same study, researchers found that 41 percent of families said they had to cut back on food and children's clothing to pay for day care.

National reports such as the Children's Defense Fund's *The State of America's Children* maintain that day care takes approximately 10 percent of an average family's income as compared to as much as 22 to 25 percent of a poor family's income.

Day care costs are particularly significant for single mothers. Women's wages often barely cover day care costs. As economy expert Timothy Smeeding, a professor of public policy at Syracuse University, observed in 2004, "Our low-income mothers work twice as hard as those in any other industrial country, but their kids are the worst off." Smeeding's study shows that among the world's **industrialized** countries, child poverty in single-mother households is highest in the United States as compared to other countries. A single income and low wages, Smeeding says, are the reasons why single working mothers may still find themselves impoverished and unable to pay for needed day care.

Is it worth the cost?

The increasing numbers of parents in the workforce, especially low income single mothers make finding quality affordable day care an important issue for today's parents. According to *The State of America's Children,* an estimated 13 million children under the age of six spend some part of every day being cared for by someone other than their parents. Yet day care is expensive and for some parents the issue of cost is a big one. Even those who can afford day care or who receive financial assistance find meeting the demand of high day care expenses to be challenging.

Financial assistance

Government assistance in paying for day care is available in the United States. Yet according to a 2000 U.S. Department of Health and Human Services report, only 12 percent of children eligible for

---

DID YOU KNOW?

Number of Hours Children Are in Day Care Per Week

Percentage of Children	Hours in Day Care Per Week
16	zero to 9
38	10 to 29
36	30 to 45
10	more than 45

Source: National Institute of Child Health and Human Development (NICHD), 2001–2003.

---

assistance are receiving help. The stark reality is that access to state monies and services can be limited or difficult to obtain. For example, the state of Pennsylvania offers financial assistance for day care when parents meet specific criteria. In 2004, a family of four is eligible for the fee assistance if the family has an income of $35,300 or less. Each adult member of the family is required to work at least 25 hours per week. Families using this assistance program are required to pay from $260 to $1360 per year as a copayment. Even when families apply for this assistance program and get approved, they may be on a waiting list until the state has money available.

ADVANTAGES FOR CHILDREN IN DAY CARE

Ongoing research on the advantages of day care cite safe supervision, socialization with same age peers, and exposure to educational information and materials as being beneficial to young children. The National Institute of Child Health and Human Development (NICHD) suggests that children in quality programs have stronger learning skills and socialization skills; they further assert that quality early learning experiences lay the foundation for later success in school.

The U.S. Department of Health and Human Services reports positive research findings of its federal Head Start Program. Studies of the program show improved measures of language, thinking, socialization, and emotional health in children after being enrolled for a year or more in the program.

Day care offers adult supervision of young children, and after-school programs benefit children of school age. A 2003 study by Brown University showed that children who return home from school but are home alone are more likely to find themselves in unsafe and even criminal situations than children who are supervised. Researcher J. L. Richardson reports that being unsupervised after school puts youths at greater risk of truancy, poor academic performance, difficult emotional issues, and substance abuse. Studies of after-school programs such as Chicago's Child-Parent Centers show that children who participate are more likely to complete high school and less likely to repeat a grade or be charged with a juvenile crime.

Children who attend day care have more exposure to socialization with same-age children. According to psychologist Ercilia Palacio-Quintin in a 2000 report entitled "The Impact of Day Care on Child Development," this exposure to social situations increases cooperative effective play. Once they are in school, children with early social experience have fewer behavioral problems.

Another socialization-related advantage of day care is that children learn to relate to those who are not the same age, advises the Office for Young Children, a child-care resource group. Interactions with older children and teachers provide modeling behavior for children along with opportunities for additional social skill development.

The Children's Defense Fund states that additional advantages of day care include improved nutrition, health screening, and access to early childhood related services for children and families.

Q & A

Question: Do day care centers provide care to children with special learning, medical, or behavioral needs?

Answer: According to the Americans with Disabilities Act, family day care and center-based day care centers must offer child care to children with disabilities. The only exception to this law relates to centers run directly by religious organizations. In the United States, the government does not legislate the policies and procedures of faith-based agencies.

SEPARATION ISSUES

The research related to attachment and separation issues in young children is contradictory. Positive outcomes related to cognitive development for children in day care are well documented by child advocacy agencies such as the Children's Defense Fund and by government agencies such as the National Institute of Child Health and Human Development. But noted experts T. Berry Brazelton and Stanley Greenspan raise concerns about young children in day care. In their well-respected book *The Irreducible Needs of Children*, they explore the critical needs of young children, especially infants, and question children's ability to bond well emotionally when in day care for long periods of time without consistent nurturing care providers.

Fact Or Fiction?

A child will be less upset if his mother leaves day care while he is busy playing than if she tells him she is leaving.

Fact: Separation issues are a key concern related to the emotional well-being of young children. Brazelton and Greenspan's review of research on attachment suggests children separate more effectively when they are prepared for the separation and placed in the care of nurturing, well-trained care providers. When parents leave without warning, separation issues may be made worse. When separation is handled with honesty and compassion, children can learn to trust care providers and that parents will return.

However, a review of the last decade of studies by Palacio-Quintin shows little negative effect, even if children attend full-time and are enrolled at young ages. The primary indicator of emotional well-being, researchers say, is having a secure attachment to a consistent caregiver.

Research evidence does not suggest that day care per se is detrimental to children's future social and emotional development. The separation and attachment concerns center on whether or not children receive nurturing and consistent care either at home or in day care.

DAY CARE ISSUES AND CONCERNS

Equal access to quality, affordable day care remains an issue for families, day care providers, and regulatory agencies. The issues and concerns surrounding day care are related to availability of day care, safety, health, and staffing.

Availability

In some areas, the biggest issue surrounding day care is that there isn't enough of it. For example, in some communities in California, there are not enough day care centers for all the children needing day care. According to the Marin Child Care Council, as many as 15 percent of all children of working parents in Marin county don't have access to care.

Safety

While safety standards may be clearly outlined by each state, compliance with these regulations continues to be an issue. The Florida Department of Children and Families, a group that inspects Florida centers to ensure child safety, found in their years of ongoing monitoring that some centers continue to use vans without car seats or seat belts. Some vans were uninsured and had no schedule for safety inspections. Monitoring activities also revealed centers that use drivers without licenses.

Safety standards are outlined federally by such organizations as the National Association for the Education of Young Children, the National Health and Safety Performance Standards, the American Academy of Pediatrics, and the American Public Health Association. The report, "State Efforts to Enforce Safety and Health Requirements," found that states often met or exceeded the federal standards. Yet the ability for states to inspect and support compliance with the regulations was found to be problematic.

In a 2000 review of the research by Ruth B. Schumacher and Rebecca S. Carlson, sexual and physical abuse can occur in both family day care and center-based day care. The report indicates that sexual abuse happens more frequently in home care and that the perpetrator in these instances is often the husband or boyfriend of the primary caregiver. When such abuse occurs at a center, the perpetrator is often one of the peripheral staff or family of staff. The report details other types of child abuse, such as hitting, which the research showed to be carried out by caregivers with unrealistic expectations of children. In centers with smaller staff size, particularly in rural centers, there was more severe abuse and abuse with a longer duration. Workers with high job satisfaction as well as workers who were trained in early childhood care were less likely to be abusive.

Health problems

Children in day care get more illnesses than children who are cared for at home. Studies reviewed by Palacio-Quitin show that the illness rate is as much as two to four times higher for children in day care. Many of the illnesses are mild health concerns such as colds, flu, and stomach and intestinal problems. Yet, some illnesses are more concerning such as measles, whooping cough, pneumonia, and cytomegalovirus (CMV). Communicable diseases are spread when sick children are in close contact with one another and when staff members and children inadequately wash hands after coming in contact with urine, feces, saliva, or nasal secretions.

Staffing difficulties

The three critical staff difficulties in day care centers are turnover, **staff ratio,** and untrained workers. The Center for the Childcare Workforce, in 2002, explored salaries, benefits, and turnover rates in day care centers throughout the United States. The average yearly turnover rate was 21 percent; some centers had a turnover rate as high as 51 percent. Salaries ranged from a starting wage of slighter higher than $5 per hour to $18 per hour, but many salaries on the whole were below $10 per hour. As reported by the Early Child Care Research Center, salaries are a good measure of staff stability; when salaries are high, caregivers stay.

Staff ratio refers to the number of children per staff member. The National Institute of Child Health and Human Development recommends staff ratios of 1:4 for infants and 1:7 for preschoolers. In both family day care and center-based day care, sensitive, responsive, and individualized interactions with children are the best measures of quality care. There is a direct relationship between appropriate staff ratios and staff being able to provide quality care. But providing better ratios is expensive. Day care agencies that strive to achieve better ratios must hire more employees, and more employees means more money spent on salaries and benefits.

DAY CARE IN THE FUTURE

Increasing numbers of parents are joining the workforce, according to the U.S. Census Bureau, and a growing body of research points to the need for quality, affordable day care for children. Child-development experts, advocates, and policy makers put forward a call to action regarding day care in the annual report, *The State of America's Children,* which discusses ways in which day care can be improved in the future. The three areas where the most impact might be made are in funding, availability of day care, and in curriculum development.

Funding and availability

The goal of improving day care funding methods should be broad-based. Although there is now some subsidized care, the ideal would be more subsidized care, to cover all eligible children. Experts and advocates call on government leaders to invest in the funding of quality day care aimed at bridging the serious gap of its availability. The Children's Defense Fund recommends adequate funding to meet the goals of providing early learning skills for young children especially those from poor families as well as providing after-school programs.

Curriculum development

Research-based and developmentally appropriate curricula should be the goal of every day care provider. According to family studies professor Dianna Chiabotti of Napa Valley College, teachers with training and education in child development provide quality care to children. The standard to attain is that all centers be accredited, and to have workers receive ongoing training.

Developmentally appropriate curricula are those in which children are exposed to information, language and social experiences that encourage a love of learning.

See also: Financial Mangement, Marital; Single-Parent Families

FURTHER READING

Brazelton, T. Berry, and Stanley Greenspan. *The Irreducible Needs of Children: What Every Child Must Have to Grow, Learn and Flourish.* New York: Perseus Publishing, 2001.

Chaudry, Ajay, and Mary Jo Bane. *Putting Children First: How Low Wage Working Mothers Manage Childcare.* New York: Russell Sage Foundation Publications, 2004.

Uttal, Lynet. *Making Care Work: Employed Mothers in the New Childcare Market.* New Brunswick, NJ: Rutgers University Press, 2002.

■ DEATH IN THE FAMILY

A death in the family means the loss of a family member and may include the loss of a child or an adult. According to statistics reported in 2004 by The Compassionate Friends (TCF), a national organization that aids grieving families, more than 200,000 infants, children, teens, and young adults die each year; 900,000 families experience the loss of a child in early pregnancy and about 27,000 face a stillbirth (an infant delivered without signs of life). In 2001, Margaret Stuber and Violet Mesrkhani of the Neuropsychiatric Institute reported that 5 percent of children will, by age 16, experience the death of a parent.

Families face the death of a loved one in many ways because every family has a different social network and engages in different rituals. These differences mean that although a death in a family is a universal event, each family copes with the loss in its own way.

The death of a relative affects everyone in the family, both young and old. It may also cause stresses in the family, as the household changes in response to the loss. There is a similarity, however, in the way adults and children grieve.

BEREAVEMENT

Bereavement is sadness about the loss of a loved one. When a death occurs in a family, the sadness experienced by both the adults and children is often a complex feeling with many responses.

Adult response to grief

When adults lose a parent, a spouse, a sibling, or a child, they may be unable, at first, to accept that their loved one is gone. Some become so depressed that they are unable to make the necessary life adjustments. The Compassionate Friends finds that when adults lose a parent, they often feel as if they have lost a part of their past. When they lose a spouse, they often feel they have lost the present, and when they lose a child, they often feel they have lost the future. TCF finds that adults who lose a sibling feel as if potentially the longest relationship of their life has ended. In this way, a sibling's death can seem like the loss of the past, present, and the future.

Among the feelings individuals experience after a family member dies are sadness, anger, anxiety, depression, and fear of being alone. Some people withdraw from friends, lose interest in eating, have trouble sleeping, or become irritable.

A landmark 1985 study in the journal *Social Work* underscored the particular strain that a child's death places on parents. Researcher T. Rando found that eventually 80 percent of these bereaved parents divorced.

Children's response to grief

Children respond to a death in the family in ways characteristic of their age. According to the Royal College of Psychiatrists in a guide titled "Death in the Family: Helping Children Cope," infants often become anxious because they pick up on the feelings of the adults around them. Infants know their routine has been altered; as a result, they may become hard to settle. Some preschoolers view death as temporary, even reversible. Young children may think that they caused the death and are therefore to blame. They may revert to behaviors more typical of younger children, experience nightmares, develop issues with toileting, or may talk about their loved one or imitate this person.

According to the guide, older children, by contrast, know that death is permanent. They know that someone who is deceased can no longer be heard or seen. They also know that all living beings die and death has a cause. Teens, the guide notes, may have intense feelings about a loss but may not show them openly. They may not be able to put their feelings into words or may be reluctant to upset others. Even though they may not show that they are upset, many teens grieve deeply. Each teen's response is unique, based on his or her personality. One teen may withdraw and feel lost, while another may feel angry. Older children may have issues with grades and friendships; some may refuse to go to school at all.

Some teens may be frightened by feelings of grief and may resist the grief process. The Dougy Center, which has provided support for more than 13,500 bereaved families, has found that teens deal with grief in constructive ways by writing about their feelings in a journal or confiding in trusted friends. Some teens try to escape the pain of a loss through substance abuse, careless sexual activity, skipping school, and engaging in other risky behaviors. These ways of handling grief have destructive outcomes.

Children of all ages may display feelings of loss sporadically over a long period of time. Parents may see anger or sadness related to the loss continue on and off for years.

Comforting children

Parents do best when they tell their children about a death and answer their questions simply and honestly. After a review of the research, the Neuropsychiatric Institute at the University of California concluded that even very young children understand that something terrible has happened when a parent dies or is seriously ill even if they are not told directly. By withholding this information, adults fail to protect children and provide age-appropriate support.

According to Dr. Alan Greene of the Stanford University School of Medicine, children as early as three who experience a loss can be encouraged to express their feelings through play or by drawing pictures, using puppets, or making up a story. Elementary school children may dramatize their feelings as a way of working through grief.

The Dougy Center advises parents to tell children when and where the funeral will be, who will attend, and what will happen at the ceremony. Children should be asked if they wish to attend. Some children view the funeral as a chance to say goodbye to the deceased. If they do not want to go to the funeral, however, they should not be forced to attend. There are other ways that children can be involved, says Greene. For example, parents can take the children later to visit the gravesite. They might light a candle together, say a prayer, or tell each other what the person meant in their lives.

Adults who wish to comfort a teen need to first sort out their own feelings so that they can better relate as companions in grief. The Center advises against lecturing a teen about the proper way to grieve. Instead it recommends listening and then offering constructive ideas about facing sadness. Teens will want to work through the process of grieving in their own unique ways, which should be honored by adults.

Fact Or Fiction?

When a family loses a loved one in tragic circumstances such as in an accident or through suicide, the family will never be the same again.

Fact: Families can grieve in healthy ways and go on to live productive, happy lives, no matter the circumstances of the loss. When families communicate with each other clearly and often about the loss, healthy grieving occurs. It is important for each person to accept the death and for family members to share with each other an acceptance of the new reality of family life. Families who grieve in healthy ways recognize that the death is permanent and means permanent changes to family structure and function. While the loss is never forgotten, healthy grief work includes a reorganization of family. Members begin to seek out new relationships and life pursuits.

ROLE OF RELIGION IN GRIEVING

Religious beliefs and participation in worship services play a role in the way families grieve. Ceremonies, customs, and rituals allow families to grieve with the support of other relatives and friends, and give grieving relatives time to remember or pray for the deceased.

When death occurs in a family, relatives and friends need to grieve. Everyone associated with the loss is touched in his or her own way. Coming together at religious ceremonies helps those who are grieving to celebrate the life of the loved one as well as find meaning in life and loss. At different ages, people react differently to the death of a loved one. Although grief stresses the family, there are ways that families can cope and can comfort children. Religious customs aim to assist families through the process of coming to terms with loss.

Q & A

Question: Why do families put themselves through a wake and funeral? These rituals seem only to make people more upset.

Answer: The rituals of wakes and funerals allow people the opportunity to express deep feelings among others who care for and about them and the person who died. Often these religious rituals and ceremonies also provide family and friends a chance to express their feelings and receive support from members of a person's faith community.

See also: Family Traditions; Religion and the Family

FURTHER READING

The Dougy Center. *Helping Teens Cope with Death.* Portland, OR: The Dougy Center, 1999.

Fitzgerald, Helen. *The Grieving Teen.* New York: Fireside, 2000.

James, John W., and Russell Friedman. *When Children Grieve.* New York: HarperCollins, 2002.

Secunda, Victoria. *Losing Your Parents.* New York: Hyperion, 2001.

Trozzi, Maria, and Kathy Massimini. *Talking with Children about Loss: Words, Strategies, and Wisdom to Help Children Cope with Death, Divorce, and Other Difficult Times.* New York: Perigee Books, 1999.

Wolfelt, Alan D. *Healing Your Grieving Heart: 100 Practical Ideas for Kids.* Fort Collins, CO: Center for Loss & Life Transition, 2000.

■ DIVORCE AND FAMILIES

Divorce is the legal ending of a marriage. During the process of a divorce, a couple's property and debts are divided. If children are involved, their **custody** and care are decided. In some cases, a former spouse may be required to provide financial support to the other, either permanently or temporarily. After the divorce is finalized, each individual can legally marry someone else.

SEPARATION ISSUES

The first step toward divorce is **separation.** Separation means moving out, starting a different household, and changing routine. Most states require that people live in separate households for a designated period of time before divorcing. When couples decide to separate, parents and children may experience emotional turmoil including depression, loneliness, and other feelings of grief. Coping is hardest when one partner wants to divorce and the other does not, if the idea is sudden and unexpected, or when friends and family members disapprove.

In addition to the emotional pain of separation, families must make many practical decisions. Who will stay and who will leave? Where will family members live? How will assets and debts be divided? Who will pay for what, now and in the future? If the couple has children, will the children live with one parent or the other? How will they share time between parents? Who will pay the children's expenses?

Marital therapists sometimes recommend that couples try a structured separation for a limited period of time before making a final decision about a divorce. During a structured separation, the couple stops living together. Partners attend regularly scheduled therapy sessions with a professional therapist and see each other at specified times. Because it puts couples in a new environment, separation may interrupt old patterns of interaction.

Trial separations may be useful for couples who are not sure if they want to divorce or in cases where there is extreme conflict between partners, including physical and verbal abuse. A separation may allow a cooling-off period of personal growth and freedom while the couple works to restructure the relationship. Stressful life events, such as the loss of a job, death of a loved one, change in jobs, relocation, or children leaving home often bring out problems in a marriage. Separation may allow the partner experiencing the stress to deal with the crisis apart from the problems in the marriage. When partners are simply unable to decide whether to divorce or not, a structured separation may help them to make a decision.

Most separations end with divorce or the couple reuniting. However, some couples choose to remain married but legally separated, either for religious or other reasons. In these cases, the legal obligations of the marriage end but no divorce occurs. Couples who are separated but not divorced must negotiate issues including child custody, finances, and maintaining separate households, but they cannot remarry unless they eventually decide to divorce.

SPLIT FAMILIES

For children of divorced parents, divorce often means living with a semi-packed suitcase, spending weekends with one parent and weekdays with the other. It may mean new friends, moving to a new home, attending a new school, and dealing with parents who are angry with one another. Economic hardship is common after a divorce, especially for families headed by women. In a 2002 study of the economic impact of family structure on children, economists Marianne E. Page and Ann Huff Stevens found that divorced parents experienced a 41 percent decline in family income in the year following a divorce. Family food consumption falls by 18 percent in the year following divorce. Using a dynamic model with longitudinal effects, Page and Huff calculated that six years later, children whose parents remained unmarried had family incomes of 45 percent lower than if the divorce had not occurred.

Divorcing families often must decide who will have **custody** or **guardianship** of the children. There are two types of custody: **physical custody** and **legal custody**. Physical custody defines where the child will live. The child might split his or her time between parents, or he or she may live with one parent and visit the other. Legal custody determines who will make decisions about how the child is raised. These decisions include medical care, religious upbringing, and schooling. These types of custody may be given to one or to both parents. If one parent has **sole custody**, he or she has both physical and legal custody of the child. Usually, the other parent has visitation rights. In **joint custody**, parents share physical and legal custody.

If parents cannot agree about custody of the children, they may seek help from a **mediator**. A mediator is a person who usually has a background in law or the behavioral sciences and specializes in helping couples resolve the issues that arise in a divorce. In other cases, a judge may appoint a child development expert to investigate the family situation and make recommendations about custody.

Decisions about custody are made on the basis of what is best for the child, instead of assuming that the child will stay with the mother. Still, most children of divorced parents live with their mothers. In 1997, according to the U.S. Census Bureau, 85 percent of the 13.7 million custodial parents were women.

When a family splits, older children may find themselves taking on more responsibility. Without two adults to share the tasks of keeping the home and earning a living, some responsibilities may fall on children. Teens especially may find themselves helping with cooking, cleaning the house, and even earning extra money to help support the family. Children may find it difficult to adjust to the constraints of a lower income and not being able to buy things that they were once able to afford.

Fact Or Fiction?

Parents feel differently toward their children after a divorce.

Fact: Immediately after a divorce, parents may be more involved in their own concerns and needs and be less attentive to their children. They may still be dealing with their own grief and pain at the dissolution of the relationship with their spouse. After divorce, parents may spend less time with their children, simply because each parent must work more hours to maintain a household. But this does not mean their feelings for their children have changed. It may seem that parents feel differently toward their children after a divorce, but this is rarely, if ever, true.

DIFFICULT DIVORCE AND KIDS

Only rarely is a divorce not marked by conflict. Often, tension and arguments between parents continue even after the former spouses have gone their separate ways. When parents cannot manage their anger at each other and bring their children into the struggle, children are torn between the two most important people in their lives.

Researchers continue to debate about the long-term effects of divorce and parental conflict on children. Some, such as psychologist Judith Wallerstein, argue that parental divorce has long-term negative effects on children's growth and development. In a 30-year study, from 1971 to 2001, of 60 divorced families in Marin County, California, involving 130 children, Wallerstein found that 10 years after divorce, 50 percent of the women and 33 percent of the men were still angry at their ex-partners and that this anger affected their relationships with their children. Memories of abandonment, terror, and loneliness were common among the children in Wallerstein's study. Many felt that they had been denied basic security while growing up and that they had "lost" their childhood by feeling the need to take care of their parents.

The negative effects seemed to grow worse over time. Ten to 15 years later, many of the children in the study had a record of illegal offenses, had engaged in sexual activity with multiple partners, and had abused alcoholic beverages. As they entered adulthood, half the children were underachieving. Financial support was limited and few had the resources to go to college. Wallerstein concluded that divorce causes serious harm to children who experience it.

Wallerstein's study, however, did not look at how children are affected by the conflict prior to divorce. The results of several other studies suggest that marital conflict has a greater effect on children's well-being than the divorce itself. For example, in 1991, sociologists Paul Amato and Alan Booth of the Population Research Center at Pennsylvania State University published "Parental Divorce and the Wellbeing of Children: A Meta-Analysis." Amato and Booth combined the results of 129 studies involving 95,000 participants. They compared children whose parents divorced to those whose parents remained married. They found that there were often problems in parent-child relationships eight to 12 years before the divorce. The lower the quality of the parents' marriage, the less close the parents were to their children at the age 18. Fathers and children were less affectionate toward each other after divorce, suggesting that the relationship between parents and children was impacted both directly and indirectly.

In 2001, Joan B. Kelly, a psychiatrist at the University of California at San Francisco, published "Adjustment in Conflicted Marriage and Divorce," a review of research on the impact of marital conflict, parental violence, and divorce on the psychological adjustment of children. Kelly looked at studies that had been published during the 1990s. She also found that parental conflict, not the separation of parents, has the strongest negative impact on children's well-being. Her summary of the research on children and divorce supports the idea that children's emotional or behavioral problems may arise from conflict between parents, before and after the divorce, more than from the divorce itself.

Kelly also notes that teens who are caught in the middle of their parents' post-divorce disagreements tend to have more problems adjusting than those whose parents do not use their children to express their conflicts. Kelly explains that, for teens, being "caught in the middle" might mean being asked to relay angry messages or requests or spy on a parent. Such children often feel the need to hide their feelings and thoughts about the other parent.

Some high-conflict post-divorce families can benefit from working with a **parenting coordinator**. A parenting coordinator works within the structure of a couple's divorce decree to help parents settle disagreements about children, and can facilitate between parents who are in high conflict. Visits should always be supervised if conflict threatens a child's well-being, if there is a risk of physical threat and abuse between parents, or if physical or sexual abuse of children is a possibility.

TEENS SPEAK

Surviving My Parents' Divorce

I had just returned home from soccer practice on a Sunday afternoon late in August when Dad called my younger brother Jeremy and me down to the kitchen. He looked so serious. My first thought was, "We must be in big trouble." Mom was sitting at the table. I could tell that she had been crying. Her mascara was in streaks down her face. That's when Dad told us that he was moving to an apartment about four miles away, and he and Mom were getting divorced. He would be leaving the next day.

It wasn't entirely a surprise. Mom and Dad had been fighting for a long time. I still have a picture of all of us, taken when my little brother was about a year old. I was four. We were at the beach near our house. Mom, Jeremy, and I were burying Dad in the sand, and he was laughing. We all looked so happy in the picture. For at least three years, I had wondered what happened to that smiling, laughing Mom and Dad in the picture. I know they tried not to fight in front of us, but still, we heard the angry voices.

The next few months were horrible. Dad moved out and Mom cried a lot. We visited Dad on weekends. It felt strange to go to his apartment and sleep on the couch in the living room. Mom started shopping at thrift stores for my clothes. I was so embarrassed. I was sure that everyone at school could tell that my clothes had come from the Salvation Army store. I was angry at her for not buying me things at department stores. Then one day, when we were at the grocery store, she didn't have enough money to pay for all the groceries. That was when I realized that she was not just being mean—she was barely able to pay for our food and other things we needed. She was going to college, and Dad had lost his job, so she wasn't receiving child support payments.

After about a year, Dad got a new job and moved to Oregon. Mom finished school, and she is an accountant at a busy office. Jeremy and I spend summers with Dad and the rest of the year with Mom in California. I still wish they hadn't split up, but I know that it was the best thing for all of us. I've gotten closer to each of them, and I've learned that I can survive really tough times.

AMICABLE DIVORCE AND KIDS

While post-divorce conflict is common, hostility between parents usually lessens dramatically after divorce. In a 1999 study of the effects of nonresident father visitation and conflict on children, Valarie King and Holly E. Heard found that three years after divorcing, only 8–12 percent of divorced couples remained in very high conflict. King and Heard analyzed data from 1,565 mothers living with children under the age of 18 years whose fathers lived elsewhere.

For children of divorce, the relatively quick lessening of hostility between parents is good news. As Kelly notes, many studies show that children whose divorced parents cooperate and mutually support each other are more likely to adjust well emotionally, psychologically, and socially. Many divorcing families have found that professional assistance such as postmarital therapy or divorce mediation helps them resolve disputes amicably, even in the early stages of divorce.

A mediator helps the couple develop a written agreement that serves as the basis of the divorce petition to the court, according to Kelly. The divorce petition spells out how the couple will divide their assets, child custody, and visitation rights; who will pay child support and how much it will be; and other workings of the divorce. Mediation emphasizes open communication, negotiation, and mutual resolution of the emotional, financial, and child-related issues. Of couples who used mediation, at least 40 percent were able to completely agree on the terms of their divorce and up to 80 percent were able to agree on at least some points. Many couples who participated in mediation say that it helped them focus on the needs of their children, gave them a chance to express their feelings and grievances, and allowed them to deal with fundamental issues in greater depth than would occur in court procedures.

Kelly notes that many studies indicate that children do better when they have a close relationship with their noncustodial parent (usually the father). According to Kelly, the frequency and pattern of contacts between fathers are related to marital and post-divorce conflict and the amount of legal conflict. She cites the work of Paul Amato and colleagues, who found that children adjusted most easily when they had frequent contact with their nonresident fathers and conflict between their divorced parents was low.

King and Heard found that the mother's satisfaction with the father's visits was a key indicator of the child's well-being. In their study, the more satisfied mothers were with the fathers' visit, the more satisfied they were overall. When mothers were dissatisfied, children had more behavioral problems and scored lower than other children on tests of adjustment and well-being. This was true even if fathers visited frequently.

In "Children of Divorce," a review of recent medical literature about children of divorce, Charles Bryner, a naval physician, observes that both children and adults experience divorce in a series of stages. These stages, argues Bryner, are similar to those Elisabeth Kübler-Ross described for terminally ill patients: denial, anger, bargaining, depression, and acceptance. However, these stages may be experienced differently by children and adults. When adults are too preoccupied with their own sorrow at the ending of the relationship, children may be forgotten and remain stuck in the denial stage.

Bryner offers the following summary of children's common feelings and actions during these five stages. During the denial stage, children often believe that their parents will reunite, a fantasy that can persist for years. In the second stage, anger, children may feel furious at their parents for not trying harder to stay together and allowing the divorce to happen. They may feel that their parents have ruined their lives and destroyed their vision of the future. In the bargaining stage, children may try to bring the absent parent home by being "perfect." They may try to get good grades at school, go out of their way to be helpful, and not cause any trouble. Young children may believe that their own misbehaviors caused their parents' divorce (for example, fighting with a sibling). A period of extreme sadness and tiredness, or **depression**, usually follows the bargaining period. The child often feels sad, tired, and listless both at school and at home. For children to move on to the final stage, acceptance, they must develop the emotional maturity and distance to recognize that their parents are happier living separately and that the divorce was in the best interests of all family members. Acceptance often does not occur until adolescence or even young adulthood.

While divorce is a stressful and painful occurrence for families, most children do eventually adjust to their parents' divorce and go on to lead happy, fulfilling lives. In *For Better or for Worse: Divorce Reconsidered,* psychologist E. Mavis Hetherington and colleague John Kelly report the results of a 24-year study of 1,400 families begun in the late 1970s. Six years after their parents' divorce, almost 80 percent of the children whose parents had divorced were as happy and as emotionally healthy as those whose parents were still together.

DIVIDING UP DAYS: WHEN DO WE SEE WHOM?

One of the most difficult decisions for most divorcing families is where children will live and whether one or both parents will care for them. Even when parents share joint legal and physical custody, it may not be practical, or best for their child, to evenly split their time between homes (for example, spending three days a week at the mother's house and four days at the father's). Geography, work schedules, and other factors all play a role in determining when and how children spend time with which parent. Each family must create custody arrangements appropriate for both parents and children. Some experts prefer the term *co-parenting* as a more accurate description of shared parental responsibilities. Arrangements, such as spending school years with Dad and summers with Mom, might be more practical for a particular family. The child's age, social network, and other needs should be taken into account when deciding who spends time with whom. Older children and teens should be active participants in choosing how and where they want to spend their time.

Holidays, birthdays, and other days of traditional celebration can create chaos in split families. Parents who share the same religion may both want to share the same holidays with their children. Children's birthdays and school vacations may be another source of conflict. Like any other aspect of post-marital family life, disputes over holidays and special occasions can be worked out amicably or can become another source of conflict. Many parents have developed workable solutions that allow everyone to share in the celebrations of these special days (for example, alternating Christmas Eve and Christmas Day). Birthdays may be celebrated twice, once with each parent. School and work vacations can be divided up in ways that work for everyone. Children, especially teens and older children, should participate in these decisions.

See also: Arguments and the Family; Families, Blended; Families, Divided; Family, The New; Family, The Traditional; Marriage and Family, Changes in; Single-Parent Families; Stepparents; Violence and the Family

FURTHER READING
Aydt, Rachel. *Why Me? A Teen Guide to Divorce and Your Feelings.* New York: Rosen Publishing Group, 2000.
Bolick, Nancy O'Keefe, and Nancy O. Bolick. *How to Survive Your Parents' Divorce.* New York: Scholastic Library Publishing, 1995.
Bonkowski, Sara. *Teens Are Non-Divorceable: A Workbook for Divorced Parents and Their Children: Ages 12–18.* Chicago: Acta Publications, 1987.
Calhoun, Florence. *No Easy Answers: A Teen Guide to Why Divorce Happens.* New York: Rosen Publishing Group, 2000.
Stern, Ellen Sue, and Evan Stern. *Divorce Is Not the End of the World.* Berkeley, CA: Ten Speed Press, 1997.

■ ELDERLY FAMILY MEMBERS

Parents or grandparents during late adulthood are considered to be elderly. Adults age 65–74 are sometimes referred to as the young-old, those age 75–84 as the middle-old, and those 85 and older as the oldest-old.

Late adulthood is often a time of transition from independence to **physical dependence** on others for activities such as walking, bathing, taking medications, or balancing a checkbook. The scale used to measure a person's ability to perform physical tasks is called the **Activities of Daily Living** (ADL). During late adulthood, physical health may deteriorate to the point where seniors are no longer able to care for themselves. According to the 2002 American Community Survey (ACS), conducted by the U.S. Census Bureau, almost half (46.1 percent) of people age 65 or older had at least one disability, physical or nonphysical. Among people age 85 or older, more than three-fourths (76.4 percent) were living with at least one disability.

DID YOU KNOW?

Life Expectancy in the United States by Ethnicity and Gender

Measure and Sex	Both Races		White		Black	
	2001	2000	2001	2000	2001	2000
Life expectancy at birth	77.2	77.0	77.7	77.6	72.2	71.9
Male	74.4	74.3	75.0	74.9	68.6	68.3
Female	79.8	79.7	80.2	80.1	75.5	75.2

Source: National Center for Health Statistics, 2001.

While many disabilities are minor, others may interfere with one's independence. The need for assistance with ADLs increases drastically with age. Data from the 2002 survey show that 5.4 percent of people age 65–74 experienced difficulty caring for themselves, as did 10.5 percent of those age 75–84 and 24 percent of those older than 85. As people move from the middle-old to the oldest-old group, the need for highly personalized care, such as assistance using the toilet or bathing, becomes three times more common.

NURSING HOMES

Many elderly people who have great difficulty performing ADLs enter nursing homes, special residential facilities that offer skilled nursing care. They are designed to care for people who need high levels of assistance with medical and personal care such as the administration of medications, moving around, or personal hygiene. Census 2000 data showed that almost 1.6 million people in the United States—4.5 percent of the population age 65 and over—lived in nursing homes.

Fact Or Fiction?

All elderly people have serious disabilities that cause them to require daily assistance.

Fact: Many of the elderly lead active, independent lives. Some continue to work, either full- or part-time, past the age of 65. Others use their retirement years to travel, pursue volunteer activities, hobbies, and other interests.

Nursing homes vary greatly in cost and quality. Many are clean, well-run facilities that offer caring, compassionate assistance to residents. These high-quality nursing homes have well-trained, professional staff that includes nurses, physicians, dietitians, physical therapists, and other licensed or certified health care providers. These facilities have safety features such as wheelchair ramps, nonskid floor coverings, grab bars in hallways and bathrooms, fire alarms, and sprinkler systems. Some residents are moderately active, even if the activity is sitting in a chair. Other residents must remain in bed all day, but they are dressed and well groomed. Well-run nursing homes also offer recreational activities, as well as healthy, attractive foods at meals. Residents have privacy for phone calls, visits of family and friends, and personal care such as bathing or dressing. They are allowed to decorate their rooms with their personal belongings. However, these facilities can be extremely costly, and private or public health insurance programs such as Medicaid or Medicare may not cover those costs.

When considering whether to place an elderly parent in a nursing home, adult children should inspect any prospective facilities carefully. Many nursing homes are little more than unsafe institutions where the elderly and dying are shut out of sight. Hazards of poor institutions include unclean facilities with no safety modifications, poorly trained and overworked staff, and inadequate care. In a 2003 report by the American Association of Retired Persons (AARP), more than one-third (36.2 percent) of nursing homes in the United States did not meet federal health and safety standards, and nearly one-third (30.5 percent) were deficient in the quality of care they offered.

In the 1999 National Nursing Home Survey, researchers concluded that the low standards of these facilities may be partly due to profit motives. About 67 percent of nursing homes are privately owned and operated. Because the owners want to make a profit, they may try to keep costs as low as possible, sometimes by providing inadequate care.

ASSISTED LIVING CENTERS

Assisted living centers are the fastest growing residential services available for older adults. Assisted living offers services tailored to those who do not require round-the-clock skilled nursing care but who do need extra help in performing daily tasks.

Usually less expensive than nursing homes, most assisted living centers provide an environment that is more like a home and less like a hospital. These facilities provide housing and care to frail older persons or persons with disabilities while maintaining an emphasis on independence and privacy.

Most assisted living centers offer private rooms or apartments along with large common areas for activities and meals. A staff is on call 24 hours a day to help with the activities of daily living such as bathing, dressing, and getting to meals, as well as housekeeping and laundry. Other services offered at most facilities are medication reminders and assistance in taking medications, transportation, security, health monitoring, social activities, and recreation. Many centers offer graduated levels of care, from transportation and social activities to full-time, skilled nursing. Quality facilities also offer care management—an ongoing assessment and reevaluation of the medical, functional, emotional and social needs of the resident.

The primary goal of assisted living is to allow the resident to live with as much independence and autonomy as possible while minimizing the risks associated with that independence. For instance, if a resident enjoys cooking but forgets to turn off the stove, the staff can provide supervision and reminders that allow the resident to enjoy that activity without endangering anyone.

ADULT DAY CARE

Adult day care centers, sometimes called adult day services, provide an alternative to residential care for the elderly. Adult day care facilities provide health and therapeutic care, as well as social activities, for physically and cognitively impaired older adults. At the same time, they offer family caregivers a break, or respite, from full-time care of aging parents or grandparents. The number of adult day care centers in the United States grew from 300 in 1978 to 2,100 in the 1980s. In 2002, there were more than 4,000 adult day care centers in the United States, according to the National Adult Day Services Association (NADSA). According to NADSA, the rapid increase in adult day care centers is due partly to an increased emphasis on home- and community-based care.

Adult daycare centers offer supervised care for people with chronic illnesses, traumatic brain injuries, developmental disabilities, and other problems that interfere with their ability to care for themselves but who live in their own homes or with a relative. Adult day care centers originated as a way of providing a break to family caregivers. These facilities continue to offer a respite for family caregivers, especially those who work or who need some time away from their loved one to complete projects, socialize, or simply take some time for themselves.

Adult day care centers generally fall into three categories:

- Social care, which offers social activities, meals, recreation, and some health-related services;
- Health care, which provides health, social, and therapeutic service for those with severe medical problems and who might otherwise need nursing home care; or
- Alzheimer's-specific adult day care, which serves only persons with Alzheimer's disease or related dementia.

Care is usually provided during weekdays and working hours, which allows family caregivers to continue working even when an elderly parent needs 24-hour care. Most adult day care centers do not provide services on weekends, although some, especially those with religious affiliations, may offer half-day services on Sundays. The range of services provided often includes personal care, transportation, meals, health screening and monitoring, educational programs, counseling, and rehabilitative services. Skilled nursing services are available at most sites, as is transportation. Some centers offer transportation at no extra cost, while others charge by the trip or number of miles.

When choosing an adult day care facility, caregivers should ask if the facility staff performs a needs assessment to determine the person's range of abilities and needs and develops an individualized treatment plan for each participant. The facility should be inspected for cleanliness and safety features. The range of activities and services offered should be clearly explained by the staff. Caregivers and the elderly patient should then determine if the adult day care center meets their needs.

A FAMILY MEMBER WITH ALZHEIMER'S

Alzheimer's disease is a progressive, degenerative brain disorder. People with Alzheimer's experience memory loss, disorientation, changes in behavior, and loss of thinking abilities. As Alzheimer's disease progresses, they gradually lose the ability to speak and move. Alzheimer's disease is most common in people over 65, although it can affect persons of any age. As people live longer, the prevalence of Alzheimer's disease is increasing. In August 2003, Rush–Presbyterian–St. Luke's Medical Center in Chicago published a study of current and future estimates of the prevalence of Alzheimer's disease in the U.S. population. The researchers estimated that about 4.5 million people in the United States had Alzheimer's disease in 2000. They predicted that 13.2 million older Americans will have Alzheimer's disease by 2050 unless new ways are found to prevent or treat the disease. The largest increases will be among the very old. Of people in that age group, 8 million may have the disease. In the middle-old age group, 4.8 million will have Alzheimer's. The disease will affect about half a million people age 65–74, about the same number as it does today.

Although no cure for Alzheimer's disease exists, some drugs can help control symptoms. People with Alzheimer's live an average of eight years after being diagnosed; some may live for as many as 20 years. The financial and emotional costs of the disease are untold. The stresses on families, children, and other caregivers are so great that Alzheimer's is often called the "family disease." The chronic stress of watching a loved one slowly decline in mental and physical functioning causes problems for everyone in the person's family and caregiving network.

A person with Alzheimer's may be unable to respond to affection and caring, making it difficult for family members to provide compassionate and consistent care. Instead of being thankful for help provided by children or other caregivers, some people with Alzheimer's disease become verbally abusive, violent, and dangerous to themselves and others. During the early stages of the disease, the person may seem perfectly all right one moment and disoriented a few moments later. Such behavior can be disconcerting to family members, for the elderly parent may appear to be getting better and then worse when, in fact, this is just a normal progression of the disease.

As Alzheimer's progresses, the stress on family members increases. A treatment program for anyone with Alzheimer's disease should take into consideration the needs of the family. Training and support groups can help family members learn how to control unwanted behaviors, improve communication, and keep the person with Alzheimer's—as well as themselves—safe. The Family Caregiver Alliance recommends that caregivers prepare themselves in specific ways for each stage of the disease. During the first stage, the emphasis should be on education, emotional support, and planning for the future.

Family members who are caring for the parent with Alzheimer's need the emotional support of other family members, friends, and other sources. Counseling and support groups can help caregivers deal with the emotional issues that arise as the parent progressively declines. The person's role in the family changes as a result of the disease, which can bring up many issues in the family. An Alzheimer's patient will gradually lose the ability to perform tasks ranging from maintaining household finances to remembering to take out the trash. Families should consult a lawyer to help them to ensure that the elderly parent is cared for by family members and that his or her finances remain in trusted hands.

In middle-stage Alzheimer's, the patient needs full-time supervision and family members need to find options for respite, in or out of the home. Safety becomes paramount, both for the person with Alzheimer's and for caregivers. An occupational therapist can offer advice about home modification and devices that can make the home safer. Family members must act as the person's medical care spokesperson, communicating with physicians and other healthcare providers and making decisions about which course of medical care to pursue. Some families may find this an appropriate time to investigate options other than in-home care.

As Alzheimer's progresses to late-stage, caregivers are faced with the end of their parent's life. If the person is still living at home or with a family, consideration should be given to placement in a skilled nursing facility. Hospice services, which are designed to support individuals at the end of life, may help to ease the burden on family members and provide dignified death. Hospice services include support groups, visiting nurses, pain management, and home care. These services are arranged through a physician, usually when the physician recognizes that the person is six months or less from the end of life.

PAYING THE BILLS

As people age, health-care costs increase and incomes go down. Findings from the 2003 MetLife Market Survey of Nursing Home and

Home Care Costs show that the average daily cost of a private room in a nursing home is $181.24—about $5,500 a month or more than $65,000 a year. A companion survey of assisted living facilities, also performed by MetLife researchers, showed that the average monthly cost of care in an assisted living facility was $2,379 in 2003, or $28,548 annually. The price of adult day care, according to the National Adult Day Services Association, averages $56 a day, which can add up to more than $20,000 annually. The Alzheimer's Association reports that 70 percent of Alzheimer's patients live at home, where three-fourths of their care is provided by family and friends. Even with family caregiving, the average lifetime cost of health care for a person with Alzheimer's is $174,000, a cost that few families can afford.

These expenses stand in stark contrast to the declining incomes of many elderly family members. Data from the U.S. Census Bureau show that in 2003, 10.2 percent of people age 65 and over lived below the federal poverty level of $9,393 per year for a single person. The percentage of people in poverty increases as they enter the middle-old and oldest-old groups. Gender also affects the likelihood that a person will live out their last years in poverty. Census 2000 data show that of people 65 and older, 7 percent of men and 15 percent of women were living below the poverty level in 2003.

Ethnicity and race are factors in the probability that an older person lives in poverty. Among people 65 and older, almost 24 percent of African Americans, 19.5 percent of Hispanic Americans, and 14 percent of Asian Americans age 65 and older were living in poverty in 2003. During that same year, fewer than 9 percent of white Americans older than 65 years of age were living in poverty.

Many people assume, wrongly, that Medicare and standard health insurance plans will cover the costs associated with in-home care, nursing homes, or assisted living centers. Unfortunately, this is not usually the case. The Family Caregiver Alliance suggests that families review their insurance coverage and investigate public and private sources of healthcare financing. When considering a facility, families should investigate exactly what costs are included in the standard monthly or daily charge, and which services—transportation, nursing care, meals, medications, laundry—will involve additional charges. Several sources of funding for long-term care exist:

- **Long-term care** health insurance plans can help people protect personal assets and inheritance while offering more options in the choice of care environments. Federal health legislation enacted in 2000 helped to make private long-term insurance an option in paying for long-term care costs without loss of personal savings, dignity, or choice. For a person age 50, the average annual premium for a long-term care policy is less than $1,000; at age 65, it is about $1,800; at 79, it is about $5,500.

- **Medicare** is a federal health insurance program for people 65 and over and certain disabled people under 65. Long-term care is not covered by Medicare nor are assisted living costs. Some short-term services such as physical therapy are paid for by Medicare. Nursing facility coverage is extremely limited.

- **Medicaid** is a federal-state program that provides health-care assistance to low-income people. Medicaid is the major payer for nursing home services. In some states, it also offers limited coverage of assisted living services and adult day care. To qualify for Medicaid, the person needing care must prove that his or her financial resources have been depleted. If the person is married, states allow the at-home spouse to retain enough from the couple's income to bring the at-home spouse's income to 150 percent of the federal poverty level for a two-person household.

- The Department of Veterans Affairs, the government agency that offers benefits and services to people who have served in the armed forces, provides care to veterans who need nursing care, both in its own facilities and through contracts with community nursing homes. All veterans qualify for these services.

ELDERLY FAMILY MEMBERS MOVING IN

While nursing homes, day care, home nursing, assisted living, and other community care services are important resources for persons in late adulthood, the most important resource an elderly person can have is a responsible and caring family. Most elderly people prefer to remain in their own homes, where they can maintain independence and privacy. Likewise, most adults prefer to live in separate homes from their parents. Both parents and grown children, if given a choice, would live close enough so that visiting is easy while maintaining separate households. Community support programs such as "Meals on Wheels," which offers free meals to homebound seniors, can help seniors to remain in their own homes.

As the care needs of an elderly family member increase, families often relocate the person into the adult child's home. Data from the U.S. census show that in 1998, about one out of 10 men and one out of five women age 65 years and older were living in the homes of their adult children.

The decision for an elderly parent to move into an adult child's home requires careful consideration of the needs of the parent, the adult child, and the other family members. Providing extensive care for someone with severe medical, functional, and cognitive problems can cause extreme stress and hardship for caregivers. Family members should openly discuss all possible options for care of the elderly parent, the role each person will play in the transition, changes in lifestyle, management of finances, and safety modifications to the home.

TEENS SPEAK

My Grandfather Lives with Us

My grandfather moved in with us about two years ago, when I was 15. Before that, I saw him once or twice a year at his home in Georgia. The last time was at my sister's wedding. He danced the whole night. So when, on a windy mid-February Chicago day two months after the wedding, an old man in a wheelchair arrived at our house, it was hard to believe that it was my grandfather. He had suffered a stroke and couldn't use his right hand or leg. I felt embarrassed for him on that first night as I watched my mother cut his meat into small pieces so he could eat it.

I helped my dad build wheelchair ramps and install bars in the bathrooms and hallways so my grandfather could get around the house. He couldn't go upstairs because of the wheelchair, so I had to move out of my room on the first floor. He was really grumpy at first. He complained about my music, my hairstyle, my clothes, and my friends.

I'll confess, I was angry. After all, I had done everything I could to make him feel at home, even given up my room. And all he could do was complain. But one evening when I was watching television and Granddad was sitting in his wheelchair, playing a solitary game of checkers, he asked me to give him the remote control. I thought he was going to change the channel, but instead, he turned the television off and asked if I had time to talk. I couldn't think of any excuses to get away. He told me he was sorry for making life harder for my family and that he was thankful for all we were doing for him. He said he had a lot of stories he would like to tell before he died, and he asked me if I would help him write them down.

That was how I started getting to know my grandfather. About three times a week, we sit down with a tape recorder and a pen and paper, and I write and ask him questions about his life. I never knew what an interesting life he had led. He told me about growing up on a farm in northern Minnesota, meeting my grandmother, fighting in Vietnam, and many other things I never knew about him. He may not be able to do many of the things he used to do anymore, but I've learned a lot about him and the rest of my family, including things my mother never knew.

When an elderly family member moves into an adult child's home, traditional roles change. The elderly parent may no longer be able to act as a parent—making decisions, giving direction and guidance, and determining the best choices for family members. The family's children may need to assist with household responsibilities and with care of the grandparent. Agreements should be developed about lifestyle issues such as bedtimes and nap times, food choices at mealtimes, and noise levels in the house.

Although the integration of an elderly parent into an adult child's home may be difficult and challenging, many adult children find it rewarding to be able to give support and care to their parents. For grandchildren, living with a grandparent can be a chance to learn about family history and family connectedness.

Q & A

Question: How can I deal with my grandparents' divorce?

Answer: Your divorcing grandparents need your support more than ever. Divorce is difficult for any couple, but for those over 60, divorce can be devastating. Late-life divorce can negatively affect the relations between parents and young adult children. In 1994, sociologist W. S. Aquilino studied 3,281 young adults whose parents divorced late in life. Aquilino found a marked decrease in the quality of parent-child relations. You may need to make an extra effort to maintain contact with both of your grandparents. Remember, they're divorcing each other, not you. Set aside some time to spend with each of them. Ask your grandparents questions about their lives. You might be surprised by what you find.

Late adulthood is often a time of transition from independence to physical dependence. These changes can be difficult for the elderly family member to accept. Nursing homes, assisted living facilities, and adult day care services offer care ranging from help with personal tasks to skilled nursing care.

When elderly parents move into their adult children's homes, the parent, the adult child, and other family members are all affected. Caregiving can be stressful, but it can also be rewarding.

See also: Day Care; Death in the Family; Family, The New; Family, The Traditional; Financial Management, Marital; Marriage and Family, Changes in; Religion and the Family

FURTHER READING

Breitung, Joan Carson. *The Eldercare Sourcebook.* Lincolnwood, IL: NTC Publishing Group. 2002.

Loverde, Joy. *Complete Eldercare Planner: Where to Start, Which Questions to Ask, and How to Find Help.* New York: Crown Publishing Group, 2000.

Pipher, Mary Bray. *Another Country: Navigating the Emotional Terrain of Our Elders*. New York: Riverhead Trade, 2000.

▪ FAMILIES, BLENDED
A family created when a divorced or widowed person marries someone who may or may not have been married before. One or both spouses may bring children from a previous marriage to the new union. Blended families are also called **reconstituted families** or **stepfamilies**.

REMARRIAGES
About half of all Americans have been or will be in a blended family at some time during their lives. In 1998, the last year in which the Census Bureau collected data on remarriages, almost half of all new marriages—46 percent—were remarriages for the husband, wife, or both. Children from previous marriages are often brought to the new relationship. Data from the 2000 census show that in that year, an estimated 3.2 million children were living with a stepparent. More than one-third of all children in the United States will live in a blended family before they reach the age of 18.

Census Bureau data of 2001 indicate that about two-thirds of people who divorce each year eventually remarry. Most remarriages occur within a few years of divorce. The median interval between divorce and remarriage is three years for women and four and one-half years for men. Whether a divorced person remarries, and how quickly, is influenced by ethnic background. The rate of remarriage is highest for whites, who also remarry most quickly. Latinos are slower to remarry, while African Americans are less likely to remarry at all. In 1998, 44 percent of white women had remarried within three years of a divorce, while 20 percent of African-American women and 23 percent of Latina women had remarried. The lower rates of remarriage among African-American women may be partly due to the lack of availability of single, economically stable African-American men.

Remarriages are slightly more likely to end in divorce than first marriages, which means that about half of the children who experience one parental divorce will experience a second. The chance that a remarriage will end in divorce is greater when one or both spouses have children from previous relationships. In "Labor Market and

Socioeconomic Effects on Marital Stability," a 1995 study of the effects of economic factors on marriages that dissolved between the mid-1960s and the mid-1980s, sociologists Jessie Tzeng and Robert Mare found that couples in which the woman is remarried are almost twice as likely to divorce as couples in which the man is the remarried partner. They hypothesized that this may be partly due to the greater likelihood that a woman who remarries will bring children to the relationship. Tzeng and Mare noted that the rate of divorce is 50 percent higher in marriages in which children are present than in those in which there are no children from previous marriages.

Fact Or Fiction?

Blended families are just like other families.

Fact: Expecting a blended family to function exactly like a biological family can lead to surprise, disappointment, and bewilderment. Parents and children can both play into this dynamic. Stepparents, having been married previously, may expect that they will quickly jump into their new parenting role, only to be surprised when stepchildren don't react to them as they do to their biological parents. Children may feel jealous of their biological parent's new spouse. Teens are likely to reject any attempt by the stepparent to act like a parent. Blended families do better when family members recognize that relationships between the individuals in blended families differ from those in biological families. Time is required to build a sense of family. The remarriage of a parent is usually accompanied by a very unstable period, which may last for as long as five to seven years. In most blended families, restabilization occurs after five years, with relationship patterns becoming more like those in non-divorced families. Blended families must create flexible family boundaries to navigate an often-complex network of custodial and noncustodial parents and extended family members. Stepparents should also recognize that they cannot replace a biological parent and may need to create their own nontraditional parenting role.

Women continue to be more likely to be the custodial parent from a previous marriage. Census Bureau data show that in 2002, 85 percent of the 13.4 million custodial parents in the United States were women.

Children's adjustment to a parent's remarriage is affected by their age, according to the American Psychological Association (APA). In a nine-year longitudinal study funded by the National Institute of Child Health and Human Development, published in the *Journal of Family Psychology*, James Bray, a researcher and clinician at the department of family medicine at Baylor College of Medicine, found that adjustment to parental remarriage seems to be most difficult for children ages 10 to 14.

Bray's results showed that before age 10, children are generally more accepting of a new adult in the family, especially if the adult is a positive influence. Children ages 10 to 14 may have had more difficulty adjusting to a parent's remarriage, partly because they are going through the emotional and physiological changes of adolescence, forming their own identities, and separating from their families. At the same time that the new blended family is trying to establish close ties, young teens are testing their independence. Still, as they experiment with issues of identity and independence, they need a stable family framework to provide continuity. Teens age 15 and older in Bray's sample fared better, in part, because they may need less parenting and have less investment in stepfamily life.

THE PERCEPTION OF PLAYING FAVORITES

Blended families involve complicated networks of relationship. A child may have relationships with a custodial mother, a noncustodial father, a stepfather, two sets of biological grandparents, stepgrandparents, siblings, and step-siblings. Half of all women who remarry will bear a child with the new spouse, adding yet another layer of complexity to family relationships. In this complex network of relationships, it is all too easy for the parent, the new spouse, and the children to appear to favor one child over another.

Several studies, including Bray's, also found that children may resist the new stepparent's entry into the family and perceive him or her as intruding into their relationship with the custodial parent or cutting off their relationship with the noncustodial parent. They may have been hoping that their parents will get back together; a parent's remarriage forces them to face the reality that their parents' marriage is over.

Tensions can create competition between the new spouse and the partner's children. Children may feel jealous of the time and attention their parent is giving to the new spouse. In turn, the new spouse may resent the time and attention the parent gives to stepchildren. Parents may feel guilty about the emotional turmoil and upheaval that children experienced at the ending of their former marriage and try to make up for it by overindulging the child. Any of these or similar situations can result in the perception of playing favorites.

Q & A

Question: How can I get along with my new stepmother?

Answer: Your new stepmother probably feels about as nervous about your relationship as you do. Ask her if you can do something together that you both enjoy. It might be taking a walk, getting an ice cream cone, or taking a drive. Just be sure that it's a setting where you'll have time to talk with her without interruptions. You may feel angry and resentful toward your stepmother; that's okay. You don't have to love her right now. Treat her with respect and let her know that you expect her to do the same for you. Remember that you don't have to choose between your biological mother and your stepmother. You can develop a special, separate relationship with each of them. You have two adult women in your life who can mentor you and help you face life's challenges.

GETTING ALONG: ISSUES FOR STEPCHILDREN

For most children, the remarriage of a parent means the introduction of not only another adult into their home but also new siblings. Children may suddenly be required to share a bedroom that was once their personal domain. **Sibling rivalry**—the competition between brothers and sisters for their parents' attention, approval, and affection—may be magnified in stepfamilies.

TEENS SPEAK

I Was Furious About Having a New Stepsister

Three years after my dad and mom divorced, he started dating Anna, who is now my stepmom. I liked Anna, but it was hard to think that my dad was dating another woman besides my mom. But when, about a year later, he told me that he and Anna were getting married and that she and her daughter Michelle were going to move into our house, I was furious.

It was the only house I had ever lived in. Dad and I had stayed there after my parents' divorce. I felt like the house was the only thing left of my parents' marriage. Having Anna in *my* house was going to be bad enough, but being required to share my space with Michelle was even worse. To me, it was simple: Michelle was an invader in my space. I stayed angry for a long time after the wedding. I made no excuses. I hated Michelle, and I told her so to her face. She told me the same thing. We fought about dumb things like whose turn it was to clean up after dinner. You might as well have declared war than have the two of us in the same room with one television. Whoever had the remote control would mastermind the channels while the other complained noisily about how lousy the show was. One day I finally got fed up and unplugged the television. Dad and Anna had to stop us before we hurt each other.

Something happened that night. Michelle and I were both crying and angry. I remember looking at her and realizing that she felt just as hurt and scared and disappointed as I did about our parents' divorcing and remarrying. I knew that no matter how miserable I made life for Michelle, she and Anna were staying. They were the family that I had, and I could accept that or fight it and make life miserable for all of us.

It's been six years now since Michelle and Anna moved in. I'll be leaving for college in the fall. And you know what? I'm going to miss her. We may not be biological sisters, but I'm glad to have her as my stepsister. After all, she knows what it's like to live through your parents' divorce and remarriage.

The first reactions of step-siblings to each other do not always predict the future. Children can seem distant, jealous, and uncertain of each other at first, then develop a relationship of trust and loyalty. Older step-siblings may become protective of younger step-siblings, who, in turn, may idolize older siblings. Relationships between biological siblings may be more contentious than between step-siblings, especially during the teenage years, according to psychologist E. Mavis Hetherington. She suggests that the difference may be due to a lack of a clear definition of step-sibling roles. Also step-siblings may not be as closely involved in each other's lives as biological siblings, which leads to less conflict.

When a remarried woman gives birth, the effect on siblings and step-siblings appears to be positive. Many couples report that having a baby improves step-sibling relationships. In *Coping with Divorce: A Risk and Resiliency Perspective*, Hetherington and colleagues present the results of "The Dynamics of Parental Remarriage," a study that found no children responded negatively to the birth of a new step-sibling. Hetherington and her colleagues suggest that the arrival of a new baby can help the two groups of children form a bond.

FINANCES: YOUR MONEY, MY MONEY

Finances, an issue in many marriages, can be an especially hot topic for remarried couples. A divorced and remarried father may need to pay child support to his ex-wife, maintain the new household, and support his new partner's children. A divorced and remarried mother may contribute her earnings to the household, receive child support from her ex-husband, and help support her new partner's children.

In 1983, psychologist Barbara Fishman published "The Economic Behavior of Stepfamilies," a study of financial arrangements in blended families. Her widely cited study is still used by sociologists, demographers, pscyhologists, and other researchers. Fishman interviewed 100 people who lived in 16 middle-class blended families. She asked detailed questions about economic decisions within the families. Fishman found two common economic patterns used by blended families, which she called the **common-pot method** and the **two-pot method**.

Couples who use the common-pot approach pool their earnings in a joint account. Those earnings may include income from employment, child support, and other sources. The family distributes resources according to the needs of each family member, not according to biological relationship. For instance, the biological child of one parent may be attending college, which puts a strain on the entire family's resources. If the family uses the common-pot approach, the cost of the child's college education comes out of the shared household resources. In reality, it may mean that the child's stepmother may put off buying items such as a new car until the child finishes college.

The couples in Fishman's study who used the two-pot method contribute an agreed-upon amount to household maintenance but keep his or her own resources for personal use or to support biological children. Pooled resources are used to pay fixed expenses such as a mortgage, gas, and electricity. The children, however, are supported by their biological parents. In the example used above, the college expenses of the father's biological child would be his responsibility and the stepmother would be free to invest her personal resources in the new car.

Among the couples in Fishman's study, the two-pot method encouraged biologically related family members to maintain loyalties and personal autonomy, while the common-pot approach helped to unify the blended family. She concluded that the financial commitment that family members make appears to reflect their commitment and the strength of interpersonal bonds in the blended family. Financial commitment to a new spouse may be slow to develop, and a financial commitment to a new spouse's children may develop even more slowly, if at all.

WHO GIVES UP THE HOUSE?

Most people who remarry face the difficult decision of who will leave an established household. In general, remarrying couples have three options: she and her children (if any) move in with him, he and his children (if any) move in with her, or they both relocate to a new home. Employment, finances, and the roominess of the living space are primary factors in deciding who gives up the house.

According to the American Psychological Association, couples who choose the third option—relocating to a new house—are taking an important step toward building a unified blended family. In contrast to the tensions that may develop when one partner and children move into the other's space, moving into a new home allows both partners and their children to start fresh.

However, it may not be financially feasible for the new couple to buy a new home. If they stay in one partner's house, they have to modify established routines. Couples should carefully discuss available options with their children, especially preteens and teens.

NEW SCHOOL?

Teens who experience the remarriage of their custodial parent are also likely to change residences, and with that change may come a change in schools. Changing schools is a stressful event for anyone, but when combined with the stresses of adjusting to a blended family, it may be especially difficult. Even if the move is only to a different section of town, moving to a new school means less interaction with friends, familiar places, and routines.

For children of divorced parents, the disruptive effect of moving to a new school may be very strong. In the November 2002 issue of the *Journal of Marriage and the Family*, Kathleen Rodgers and Hilary Rose, researchers from Washington State University, demonstrated that the ability of teens to adjust to divorce—which they call adolescent resiliency—is strongly affected by the support they receive at school. The researchers studied 2,011 teens who lived in intact families, blended families, and single-parent families. The researchers evaluated the teens' level of parental support and nonfamily support and asked about risk-taking behaviors such as the use of alcohol or tobacco. While parental support and monitoring helped to decrease teens' self-destructive behaviors, nonfamily support was at least equally as important. Significantly, of all the nonfamily factors that the researchers examined, attachment to school had the greatest effect on a teen's mental well-being.

Teens *can* and do cope with the changes that a move to a new school brings. Attending a new school does not necessarily mean losing friendships. Visits with friends from the old school can help to ease the transition. Teens may feel embarrassed about the divorce and remarriage of their parents, but there is no reason for them to feel this way. It's almost a given that many other teens at the school also come from blended families.

The challenge of making friends at the new school is a big concern for many teens. At a new school, teens may have to go out of their way to introduce themselves to others. Indicators of shared interest are good places to start conversations. Getting involved in sports and other extracurricular activities can also help teens make new friends and adapt to a new school.

NEW STATE?

A parent's remarriage may mean that teens must relocate to a new state, far from friends, the noncustodial parent, and other family members. Moving far away from familiar people and places may bring up feelings of anxiety, sadness, and anger for all family members. Teens and preteens may resist moving away from a familiar home. This resistance is not mere stubbornness. According to the *American Psychological Association*, such resistance often reflects the important developmental work that they are doing in their lives. One aspect of this developmental work is learning how to form long-term relationships, including romantic ones. The prospect of moving seems to tear apart the ties that they have carefully been forming. Having to move because a parent remarries is also a harsh reminder that the teen is not yet an independent adult. When a parent's remarriage is accompanied by a move, the changes can seem overwhelming.

Parents and children of all ages can work together to make the move to a new state the first step toward creating a unified new blended family. According to TeenGrowth.com, a physician-reviewed Web site for teens, teens adapt better to a family relocation when they are involved in the move from the start. Many teens are adept internet users and can cybersurf to research the new community. Anxiety about the move may be lessened if the family visits the new home and becomes familiar with the new community and its resources.

Before the move, parents can schedule frequent family meetings to talk about the upcoming relocation and the changes it will bring for each member of the family. Each person should have a chance to express his or her feelings without criticism.

After the move, telephone calls, e-mails, letters, and visits from friends at the old school can help family members make the transition smoother. For some older teens—seniors in high school, for example—the best alternative might be to stay behind with a trusted family friend or relative for a year.

A blended family is created when a divorced or widowed person marries another person who may or may not have been married before. About half of all Americans have been or will be in a blended family at some time during their lives. Because children most often live with their mothers after divorce, most blended families include a biological mother, her children, and a stepfather. In this complex network of relationship, tensions and anger can erupt between family members. Couples who pool financial resources tend to display greater commitment. When parents remarry, teens and other family members may need to move. While these changes can be difficult, teens who actively participate in the move and maintain contact with their established lives, can eventually adjust.

See also: Arguments and the Family; Divorce and Families; Families, Divided; Families, Racially Mixed; Family, The New; Family, The Traditional; Financial Management, Marital; Marriage and Family, Changes in; Single-Parent Families; Stepparents

FURTHER READING

Block, Joel D., and Susan S. Bartell. *Stepliving for Teens: Getting Along with Stepparents and Siblings.* New York: Price Stern Sloan, 2001.

Bray, James H., and John Kelly. *Stepfamilies: Love, Marriage and Parenting in the First Decade.* New York: Broadway Books, 1999.

O'Connor, Anne. *The Truth about Stepfamilies: Real American Families Speak Out about What Works and What Doesn't When It Comes to Creating a Family Together.* New York: Avalon, 2003.

■ FAMILIES, DIVIDED

Conflict between family members that leads to short or long-term alienation of family members from each other is known as estrangement.

Conflicts may involve only two individuals, or family members may "take sides." Estrangement may last for days, weeks, years, or generations. Often, however, long-lasting divisions in families can be avoided or healed.

WHY FAMILIES DIVIDE

Divisions in families arise as a result of interpersonal conflict. Although definitions of interpersonal conflict vary, some sociologists define *interpersonal conflict* by focusing on actions—for example, "an interpersonal process that occurs whenever the actions of one person interfere with the actions of another." Others focus on the philosophy behind conflict, defining it as "interactions between persons expressing opposing interests, view, or opinions."

Divisions in families are often the result of intolerance. Family members may disapprove of each other's lifestyle choices, choice of mate, religious preferences, or educational choices, to name a few topics of frequent conflict. The decision to marry outside one's religion, race, nationality, or **ethnicity** may lead to long-term feuds between family members. Many families have broken apart when dividing a parent's estate. For instance, two sisters may become estranged over what one feels is the unfair division of their recently-deceased mother's belongings. The conflict may focus on a specific item, such as a cherished heirloom piece of jewelry, but the estrangement may really be about the lifelong dynamics between the sisters. The sister who did not receive the jewelry may feel that it is just another way in which her sister was always preferred by her mother and may overreact with anger, resentment, and estrangement.

Teens and parents may be especially vulnerable to conflict that is bitter and long-lasting. Emotions often run high for both teens and parents. Teens are working to establish their own identities and separate from their family. They are forming their own relationships, asking questions about the purpose of their lives, and forming their own beliefs and value systems, which may be markedly different from those of their parents. They are becoming more independent. Parents may react with fear and anger to teen's normal developmental process and his or her experiments with identity and separation from the family. These efforts may result in a reactive, rather than a responsive, cycle of fighting between the teen and his or her parents. The fight may seem to be about the teen's hairstyle or choice of clothing. In reality, the clothing or hairstyle may symbolize the real source of conflict—the teen's attempt to differentiate from the family, and the parents' resistance to those attempts.

COMPROMISE

Often, conflict can be resolved through **compromise**. In a compromise, both sides agree on a mutually acceptable solution that is not exactly what either wanted but is fair and meets each person's minimum needs. Both get some of their wishes fulfilled, but neither is totally satisfied. For instance, Tony may want to go to an American-style restaurant and Joan may prefer to go to a Chinese restaurant; they could compromise by going to a restaurant that serves both types of food. Compromise involves negotiation, a clearly thought-out approach to solving problems and considering all options. When negotiating a compromise, family members state their positions, exchange information in an objective manner, and work toward an acceptable solution.

NEW ALTERNATIVES

If intolerance is the tool that divides a family, tolerance is the key to mending family ties. Tolerance may start with education or acceptance of the other's beliefs and exploring alternative solutions. In many cases, feuding family members can use **integrative agreements** and accommodation to find creative ways to resolve the problem and restore peace.

In integrative agreements, a solution is found in which both parties can achieve their original goals and aspirations. While difficult to achieve, these types of agreements allow each party to pursue central goals while working within the boundaries of the other person's core goals. For instance, a teen and parent may be at odds about where the teen will go to college. They can start by identifying each other's central goals. The parent's central goal for both may be for the teen to attend a college of high academic standing at a reasonable price. The teen's central goal may be to go to a more expensive school because it has an excellent program in veterinary medicine, which she wants to study. The teen and parent may agree that she will start her studies at an in-state college, where tuition is less, take a part-time job, and then apply for scholarships that will allow her to transfer to the school she wants to attend. Integrative agreements require flexibility and **logrolling**, or making concessions on one issue if the other person will make concessions on another, while still maintaining commitment to central goals.

Fact Or Fiction?

Avoiding fights is the best way to handle disagreements.

Fact: There are "good" fights and "bad" fights. In good fights, the two people remain respectful of each other, listen carefully, validate the other's feelings, and own their own feelings. In bad fights, the two people go at each other mercilessly, with no restraints. Bad fights also occur when one or both people act manipulatively or lie. "Good" fighting is no easy task. It requires self-discipline, genuine caring about the other person, and self-awareness. It requires the ability to recognize and honestly state one's own feelings. But the potential rewards are great. Conflict, instead of leading to lasting feuds and divisions in families, can instead become a chance for everyone involved to grow closer, learn more about each other, and learn more about themselves. Instead of being something to be avoided at all costs, fighting fair can present a challenge and an opportunity for personal growth.

Caryl Rusbult, professor of psychology at the University of North Carolina at Chapel Hill and colleagues describe an alternative method of handling conflict, which they call accommodation. In accommodation, a person does not respond destructively to another person's destructive actions, but instead reacts in a constructive manner. Constructive responses might be loyalty, which involves optimistically waiting for conditions to improve, defending the partner in the face of criticism, or continuing to show signs of involvement. Another constructive response is to give voice to the issue by discussing it with the partner, changing behavior to solve the problem, or consulting a therapist or friend. Destructive responses might take the form of neglect, in which the offended person withdraws, avoids discussion of the problem, or nags the other person about unrelated issues. Exit is an actively destructive response in which the offended person leaves, threatens to end the relationship, or engages in abusive acts such as yelling or hitting.

According to Rusbult, people who are able to accommodate are usually responding out of **effective preferences**. Effective preferences are the actions people want to take when they focus on broad concerns, such as the long-term consequences of their actions and the implications for others. In contrast, **given preferences** are the actions people want to take when they focus only on short-term, self-centered, immediate reactions to an event. When accommodation does occur, it is likely to set in motion a positive cycle of increased trust and willingness to accommodate.

BEING FAIR AT ALL TIMES

Conflict is an inevitable part of life. When people who know each other closely and intimately fight, conflict can be difficult and devastating. Family members know enough about each other to "fight dirty," whether consciously or unconsciously. When families fight, it is especially important that they fight fair. Experts in conflict resolution offer a few suggestions for fighting fair and accomplishing goals:

- Set a time and place.

- Feuding family members should agree on a neutral place and a time that works for everyone. Launching into a fight unexpectedly makes it more likely that things will escalate.

- Establish ground rules. Ground rules should be established in the beginning. They might include allowing everyone to have their say, no interruptions, a system of signaling the wish to respond, and other principles of fairness.

- Be respectful. When feelings are hurt and anger is high, it is difficult to act respectfully toward another. But it is also the most important time to show respect to the other person. Avoid belittling, criticizing, or making fun of the other person. Blanket statements such as "you always" can lead to more animosity.

- Tackle the problem, not the person. The problem should be clearly defined in concrete terms. Who did what? When did they do it? How does it make the other person feel? Give everyone a chance to describe their feelings using statements that begin with "I." Do not seek to shame, belittle, or punish the other person. Name calling or attacking sensitive issues in a spirit of ill will, hatred, revenge, or contempt—"You are such a slob. Can't you ever pick up after yourself?"—will only deepen the conflict. Define the conflict as a problem to be solved by both people working together, not a war to be won.

- Communicate clearly. Each person should spend at least as much time listening as talking. Everyone should have a chance to say what they need to without interruption. Restate the other person's position to increase understanding: "So what I hear you saying is that you were frightened when I didn't come home until after 2:00 this morning?" Asking questions can help ensure that listeners understand before they explain their positions.

- Be creative. What solutions might there be that no one has thought of? Family members should take turns offering ideas for ways to develop or find workable solutions.
- Write a letter of agreement. Whatever solution is reached, it should be explicitly stated, written down, and shared with all family members.
- Reassess the agreement in a few weeks or months. How is it working? Does it need to be modified in any way? Does everyone still feel it is fair?

Q & A

Question: My father and I fight constantly about the way I keep my room. We haven't spoken since our last fight two months ago. How can I make peace with my father?

Answer: You might want to start by writing your father a letter in which you tell him about your desire to make peace with him. What do you want to say to him about your room? Is it really the state of your room you're fighting about, or are you two fighting about your ability to choose how to maintain your personal space? You may wish to consult a professional therapist or mediator for help in resolving these issues.

MAINTAINING CIVILITY

Laura Davis, author of *I Thought We'd Never Speak Again*, suggests that reconciliation is an ongoing continuum with a spectrum of possible outcomes. According to Davis, the most desired and most difficult to achieve is a deep and transformative reconciliation in which intimacy is reestablished, past hurts resolved, and family members feel closeness and satisfaction.

For example, one family member may be able to change his or her expectations so that interaction can occur with another family member in a positive and caring manner, whether or not the other person makes significant changes. In the third and most difficult type of resolution, much remains unresolved and ambivalent feelings are still present. Both people "agree to disagree" and establish ground rules that allow them to have a limited but courteous relationship. When they realize that no viable relationship is possible, the only option is to find resolution within themselves.

When violations in families are deep, such as in cases of physical or sexual abuse, or the parties cannot create a workable solution, an atmosphere of mutual civility may be all that is possible. Politeness and respect are integral to any interactions. Davis suggests that family members agree on "terms of engagement," or rules the two parties agree to so they can interact peacefully in limited circumstances. Terms of engagement might include avoiding discussions of certain volatile topics, requests that certain types of jokes or stories not be told, boundaries about touch, discussions about where, when, and how interactions should take place, or conditions under which family members are allowed to visit. In extremely difficult and conflicted situations, families should consider professional mediation.

Divisions in families arise as a result of interpersonal conflict between family members. Disputes over deeply held beliefs or values can lead to long-lasting alienation of family members from each other. Teens and parents may be especially vulnerable to divisive conflict, partly because teens are working to establish their own identities and separate from their family. Parents may react with fear and anger to teens' efforts to gain independence. But conflict does not always have to lead to estrangement. Resolving conflict usually requires effort, compromise, and agreement from all family members. By learning to fight fair when disputes do arise, family members can often preserve their relationships with each other, even if they cannot completely agree on a particular issue. Even when disputes cannot be reconciled, politeness and respect can help to preserve family relationships.

■ FAMILIES, RACIALLY MIXED

Families in which members are of different races are considered racially mixed. In an **interracial marriage,** the husband and wife are of different races. Children born to interracial couples are **biracial,** meaning a mixture of more than one race. In 2000 the census showed that more than one in six adopted children in the United States are a different race from their parents. William Frey, a census analyst from the Brookings Institution in Washington, says that about one in 15 marriages in the United States is interracial. That percentage, according to Frey, is up from one in 23 in 1990.

Most scholars today regard race as a meaningless concept in science because human beings, regardless of their race, are more alike than different. Race, however, has social importance. Because it is a social concept, its meaning varies with the time and the place. For example, the 1870 census divided the population into five races: white, colored (blacks), colored (mulattoes or mixed race), Chinese, and Native American. By 1950, the census categories reflected a different social understanding: white, black, and other.

In 1980, the U.S. census categories reflected the arrival of new groups as a result of a change in the nation's immigration laws. The census now labeled race categories as white, black, Hispanic, Japanese, Chinese, Filipino, Korean, Vietnamese, American Indian, Asian Indian, Hawaiian, Guamanian, Samoan, Eskimo, Aleut, and other. In England that same year, the categories were white, West Indian, African, Arab, Turkish, Chinese, Indian, Pakistani, Bangladeshi, Sri Lankan, and other. In South Africa in 1980, there were only four racial categories: white, African, "coloured" (mixed race) and Asian. Each of these systems of racial classification reflected a different social, economic, and political reality. As social situations change, so do racial categories and other understandings of a racially mixed family.

According to the 2000 census, 7 million persons in the United States identified themselves as belonging to more than one race. This number represented slightly more than 2 percent of the population. The 2000 census was the first census to allow individuals to identify themselves as belonging to more than one race. Researcher Donna Nakazawa estimates that by the year 2030, as many as 10 percent of the United States population will consider themselves multiracial.

ACCEPTANCE BY SOCIETY

Although the number of racially mixed families is on the rise, interracial marriage continues to be a source of conflict among some family members and friends. Researcher Peggy Gillespie believes that the debate over adding multiracial categories to the U.S. census forms in 2000 illustrated the deeply embedded role race plays in American life and the way it continues to divide the nation.

Transracial adoption, the adoption of a child of one race by parents of another, has also generated controversy, debate, and discussion. As recently as 1987, 35 states had laws prohibiting the adoption of African-American children by white families. In 1996, President Bill Clinton signed into law a bill that made it illegal to prohibit adoptions based on race.

TEENS SPEAK

I Didn't Even Notice I Was Different

When I was younger, I didn't even notice that I was a different race than the other kids in school. But when I hit fifth grade everyone started to make jokes about my being adopted. At first it didn't really bother me because my parents had always told me how I came to live in my family. After a while the teasing stopped, probably because I tried not to show them that it bothered me. But it did make me more aware of how I am different and how I am the same as everyone else. My parents have always taught me about the country I was born in. I am actually pretty lucky to know so much about life there and life here. I wouldn't change my story; I think I am more open-minded about other people. And I know I don't judge people as much as others judge me. It really helps to have parents that love and accept you for who you are and not how you look.

Both transracial adoptions and interracial marriages are helping to break down racial barriers. Adam Pertman, an adoption expert, attributes an increase in biracial births to the 1967 Supreme Court decision in the case of *Loving v. Virginia*. The decision declared state laws banning interracial marriage unconstitutional. Experts on racially mixed families also suggest that increased interaction among the races at schools and in the workplace further contribute to a greater acceptance of these kinds of families.

Francis Wardle is executive director of the Center for the Study of Biracial Children and adjunct professor at the University of Phoenix–Colorado. He believes that multicultural education in workplaces and schools, teacher training related to issues of diversity, and the promotion of antibias programs nationwide have also led to greater acceptance of racially mixed families.

WHERE DO WE FIT?

Although researchers have documented greater acceptance of racially mixed families, some children still grapple with issues of identity. According to the Center for the Study of Biracial Children, many children are uncertain as to which race they belong. As children mature, they become curious about their racial background, particularly if they must contend with prejudice about their own appearance or the appearance of their parents and siblings. By the time they reach adolescence, children want to know where and how they fit into various social groups and communities. In a study that examined issues in racially mixed families, Elias Cheboud and Chris Downing, researchers from the Capital Region Race Relations Association, found that many children begin to feel societal pressure to choose the identity of one race over another during adolescence.

Even adults may feel that they do not fit in, according to Cheboud and Downing. While few multiracial families feel totally secure, fitting in is becoming easier, experts say. Biracial activist Matt Kelley insists that most families can fit in without choosing sides.

Q & A

Question: How do most biracial children identify themselves?

Answer: As a result of a trend toward increased tolerance nationwide, children are more open about their multiracial background, according to Francis Wardle, executive director of the Center for the Study of Biracial Children. While identity issues may continue for some biracial children, more and more children feel comfortable identifying themselves as racially mixed or talking freely of their experience growing up in a racially mixed family.

IMPACT ON TEENS

While some teens struggle with issues of identity relating to their multiracial background, many do not. In fact, some teens say that the expectation that they will have difficulty is problematic in and of itself. Teens who seek support at the Center for the Study of Biracial

Children say that it is frustrating when people expect them to have problems just because of race. Most often the issues they struggle with have more to do with being a teenager than with anything else.

But other teens are uncomfortable with the way their peers react to their biracial identity. They point to feelings of rejection from their peer group, not being taken seriously by others, being subjected to intolerant remarks, and exclusion from social events as particularly troublesome.

The identity issues and the feelings of exclusion that some biracial children describe can lead to behavioral problems, according to the Oregon Alliance of Children's Programs that is part of the juvenile justice system. The group conducted a survey in 2002 that shows that the fastest-growing segment of youths entering the criminal justice system are multiracial youths. The survey also found that many of the children that enter the system have been victimized in some way. Kelly, founder of the Maven Foundation, a nonprofit organization aimed at raising awareness about multiracial children and their concerns, says more resources need to be created that celebrate multiracial youths and inform parents and educators about their issues.

With numbers of biracial teens on the rise, many teens date people of other races. Some of these teens cannot understand why their parents who are accepting of racially mixed friendships draw the line at interracial dating. This phenomenon, experts say, illustrates how much further society needs to go to accept racially mixed relationships of all kinds.

See also: Adoption; Family, The New

FURTHER READING

Dalmage, Heather M. *Tripping on the Color Line.* New Brunswick, NJ: Rutgers University Press, 2000.

Gaskins, Pearl. *What Are You?* New York: Henry Holt Company, 1999.

Nakazawa, Donna Jackson. *Does Anybody Else Look Like Me? A Parent's Guide to Raising Multiracial Children.* New York: Perseus Publishing, 2003.

Reginald, Daniel G. *More Than Black.* Philadelphia: Temple University Press, 2001.

Root, Maria, and Matt Kelley, eds. *The Multiracial Child Resource Book.* Seattle: Mavin Foundation, 2003.

■ FAMILY, THE NEW

The traditional family in the United States has long been a nuclear family—two parents and their unmarried children. Today, fewer children live in such families. More and more children grow up in extended families, single-parent families, blended families, alternative families, or culturally or racially mixed families. An extended family consists of three or more generations. Alternative families may include parents who are gay or lesbian, bisexual, or transgender. In a culturally or racially mixed family, family members may differ from one another in language, ethnicity, religion, or race.

EXTENDED FAMILIES

An extended family consists of three or more generations who share a household. One example of an extended family is one in which a widowed grandmother lives with her married daughter, son-in-law, and grandchildren. The grandmother may help to raise the children while the parents are working. Extended families may live together for a variety of reasons—to save money, help raise children, or care for a member who is ill. Sometimes grandparents take care of their grandchildren full time if the children's parents cannot.

The 2000 U.S. census showed that 2.3 million households had an adult living with a parent. This arrangement is most common among immigrants and in cities with housing shortages and high costs.

In the United States, according to social worker George W. Doherty in his report *Extended Families*, immigrant families are often extended by choice and necessity. His research shows, for example, that many Mexican-American parents rely on the support of their extended family. Family members share not only child care, but also the care of elderly relatives.

TEENS SPEAK

It's Different Growing Up in an Extended Family

I'm Chinese American, and I can tell you that leaving home at a certain age is not a part of Chinese culture. The Chinese believe that a child's leaving home is based on his or her maturity. My parents believe that it is better to not leave home until you marry! Otherwise you are not being respectful. Your parents would think you don't love them. Even when you graduate from college, your parents still must take care of you. So I can't move out until I marry, even though I've told my parents that they will save money if I leave. I have told them many times that I will always love them—even if I leave home.

In a statement in 2003, President George W. Bush praised families who choose to take care of elderly or ill relatives at home:

Millions of Americans make extraordinary efforts every day to care for loved ones who are elderly, chronically ill, or disabled. These caregivers make many sacrifices to improve the lives of their loved ones. Through their love, dedication, and courage, these compassionate children, parents, spouses, grandparents, and extended family members strengthen and preserve the importance of family and reflect the true character of our nation.

Living in an extended family can be difficult because individuals have less privacy and less independence than in a nuclear family. It may also be hard to provide everyone with the attention he or she requires. According to a 2001 guide to extended family relationships published by *Resources for Living*, a counseling group that works with many such families, these tensions can be reduced by setting clear boundaries.

ALTERNATIVE FAMILIES

Alternative families are those created by unmarried heterosexual couples, homosexual couples, bisexuals, or transgender persons. Children in such families may be a result of artificial insemination or adoption.

Q & A

Question: Are gay people allowed to adopt?

Answer: Many state laws allow any adult person to adopt. However, even in those states, courts may not be willing to allow gays to adopt.

States that do not permit gays or lesbians to adopt are Florida, Mississippi, and Utah.

According to the U.S. Census Bureau, in 1998 about 167,000 gay parents were rearing children under 15 years of age. The 2000 census reported that 94,000 adopted children were living with single parents who had never been married.

Because the state does not always recognize relationships in alternative families, these families often have to draw up legal documents that protect the rights of family members to inherit property, participate in medical decision making, and share in the guardianship of children.

For example, prior to starting a family, lawyer Elizabeth Schwartz suggests that prospective gay parents make a formal agreement in which they spell out their intent to cooperate with each other in rearing a child. Schwartz also advises these parents to formally state what their respective monetary contributions will be and what should happen if one partner dies or the couple decides to separate.

Parents in alternative relationships often experience discrimination by the larger society and even their own families. Many turn to parenting groups and other support systems to help them make up for that loss.

Fact Or Fiction?

It is safer for children who are part of an alternative family to remain silent about their parents.

Fact: According to the Family Pride Coalition's *Issues and News* 2004, children in alternative families do need to be careful before they speak openly about their living arrangements. Doing so in some situations may be dangerous. However, not talking about their families may imply that something is wrong with the way they live. It is crucial for schools to foster safe places for children to talk about their families and to know that their families are okay.

According to a review of research in the 1990s by Geri R. Donenberg, a professor of psychiatry at the University of Illinois at

Chicago, children reared in alternative families, such as those headed by gays and lesbians, are very similar to those who grow up with heterosexual parents. For example, the American Academy of Pediatrics studied children of gay parents in 2002 in terms of the psychosocial aspects of family health. The group found no significant differences between children of gay parents compared to children of heterosexual parents.

CULTURALLY AND RACIALLY MIXED FAMILIES

In a mixed family, family members differ in race, culture, and/or religion. Interracial and multicultural families have much to share but may also have to overcome many challenges in order to understand each other.

According to the 2000 census—the first to allow Americans to define themselves as multiracial or multicultural—7 million people described themselves as multiracial, about 2.4 percent of the population. Current projections by the Census Bureau suggest that by 2050, people of European descent will constitute about 53 percent of the population, while Hispanics, African Americans, and Asians will make up 25, 14, and 8 percent respectively.

Some multiracial and multicultural families experience discrimination and intolerance. As diversity has increased in the United States, so has acceptance of these families.

To summarize, not all families have the same living arrangements. Families in the United States today include extended families and alternative families as well as culturally or racially mixed families.

See also: Families, Racially Mixed; Gay Parents; Religion and the Family

FURTHER READING

Boenke, Mary. *Trans Forming Families: Real Stories about Transgendered Loved Ones*. 2nd edition. New Castle, DE: Oak Knoll Press, 2003.

Coontz, Stephanie. *The Way We Really Are: Coming to Terms with America's Changing Families*. New York: Basic Books (Perseus), 1997.

Howey, Noelle. *Out of the Ordinary: Essays on Growing Up with Gay, Lesbian, and Transgender Parents*. New York: St. Martin's Press, Stonewall Inn Editions, 2000.

Root, Maria, ed. *The Multiracial Experience*. Thousand Oaks, CA: Sage Publications, 1996.

■ FAMILY, THE TRADITIONAL

A traditional family consists of a married couple and their unmarried children; it is sometimes also called a nuclear family. Parents generally play traditional gender roles, with the man assuming responsibility for financially supporting the family and the woman for maintaining the household and caring for the children.

Many factors—including a high divorce rate, changing economic conditions, and the increased participation of women in the labor force—have combined to make the traditional family only one of many family structures in the United States today. As family forms become more diverse, the traditional family is becoming less common.

DO THEY STILL WORK?

The average life cycle of the traditional family can be inferred from census and other data. When the couple marries, the man is 26 and the woman is 24. Two years later, the woman gives birth to the first of the couple's two children. The second child is born two years later. For the next 20 years, the husband works outside the home, while the wife cares for their home and children. When the youngest child leaves home, the wife is 48 and the husband is 50. They become "empty nesters." The man continues to work until he is 65. He is about 74 years old when he dies. The woman will probably live five years longer than he did, dying at 79.

In the 1950s, about two-thirds of American children grew up in families that fit this portrait of a mother, father, and their children. In a traditional family, gender roles for husband and wife were clearly defined. The husband provided the income; the wife stayed home and cared for the family. The children spent their days in school. Not only was the husband the breadwinner, but he was also responsible for tasks defined as "man's work." "Man's work" usually included handling the family finances, making home and car repairs, and acting as the chief disciplinarian for the children. The wife was expected to perform "women's work," which usually included cleaning the house, cooking, sewing and mending, and child care. Children were expected to attend school and to spend their free time in play.

By 2000, this picture had changed. The percentage of married-couple households dropped from 78 percent of all households in 1950 to just 52 percent in 2000. According to census data, more people are opting to live alone and many others are delaying marriage and childbirth. The percentage of households occupied by one person increased from 11 percent in 1950 to almost 26 percent in 2000. Family size also decreased in the late 1900s. Between 1970 and 2000, the number of households with five or more people dropped from 21 percent to 10 percent. The percentage of married couples with children also declined. In 1960, about 60 percent of married couples had at least one child; by 1990, less than half had a child.

Data from the National Center for Health Statistics (NCHS) also show that the divorce rate increased between 1950 and 1980, leveling off in the 1990s. By 2000, almost half of all marriages ended in divorce, with 20 percent of marriages ending within three years. The high divorce rate means that more than 60 percent of children live in a single-parent household before they are 18. Blended and reblended families are becoming more common as divorced parents remarry—half of them more than once. Census Bureau data also indicates that **cohabitation**, the practice of living together without marriage, is becoming more common. In 2003, 5.5 million unmarried couples were cohabiting, many of them with their biological children. Of these couples, 4.9 million were heterosexual and just under 600,000 were homosexual.

Other data from the NCHS show wide fluctuations in the **fertility rate**—the average number of children a woman has in her lifetime. In the late 1950s, the average woman gave birth to 3.5 children. The fertility rate dropped to a low of 1.8 births per woman in 1972, then climbed slightly and stayed at between 2.0 and 2.1 births from the early 1990s through 2003. The percentage of unmarried women who gave birth to children climbed from 5 percent in 1960 to 34 percent in 2002.

Gender roles are also becoming more fluid as more and more married women enter the workforce. According to a report issued in November 1999 by the National Opinion Research Center at the University of Chicago, attitudes toward married women's participation in the workforce changed dramatically in the last quarter of the 20th century. In 1972, 67 percent approved of a wife working even if her husband could support her. By the 1990s, that percentage rose to 83 percent. In 2003, according to the Bureau of Labor Statistics, both husband and wife worked outside the home in 50.3 percent of married-couple families. Married women today are more likely to pursue careers as part of their life goals, while men are spending more time with their children and performing household tasks. The percentage of households in which women work outside the home and men are the primary caretakers of children rose from 2 percent in 1972 to almost 7 percent in 2003.

Sociologists and demographers attribute many of these shifts to changes in norms, values, laws, the economy, and the health of the elderly. As divorce, single parenthood, and remarriage become more common, the traditional family becomes only one of many possible family types. In November 2000 sociologist Jay D. Teachman and his colleagues at Western Washington University published the results of a study that examined the effects of economic patterns on marriage and family stability. The study, which appeared in the *Journal of Marriage and the Family*, suggests that a woman's income is becoming more important as a source of economic stability. Teachman's research builds on earlier work by other researchers, including sociologists and demographers. These researchers maintain that as women achieve greater economic independence, they are less likely to stay in unhappy marriages. Another factor is cited by sociologist Valerie Oppenheimer. She points out that men's earning power has declined, leaving fewer families able to survive on the income of a single wage earner.

DO THEY STILL EXIST?

The traditional family may be a rapidly disappearing entity. According to data from the 2000 census, fewer people are living in nuclear families today than ever before. In 1970, married couples who lived with their own children made up 40 percent of households in the United States. By 2000, that number had dropped to 24 percent. This figure includes blended families, so the percentage of families that include a father, mother, and their mutual offspring is probably even lower.

TEENS SPEAK

I Thought Families Didn't Come Any More Traditional Than Mine

My family is what the experts would call a "traditional family." My parents just celebrated their 25th anniversary. They married when they were both in their early 20s. For as long as I can remember, my father has worked—he's an emergency room physician at the local hospital—and my mother has taken care of our house, my brother, my sister, and me. She cleans the house and drives us to soccer practice, piano and ballet lessons, and everywhere else we go.

To someone looking in from the outside, families don't come any more traditional than mine. In comparison to my friends' families, we're almost "embarrassingly normal." About half of my friends' parents have divorced at least once. Some of my friends live with just one parent, stepparents, step-stepparents, or grandparents. My friend Michelle has two mothers.

But anyone living in my family would quickly see that we are rather nontraditional. Not only does my mother clean the house, she also does most of the home and car maintenance. She changes the oil on both her car and dad's, fixes leaky faucets and other problems around the house, mows the lawn, and takes out the garbage every week. She's also an environmental activist. I started going to peace rallies when I was still in my stroller. Dad couldn't fix a leaky faucet if you offered him a million dollars, but he loves to cook. He does most of the cooking whenever he's not working a 24-hour shift at the hospital. He also loves, believe it or not, to sew. He made most of our clothes when we were younger, and he still sews curtains and other things for the house as well as the tents we use each summer for our family vacation.

According to Stephanie Coontz, professor of history and family studies at Evergreen State College in Olympia, Washington, the question might not be whether the traditional family still exists but whether it ever existed at all. In *The Way We Never Were: American Families and the Nostalgia Trap*, Coontz argues that the portrait of the 1950s traditional family was true for very few people. Coontz points out that during the 1950s, divorce rates were low, but more than 2 million people lived separately while remaining legally married. Married women were more likely to suffer depression and anxiety than working mothers. Many states did not allow married women to sign contracts, secure credit cards or loans, or serve on juries.

Unmarried mothers were forced to marry or they were shipped off to another town to give birth and then give their babies up for adoption. The number of pregnant brides doubled in the 1950s, while the number of infants born to unmarried mothers and available for adoption rose 80 percent between 1944 and 1955. Coontz suggests that the post–World War II economic boom led to a strong labor market and relatively high wages for men. In this economic environment, many men could support a family and buy a home without help from other family members. Still, 25 percent of the population lived below the poverty line, and one-third of white American families could not subsist on the income of only one working adult. Children were more likely to go hungry, and people over 65 were twice as likely to be poor as they were in 2000. Coontz also points out that the discrepancy between the myth of the American nuclear family and the reality of family life was even more apparent for people of various ethnic backgrounds. More than half of all African-American families lived in poverty, even when both parents worked.

Fact Or Fiction?

"Latchkey children" suffer greatly.

Fact: About 5 million children between the ages of five and 13 are home on a regular basis without direct adult supervision. Most of these children are the sons and daughters of white, middle-class parents who live in suburban or rural areas. These "latchkey children"—the name comes from the fact that they often carry a house key so they can let themselves into their homes—may experience both positive and negative effects. Latchkey children may be more independent and self-reliant, have less stereotypical gender-role expectations of mothers, interact more with friends, help out more with household duties, and be better able to care for themselves than children who always have an adult in the house. However, they also may be fearful and apprehensive at being left alone, especially if they are left alone in an environment in which crime is high.

For most of the last 2,000 years, mothers have spent almost as much time in paid employment as they have raising children. Coontz argues that the idea that women's main function was to mother was a relatively recent one. Not until the 19th century did white, middle-class women withdraw from the workforce, prompted partly by a cultural ideal that equated womanhood with motherhood and a woman's leisure time with her husband's success. Women in low-income families have always worked outside the home, usually for lower wages than men. Children also contributed significantly to family incomes. Coontz suggests that after child labor laws were imposed in the 1960s, married women immediately began to reenter the workforce. By 1997, only 15 percent of families were supported solely by a male.

SINGLE-BREADWINNER FAMILIES

Families in which only one spouse works are becoming the exception, not the rule. Census Bureau data shows that in 1960, 42 percent of all families were supported solely by a male. By 2003, the male was the sole breadwinner in only 20 percent of families.

The financial adjustments

Most families that depend on a single earner have a limited income. If one spouse has been working and decides to leave the labor force to care for the couple's children, the family faces a drop in income at the same time that it encounters the increased expense of a child in the household. While families in which the working partner earns high wages may not experience a dramatic drop in income, most families in the middle-income range may have more difficulty adjusting to a lower income level. For families in lower-income brackets, it may not be financially possible for one spouse to stay at home.

Single-income living usually requires careful budgeting and planning, starting with the calculation of the lost income. According to experts, those considering whether to become a single-income family should calculate the net income that will be lost when one spouse leaves work after subtracting taxes, the costs of child care, commuting, work clothes, meals out, and extras like office parties and gifts. The reduction in income may affect all family members.

Income-earning spouses in single-earner families may feel that the income that they contribute to the family belongs to them. When both partners work and contribute financially to a family, money is often shared equally. But when only one spouse is contributing financially, that spouse may feel entitled to make financial decisions without consulting his or her partner. Conversely, the person who is not working outside the home may feel he or she needs to ask permission to spend money, even on necessities. The change in the couple's financial relationship may be a source of stress to both partners.

The couple's choice may be affected by the number of children in the household. The more children a couple has, the greater the child-care demands and the more expensive it is to provide child care. In a 1996 study published in the *Journal of Marriage and the Family*, sociologist Stacy J. Rogers examined the effect of mothers' work hours on marital quality. She found that full-time employment of mothers in large families was associated with less marital happiness and more conflict.

In 2004 Rogers published another study of family economics— "Dollars, Dependency, and Divorce: Four Perspectives on the Role of Wives' Income"—in *Journal of Marriage and the Family*. After interviewing 2,033 couples in 1980 and again in 1983, 1988, 1992, and 1997, Rogers found that the greater the difference between spouse's incomes, the greater the chance that couple would divorce. Conversely, couples that were happy and equally rewarded by their work were less likely to divorce. Rogers concluded that when women are employed, the increased family income can enhance marital stability and contribute to the family's economic security.

Cultural pressures
In a society that equates individual identity with work, being a stay-at-home parent can be challenging for both men and women. According to the National Association of At-home Mothers, parents who choose to stay home and devote their energies to raising children and maintaining a home may be pressured from friends and family to work outside the home. They may also face questions about their decision to become "full-time parents."

Women who choose to focus their energies on their family and home may be stigmatized, in an odd reversal of cultural stereotypes of the 1950s. In the 1950s, the married mother who chose to work was often considered selfish and inattentive to her children. In 1947, a best-selling book, *The Modern Woman*, claimed that the idea of the independent woman was a "contradiction in terms," and warned that women who wanted equal economic and educational opportunities were engaged in a "ritualistic castration" of men. While most of this myth has been dispelled, women who choose employment may still experience criticism for spending less time with their children. But the married mother who chooses not to work may also find herself apologizing for being "just" a mom.

Men who choose to stay at home may find the adjustment even more difficult, mostly because men have been reared to identify themselves as providers for their families. Since the 1960s, researchers have been examining the ways that married women's participation in the labor force affects families. Many of these studies, including a 2001 study of the effects of wives' income on marital stability and happiness by sociologists Stacy J. Rogers and Danielle D. DeBoer, indicate that the ability to financially support a family continues to be an important aspect of men's well-being. Rogers and DeBoer's study, "Changes in Wives' Income: Effects on Marital Happiness, Psychological Well-being, and the Risk of Divorce," was published in the *Journal of Marriage and the Family*. The researchers found that when women's incomes rose, their marital happiness and well-being increased. However, when women contributed a greater percentage of the total household income—40 to 50 percent—men's well-being decreased, even when the men did not subscribe to traditional gender roles. Rogers and DeBoer concluded that the decrease in men's well-being reflected continued emphasis on men as the family breadwinner, despite increasing support for nontraditional gender roles by both women and men.

WHO STAYS HOME?

Traditionally, the man has been the primary economic provider in the family, while women assumed responsibility for child care and household tasks. While this division of labor is still prevalent in traditional families, other families in the United States today opt for different arrangements—including one in which the woman works and the man stays home. As gender roles become less defined by gender, so does the division of labor within households. The Census Bureau reports that in 2002, 105,000 fathers stayed at home to care for their children under the age of 15. These fathers chose not to work primarily so they could care for the children while their wives worked outside the home.

For the most part, however, it is women who stay home to care for the children. The gender wage gap may affect the family's decision about who stays home. Estimates from the Institute for Women's Policy (IWPR) research show that women earn only 71 cents for every dollar that men earn, often even when they are employed in similar jobs. IWPR's analysis of census data showed that even during the peak earning years of ages 45–54, women earned 68 percent of what men earned in 1998.

That discrepancy persists even after factors such as education and work experience are taken into account. Data compiled by the American Federation of Labor–Congress of Industrial Organizations (AFL-CIO) show that in 2003, women in professional and technical occupations earned almost 27 percent less than men, while women in sales occupations earned 38 percent less. One of the largest differences was among physicians. Female physicians and surgeons earned 41 percent less than their male counterparts. According to a 2004 study from IWPR, *Still a Man's Labor Market: The Long-Term Earnings Gap,* on average a woman who was in her prime earning years between 1983 and 1998 earned $273,592 during that 15-year period; the average man earned $722,693. IWPR researchers say the male-female wage gap appears to have three underlying causes. First, women are more likely to work in lower-paying jobs such as nursing and teaching. Second, women may not work as many hours per week as men. Third, women are less likely to advocate for increases in their own pay.

In every single-income family, the decision of who will stay home is a very personal one. The woman may be a more skilled worker or more highly educated than the man, she may have a job that pays more and has better benefits, or she may want to work because she finds that work contributes to her own well-being and ability to mother. The man may identify strongly with the traditional male role of provider and be unwilling or ill-suited to being the primary child-care provider.

SHARING RESPONSIBILITIES

For many couples, the home is becoming a place of shared responsibility and caring, rather than the site of "women's work." In a 1987 study of 640 white, middle-class parents, psychologist Rosalind Barnett and sociologist Grace Baruch examined factors that affected fathers' participation in child care. They found that a father's participation in child-care tasks was linked to a number of variables. The more hours the mother worked per week, the more likely he was to assist with child care. A mother who expected help from her husband got more help than those who did not expect and ask for the help. Fathers who were unhappy with the fathering they had received as children tended to be more involved in caring for their own children. Those fathers also spent more time with their children when they were small and devoted more time to their sons than to their daughters. As the number of children in the family increased, so did the percentage of time that fathers interacted with their children. Finally, fathers who were employed but worked fewer hours spent more time caring for their children. However, unemployment made it less likely that fathers would spend time with their children.

Although the difference between the amount of time women and men spend performing housework and child care is decreasing, women still do more family work than men. Several studies, including a 2001 study of the relationship between domestic labor and marital satisfaction published in the *Journal of Marriage and the Family*, show that both employed and unemployed women in all income brackets spend significantly more time doing housework and caring for children than men do. Sociologist Daphne Stevens and her colleagues at Utah State University found that whether they work outside the home or not, women tend to have more responsibility for children. Women are more likely to plan and carry out decisions regarding children's care and to spend more time caring for their children. Yet the researchers found that the happiest couples didn't necessarily divide household tasks equally. The happiest couples in their study had developed a mutually agreed-upon division of household labor and financial responsibilities. That agreement, not the 50/50 division of household labor, had the most influence on marital happiness.

Men and women are more likely to share home responsibilities when they are somewhat egalitarian in their beliefs about gender roles in relationships. Yet segregation of home responsibilities seems to persist even in egalitarian relationships.

Q & A

Question: Can a woman be a feminist and still be in a traditional family?

Answer: Feminists do not object to women's traditional roles within families but believe that women should be able to choose whether or not to play those roles. Many feminists argue that the work that women have traditionally done should be valued as much as the work that men traditionally do. For instance, if a husband wants to stay home and take care of his children instead of pursuing a career, that choice should be recognized as valid and valuable. Likewise, when women choose to stay home and provide care to their children, their activities should be recognized as equal in importance to her husband's work outside the home.

This segregation of tasks may stem partly from gender-role stereotypes, which deeply affect both men and women. Men or women who consciously or unconsciously hold traditional gender-role beliefs may inhibit one another from sharing household tasks. Even men who want to spend more time with their children may find that their wives are reluctant to give up the control. The mother may see family work as her domain. Some women act as "gatekeepers," preventing men from more involvement with children and household tasks. After studying this phenomenon, sociologists Sarah Allen and Alan Hawkins defined maternal gatekeeping as "a collection of beliefs and behaviors that ultimately inhibit a collaborative effort between men and women in family work by limiting men's opportunities for learning and growing through caring for home and children." In a 1999 study of 1,500 women published in the *Journal of Marriage and the Family*, Allen and Hawkins found that 25 percent engaged in some kind of gatekeeping behaviors. Such gatekeeping activities, they argue, provide barriers to fathers' involvement in housework and childcare.

Once the most common family structure, the traditional family—consisting of a mother, father, and their biological children, in which the father is the breadwinner and the mother cares for the home and children—has become increasingly less common in the United States. The decrease in the percentage of traditional families stems from many factors, including increasing rates of divorce, single parenthood, and remarriage; women's increased participation in the labor force; and changing gender role expectations. Families in which only one spouse works are becoming the exception rather than the rule. As more married women work outside the home, taking on some of the financial responsibilities for the family, many couples are dividing household tasks more equally.

See also: Day Care; Divorce and Families; Families, Blended; Families, Racially Mixed; Family, The New; Family Traditions; Marriage and Family, Changes in; Single-Parent Families

FURTHER READING

Barnett, Rosalind. *Same Difference: How Gender Myths Are Hurting Our Relationships, Our Children, and Our Jobs.* New York: Perseus Books, 2004.

Coontz, Stephanie. *The Way We Never Were: American Families and the Nostalgia Trap.* New York: Basic Books, 2000.

Hochschild, Arlie Russell. *The Second Shift.* New York: Penguin, 2003.

Presser, Harriet. *Working in a 24/7 Economy: Challenges for America's Families.* New York: Russell Sage Foundation, 2003.

■ FAMILY RULES

Family rules are the guidelines for interaction within a family. Rules, limits, and boundaries are necessary for any group of people to live and work together effectively. Rules guide communication and help individuals know what is expected of them and how to treat one another. In family life, parents are responsible for conveying rules of behavior to their children. When rules are clear and communicated effectively, children learn the skills they need to function effectively at home, in school, and in the community. Knowing what to expect and how to act in various settings helps children feel safe and secure.

WHO IS IN CHARGE?

The word *authority* has many meanings. In relation to family life, parents are the authority. They have the power to influence the actions of their children. As the authority figures in the family, parents are responsible for teaching their children to accept limits and act in acceptable ways. As the authority figures, parents make rules, enforce those rules, and guide behavior. Other authority figures in a family may be grandparents or other adults who provide similar guidance.

Jane B. Brooks, author of *The Process of Parenting*, says that children are more likely to follow rules when parents define the rules and clearly communicate those rules to their children. Much research exists describing the ways in which parents set and enforce rules. Researcher Nancy Darling reviewed current research on the role of rules in family life in an article entitled "Parenting Style and Its Correlates." She highlights three approaches to setting rules and enforcing them. The three are generally known as an authoritarian style, a permissive style, and an authoritative style. Each style is characterized by the way in which parents respond to their children emotionally and how parents try to control their children's behavior.

Authoritarian parents tend to be demanding and directive but not responsive. They clearly state family rules and enforce them. Children are expected to obey or accept the consequences of not following the rules. They have little input into those rules. Parents with an authoritarian style provide their children with strict boundaries with little focus on the expression of feelings related to those rules.

Permissive parents are more responsive than demanding. They place more emphasis on the feelings related to the rules and less on establishing firm boundaries. Parents who are permissive are often willing to negotiate the rules with their children and are likely to place little emphasis on strict enforcement of rules.

Authoritative parents are both demanding and responsive. In families where this style is present, the children know and understand their family's standards of behavior. The children are likely to have some input into rules and family decisions, but adults have the ultimate authority.

The research on parenting style reveals that the way in which rules are established and enforced is a strong indicator of how well a family functions. It also predicts children's well-being in a wide spectrum of environments and communities. Both the way that parents respond to their children and the way they direct or correct behavior are important components of good parenting. Authoritative parenting, which balances clear firm expectations for behavior with a high degree of emotional responsiveness and recognition of children's individuality, is one of the most consistent predictors of social competence from early childhood through adolescence.

Fact Or Fiction?

Spanking is effective because it stops children from misbehaving.

Fact: While children may stop the misbehavior immediately after a spanking, experts say that it does not change future behavior. Noted development expert Penelope Leach says that when children are spanked parents may be sending the unintended message that aggression in certain circumstances is acceptable. In fact, in a longitudinal study that examined the effects of spanking, children were found to have more behavioral difficulties over time if they were spanked.

Jane Brooks, in her book *The Process of Parenting*, suggests that behavioral management techniques such as providing logical consequences, giving limited choices, and modifying the environment are more proactive and less reactive ways to guide behavior. Sharing expectations for behavior in advance of difficult situations and helping children to make better age-appropriate decisions the next time he or she faces a problem are more effective ways to coach behavior than spanking.

BEING FAIR

Fairness is a universal concern in most families. Most children know if each member is treated equally and whether everyone has the same opportunities and privileges. Rick Lavoie, a parenting expert, maintains that fairness in family life teaches children important lessons. He does not believe that fairness means that everyone is treated the same. He believes it is more accurate and in many cases more helpful to define fairness as everyone getting what he or she needs. His premise is that every child is unique and therefore has unique needs. The struggle for parents, according to Lavoie, is managing the inevitable conflict that treating children fairly yet differently often brings.

Q & A

Question: What are some specific rules that many families have?

Answer: Typical expectations for behavior may be negotiable, such as which coat to wear in winter. These are rules children may have input into. Other rules may not be negotiable such as wearing a coat in winter. Nonnegotiable rules often fall into two categories: those related to safety and those related to respect. Some examples of safety rules that may change with a child's age include: two-year-olds and car seat safety, 10-year-olds and bicycle safety, or 17-year-olds and driving safety. Although some rules change with age, others remain the same regardless of age. Examples of respect rules that stay the same regardless of age might be those rules related to lying or aggressive behavior.

BEING CONSISTENT

Consistency in parenting is an important element in modifying behavior. When parents want children to follow rules, it is important to enforce those rules regularly. If a particular behavior such as hitting a brother or sister is unacceptable today, it must be unacceptable tomorrow, next week, and next month. While it is nearly impossible to enforce every rule at all times, it should be parents' goal to do so. Susan M. Ward, author of *Why Consistency Is Important*, says consistency teaches children cause and effect. They learn that if they act in a certain way, there will be certain consequences. When children become capable of recognizing cause-and-effect relationships, they can begin to predict the impact of certain actions. Ward believes that kind of consistency helps children feel safe and secure because they can begin to predict the outcome of their own actions.

See also: Family Traditions; Media and the Family; Pets in the Family; Teens in Trouble

FURTHER READING
Brooks, Jane. *The Process of Parenting*. New York: McGraw-Hill, 2004.
Faber, Adele and Elaine Mazlish. *How to Talk So Kids Will Listen and Listen So Kids Will Talk*. New York: Perigee Books, 1999.
Griffin, Lynne Reeves. *The Promise of Proactive Parenting: Sea Change*. San Diego, CA: Aventine Press, 2004.
MacKenzie, Robert J. *Setting Limits with Your Strong-Willed Child: Eliminating Conflict by Establishing Clear Firm and Respectful Boundaries*. New York: Three Rivers Press, 2001.

■ FAMILY TRADITIONS

Family traditions are routines, practices, and beliefs that are passed from generation to generation. Family traditions are powerful organizers of family life. A 50-year review of research by the American Psychological Association found that family traditions are alive and well in American family life and are linked with marital satisfaction, a sense of identity among family members, children's health, academic achievement, and strong family relationships.

The collection of research studies suggests that the need to bond with other family members is a universal desire among people. Vern Bengtson, professor of gerontology and sociology at the University of Southern California in Los Angeles, maintains that families provide their members with support and a sense of identity. Family members use traditions and rituals to connect with one another in positive and encouraging ways. While traditions tend to be enjoyable and family members often look forward to them, they also offer stability during difficult times and times of change.

TEENS SPEAK

Thanksgiving Dinner Is My Favorite Family Celebration

In my family, we spend Thanksgiving with my father's side of the family and Christmas Eve with my mother's. Every year both events are like small weddings with 25 to 50 people. The only thing there that seems to be more of than people are pies.

After the huge meal, all the cousins go outside to play after the huge meal. The older cousins serve as combination babysitters/team leaders in our intricate role-playing games. The farm serves as our stage to recreate favorite television shows or reenact exciting adventures. The barn is our castle, cave, or home. The farm equipment, with a little imagination, becomes racecars, boats, or space ships. I love playing these games even though many of them are too young for me now. But it's really fun to play with my younger cousins and to see them learning the games that the older cousins have been playing for years.

I love these traditions. I have such nice memories of holidays spent with my cousins. I really look forward to the next holiday, especially Thanksgiving. When I have a family of my own, I want to pass on some of these traditions to my own children.

DESCRIBING FAMILY TRADITIONS

Traditions can be described as practices in which families have engaged previously and will continue to engage. They are practices that the family values and respects. According to Susan Coady, a professor of family relations and human development at Ohio State University, traditions are characterized by predictability, regularity, and the commitment of family members. Traditions are specific to a family's cultural, religious, and racial background. Although culture, religion, or membership in a particular ethnic group might influence the occasions a family celebrates, each family individualizes the way in which it celebrates those occasions.

William Doherty, professor of family social science at the University of Minnesota, writes that family traditions are intentional ways families create patterns of connection. Doherty says that in order for a practice to truly be a family tradition, family members must be involved in the tradition in a deliberate way. The tradition must also have a special significance to family members. And to become a tradition, the practice must be repeated on a regular basis.

In a study of 28 families, Lloyd Newell found that in each family interviewed, members described a religious link to its traditions. Whether it was a faith-based holiday that brought families together or simply a set of long held beliefs or values, families made a connection between their traditions and their faith.

Fact Or Fiction?

The traditional family reunion started during medieval times in Europe.

Fact: Family reunions are gatherings of people who descend from common ancestors. While some reunions bring together family members who simply haven't seen each other in a while, some gatherings include family members who may not know each other at all. According to researchers, such reunions originated in North America in the late 1860s. Historians believe that the reunions began in response to the traumatic family losses during the U.S. Civil War and may still be seen in African-American families as an affirmation of the end of slavery.

Family reunions became popular around the turn of the 20th century. In the 1960s, during the Vietnam War, President Lyndon B. Johnson asked Americans to hold family reunions as a way to foster national unity. Today, family reunions continue as a way to celebrate family history and draw together family members who live great distances from one another.

WHERE DO WE GO FOR THE HOLIDAYS?

Traditions, rituals, and routines can be seen in the way families celebrate holidays. According to a national poll conducted in 2001 by Harris Interactive/Modern Woodmen of America, wanting to be with family at the holidays is one of the major reasons people attend family gatherings. Celebrating religious holidays was important to 85 percent of those polled. In that same poll, 90 percent said they had attended a holiday event with family in the past three years, with 36 percent citing Thanksgiving and Christmas as the favorites.

Welcoming others into one's homes or traveling is part of the sharing of family traditions. Yet, many people claim that doing so is not easy. According to the same poll, 90 percent of Americans agree that spending time with extended family is important, but 75 percent say that getting together can be difficult.

Stressful travel is the challenge described by those who return home for the holidays. According to the American Automotive Association (AAA), approximately 37 million Americans travel 50 miles or more over the Thanksgiving weekend. AAA claims that slightly more than 30 million Americans travel by car and slightly more than 4 million travel by airplane. For those that host or entertain family on such occasions, preparation, including cooking and cleaning, top the list of challenges to sharing family traditions.

HONORING OLD TRADITIONS

Some family traditions center on national or religious holidays. Many families also have personal practices or interpretations of their heritage and these family rituals are unique. Traditions may be written down, but more often they are passed orally from one generation to the next.

Many traditions have evolved from cultural, religious, and recreational activities that families have adopted over the years. Some family traditions celebrate the past and connect family members to their roots. Honoring old traditions, experts say, builds a shared understanding of family heritage and a sense of community. Sharing unique memories and reflections is an important part of family life.

Traditions are also important because they keep the generations in contact with one another. In her multigenerational research on family traditions, Susan Coady of Ohio State University interviewed three generations of women. The oldest generation described its traditions in great detail. The youngest women who were of college age shared the fewest details. The researcher found it interesting that the middle generation expressed the most dissatisfaction with their family's traditions. This middle generation, she remarks, is usually the bridge between the youngest and oldest generations and therefore the most active in keeping the family traditions alive.

CELEBRATING NEW TRADITIONS

As families change, traditions change. As new family members are added through marriage and the birth of children, the dynamic of family life changes. Coady's research found that in the early years of a new marriage, couples begin to sort through the traditions that each has brought from his or her family of origin. Together, they begin to examine their individual family histories and negotiate what their new traditions will be.

Traditions are important to families with young children, because the parents are at a stage in life when they want to establish their own traditions and perhaps break away from those of previous generations. For example, when children begin to anticipate the traditions of Christmas, their parents may prefer to celebrate Christmas in their own home instead of traveling to their parents' homes.

More often than not, traditions within a family evolve slowly over time into new traditions with few, if any, dramatic breaks with the past. Yet even small alterations in the rituals and routines of family holidays or activities may lead to significant changes in traditions.

Q & A

Question: What is meant by "rites of passage"?

Answer: Rites of passage are ceremonies or observances associated with the transition from one place or stage of life to another. Rites of passage may be formal, such as the Jewish ritual called a bar mitzvah or bat mitzvah. It signifies the beginning of a boy or girl assuming adult responsibilities in Judaism. Other rites of passage are informal, such as the recognition that a child may be old enough to have a later bedtime or learn to drive a car. Rites of passage, when celebrated or acknowledged, help children and adults understand and respect the responsibilities and privileges that come from moving to a new developmental stage.

INCLUDING RELATIVES IN TRADITIONS

At the core of the celebration of family traditions is the desire to include treasured friends and relatives. Numerous family customs include aunts, uncles, and other extended family members and special guests.

While many families look forward to time spent together, for some family members, time spent with relatives can be challenging. The Mayo Clinic says that distance, extended family obligations, finances, work responsibilities, health concerns, scheduling conflicts, religious differences, and personality issues may contribute to the high levels of stress some family members may experience when they participate in family traditions. Honest, open communication and compromises, experts say, are the key to keeping healthy family traditions alive and enjoyable.

Given the strength that family traditions bring to family life, Susan A. Lieberman of Rice University in Houston, Texas, believes that families today need tradition now more than ever before. "The world is changing so rapidly now, and traditions give us an anchor. Traditions make you feel good as a family. These indelible memories bring character and texture to our lives."

See also: Death in the Family; Family Rules; Religion and the Family

FURTHER READING
Doherty, William. *The Intentional Family: How to Build Family Ties in Our Modern World.* New York: Avon Books, 1999.
Lieberman, Susan Abel. *New Traditions: Redefining Celebrations for Today's Family.* New York: Noonday Press, 1991.
Pipher, Mary. *The Shelter of Each Other: Rebuilding Our Families.* New York: Ballantine Books, 1996.
Pleck, Elizabeth Hafkin. *Celebrating the Family: Ethnicity, Consumer Culture, and Family Rituals.* Cambridge, MA: Harvard University Press, 2000.

■ FINANCIAL MANAGEMENT, MARITAL

Marital financial management involves the organization of a family's money, property, and other wealth. When a couple marries, they make a financial and legal commitment to one another. The couple shares the financial and legal benefits of the union. Those benefits may include being entitled to one another's work benefits such as health insurance and pension. Good financial management requires two people willing to learn about finances and to be responsible with money.

Some couples draw up a **prenuptial agreement** prior to marriage. It is a legal agreement arranged before marriage stating who owns property acquired before marriage and during the marriage and how property will be divided in the event of divorce. Many couples prepare **wills**. These legal documents express a person's wishes regarding the disposal of his or her property after death. In the event of an emergency, a husband and wife are often encouraged to keep good records regarding their finances and provide one another with **power of attorney**. A power of attorney is a legal document that authorizes another person to act on one's behalf. Other financial management considerations in marriage include the process of changing one's name, opening bank accounts, paying family bills, acquiring stocks and bonds, and managing debt and credit cards.

PRENUPTIAL AGREEMENTS

Some couples, prior to marriage, draw up a contract detailing what each is bringing to the marriage and how, in the event of one's death, these assets are to be distributed. Such agreements protect funds each individual had prior to the marriage. While most couples enter into a prenuptial agreement to protect separate property and money, some couples enter into one to protect themselves from each other's debt. According to Lee Borden, a noted lawyer specializing in these arrangements, remarriage, blending families, and high divorce rates are the reasons some couples feel more financially secure entering into a marriage with a prenuptial agreement.

WILLS

A will is a legal document stating what should happen to the money, property, and belongings of a person after his or her death. A will shows how to distribute the property of the deceased, and how children of the deceased will be provided for. As assets grow during a marriage and the family expands and changes, couples are encouraged to review their wills from time to time to see if alterations need to be made.

DID YOU KNOW?

Legal Documents for Unmarried Couples

Did you know that unmarried couples can obtain some of the rights of married couples by arranging for certain legal documents? Among the documents that may afford unmarried couples similar rights as married couples are the following:

Power of Attorney for Health Care Decisions
Power of Attorney for Financial Decisions
Living Together Agreement
Will

Source: Alternatives to Marriage Project, Albany, NY: 2004.

TAX BENEFITS

Income tax is a tax on earnings payable to city, state, and/or federal governments. Married couples may file tax returns separately or together. Many couples enjoy tax benefits when filing returns jointly. The way a couple is taxed differs from the way a single person is taxed. In most cases, couples save money by filing tax returns together. Another benefit of filing a joint return is the tax credits that are offered to married couples. However, if couples file taxes together, they are responsible for one another. If one spouse doesn't pay what is owed, the other spouse must pay for both.

INSURANCE BENEFITS

Life insurance is paid to a stated family member in the event of the death of the person insured. Most state laws allow a spouse a portion of the benefits from a spouse's life insurance policy, even if the policy was purchased prior to the marriage. These laws are complex, yet often they override the recipient actually named in the policy, paying some, if not all, monies to the surviving spouse.

Some couples make sure that they each carry enough life insurance during their marriage to handle potentially difficult financial situations that may result from the death of one spouse. Many purchase policies large enough to pay a mortgage or provide day care for young children in the event of either spouse's death.

SOCIAL SECURITY BENEFITS

Monthly benefits are paid to eligible people from a federal government agency called the Social Security Administration. Those that are eligible include individuals over the age of 68 who have worked for ten years or more and paid into the Social Security system, their spouses, and dependent children as well as disabled persons of any age. The rules and regulations are complex. Yet, it is an important benefit that married couples can share if eligibility criteria are met.

Couples can also receive veteran and military benefits, including special loans. Such benefits may be used to pay living expenses, help pay for education, or medical care.

PENSIONS

A pension is income paid after retirement. Some companies offer their employees pension plans so that when workers retire they receive a monthly income. A number of large companies offer **profit sharing**.

Profit sharing is a plan in which employers share their profits with employees at the employer's discretion. The compensation may be stocks, bonds, or cash and can be paid immediately or deferred until retirement. According to the Center for American Progress, a non-profit financial information organization, because few employees stay at one job for all of their working life, many people today purchase private pension plans. These plans play an important financial role for couples in planning for retirement.

PROPERTY

Property that is obtained by either spouse individually or the couple together during a marriage is considered marital property. The time frame starts the day the couple marries and lasts until the date that the couple begins to live apart. Nine states are known as **community property states**: Arizona, California, Idaho, Louisiana, Nevada, New Mexico, Texas, Washington, and Wisconsin. The Commonwealth of Puerto Rico is also a community property jurisdiction. In each of these places, all property obtained during the marriage—other than a gift or inheritance—belongs equally to each spouse. Even if one spouse earned all of the money used to obtain the property, the government views the property as belonging to both parties. While these laws differ, each is based on the idea that both spouses contribute equally to the marriage and therefore all property obtained during the marriage is the result of their combined efforts.

Each person owns the property he or she brought to the marriage separately, unless the owner wants the property to be jointly owned. Lawyers can help couples clarify arrangements so that in case of death, it is clear which property is separately owned and which is jointly owned.

WORKER'S COMPENSATION

Worker's compensation is a payment received for injury on the job. This state-governed system addresses injuries that are work-related. Under the system, employers pay the cost of medical treatment and lost pay that results from a worker's job-related injury or disease, regardless of who is at fault. In return, the employee gives up the right to sue the employer, even if the injuries are due to carelessness on the employer's part.

If a person receiving worker's compensation dies, his or her spouse is due the worker's compensation benefits owed to the deceased.

NEXT-OF-KIN PRIVILEGES

The term **next-of-kin** refers to a person's closest living relative either by blood or by marriage. In marriage, the term has legal significance. It has become a term that describes those individuals who are most closely related to the deceased and therefore eligible to inherit his or her money and property. Laws have been established to clarify the rights of a person's next-of-kin.

Some next-of-kin privileges relate to visitation when the individual is ill or hospitalized. For example, the wife of a terminally ill man can remain with him in intensive care at the hospital. She is allowed to make medical decisions regarding his care when he is no longer able to make these decisions. The hospital will follow her instructions for the after-death procedures, and she has the authority to make burial arrangements. Visitation of a relative convicted of a crime and sent to prison is also covered in next-of-kin privileges.

RECORD KEEPING

Keeping financial information organized and accessible is an important aspect of financial management. Some couples use files for most papers and safe deposit boxes held at a bank for particularly important papers. Documents that require safekeeping include the marriage certificate, car titles, proof of property held prior to marriage, social security cards, canceled checks, birth certificates, adoption records, credit card charge slips, copies of tax returns, insurance policies, property deeds, stocks and bonds, military discharge papers, veteran's benefits, death certificates of family members, divorce and custody agreements, passports, and children's immunization records. Couples sometimes keep copies of these documents in more than one separate location in case of fire.

Q & A

Question: If one spouse is responsible for paying all the bills each month, how will the other spouse know the couple's financial situation?

Answer: Early in a marriage, experts recommend coming up with a system for paying bills and another system for communicating the family's financial picture to one another. Financial experts recommend regular discussions about current finances as well as regular discussions about financial goals.

OTHER FINANCIAL CONCERNS
Changing a name

Many women change their last names to the last name of the person they are marrying, while others prefer to keep their maiden or family name. Legally speaking, either decision is acceptable. Whether a name is changed or not, it is best for women to sign all papers during the marriage with only one name.

Assets

Stocks and bonds purchased before the marriage are not community property unless the person wishes to have them be jointly owned. Many people have separate bank accounts prior to marriage but open a joint account when they marry. Whether or not couples maintain separate accounts or opt for a joint account is a matter of personal preference. Yet, once couples deposit money into a joint account, the money becomes the property of both people.

Debt and credit cards

Before a couple marries, each may have his or her own credit report. Regardless of how good either party's credit rating, it does not affect anyone else's rating. However, when a couple marries and tries to secure a loan to buy a house or other property, the bank will look at both ratings. Partners who live in a community property state find that all of the debts one spouse may incur during their marriage are considered the other spouse's debts as well. For example, if one spouse buys a car and then doesn't keep up the payments, the bank can make the other spouse pay for the car. If one spouse applies for credit, the other spouse's debts may hinder his or her chances of receiving credit.

Financial advisers strongly suggest that before couples marry, they discuss how they will handle their finances during their marriage. They should consider how they will divide expenses, make purchases, and manage long term financial planning.

Given the complexity of financial management, it's easy to see why many couples disagree about money. Ruth Hayden, a financial educator, offers practical methods for financial management in her 1999 book *For Richer, Not Poorer: The Money Book for Couples*. Hayden suggests that spouses meet each other halfway, with feet firmly planted in security while still stretching to make compromises.

Frequent communication and the setting of financial goals are the key to a strong financial plan, Hayden says.

Fact Or Fiction?

A person needn't be concerned with financial management in marriage until he or she is an adult.

Fact: Managing money is a skill that can be learned. Experts say that early positive experiences in managing money provide a strong foundation for managing money later in life. Teens can learn about managing money by watching the way in which the people around them manage money. Observing how parents spend and save teaches teens valuable lessons. When teens manage small amounts of their own money, they also learn important lessons on the value of managing money well as well as the consequence of various spending decisions.

Child support

Every parent has a legal requirement to support his or her children. Money paid by a parent to help support children who are not living with him or her is called **child support**. Child support can be paid voluntarily or be ordered by a court. The support may come in different forms including a one-time payment, regular installments paid directly to the custodial parent, or regular deductions from a paycheck paid directly to the custodial parent. Child support can be costly and may create conflict between parents caring for children but living apart.

Power of attorney

If one spouse becomes too ill to manage legal and financial matters the other spouse may need to have the legal right to manage the household. But to do so, the spouse may need a document called a "power of attorney." For example, if a person needs to sell a car that is jointly owned and his or her spouse is seriously ill, then this document provides a way to make the sale. Many couples who are facing the onset of a serious illness get legal assistance in drawing up a power-of-attorney document.

Health insurance

Families vary in the way they handle health insurance. In some families, one person will carry the medical coverage for the entire family through his or her employer. Not all employers offer insurance and both spouses may not work. So, this decision is often based on the type and cost of coverage offered by the employers of the working spouse or spouses.

Financial management in marriage is complex. The more a couple learns and plans together for a strong financial future, the more they can enjoy the financial and legal benefits of their marital status.

When managing finances, couples may benefit from keeping good records, reading about financial planning and obtaining the support of professionals in financial management and the law.

See also: Day Care; Death in the Family; Gay Parents

FURTHER READING

Bach, David. *Smart Couples Finish Rich*. New York: Broadway Books, 2002.

Barnhill, Julie. *Til Debt Do Us Part*. Eugene, OR: Harvest House Publishers, 2002.

Burkett, Larry, and Michael E. Taylor. *Money before Marriage: A Financial Workbook for Engaged Couples*. Chicago: Moody Publishers, 1996.

Gibson, Robert C. *First Comes Love, Then Comes Money: Basic Steps to Avoid the #1 Conflict in Marriage*. Green Forest, AR: New Leaf Press, 1998.

■ GAY PARENTS

Gay parents are those who are **homosexual** in their sexual orientation—that is, they are attracted to people of the same sex. **Sexual orientation** refers to one's enduring romantic, emotional, or sexual attraction to a person of the opposite sex and/or one's own sex. People who are **heterosexual** are attracted to the opposite sex. People with a homosexual orientation are referred to as gay (both men and women) or lesbian (women only). A person who is **bisexual** is attracted to both men and women. A person who is **transsexual** has an overwhelming desire to live his or her life as a member of the opposite sex.

Bisexual and transsexual persons can also be parents. Their issues are similar to those of gay parents and are often discussed together.

The concept of sexual orientation refers to more than sexual behavior. It includes the way in which a person describes his or her identity. Some individuals may identify themselves as gay, lesbian, or bisexual without engaging in any sexual activity. Individuals may become aware at different points in their lives that they are heterosexual, gay, lesbian, bisexual, or transsexual.

According to the 2000 census, many gay couples have children and research shows that these families have much in common with other families. Yet, gay families still face discrimination by those who believe that exposure to gay men and women will in some way harm a child's development.

CHILDREN IN GAY PARTNERSHIPS

Current estimates indicate that between five and six million gays in the United States have children. Research published by the *Journal of Homosexuality* suggest this number may be low, because many people conceal their sexual identity out of fear of losing custody of their children or visitation rights. According to the 2000 U.S. census, of those who reported a gay partnership, 33 percent of lesbians and 22 percent of gay men had children living with them.

The majority of gay parents had their children in a heterosexual relationship. Following divorce or separation they entered into a gay partnership and their children from the previous relationship were included in their new family. In other families, one or both gay parents have adopted the children. Some lesbians have children through **artificial insemination** (the placement of sperm into a female reproductive tract by means other than sexual intercourse). Data from the 2000 U.S. census also reveals that approximately 3 million children have gay parents.

In a 2001 study, developmental psychologists Suzanne Johnson and Elizabeth O'Connor polled participants about how gay parents came to have their children. In families where the children were born into the relationship, 88 percent of lesbians used artificial insemination and 85 percent of gay men adopted their children.

According to a 2002 report by the American Academy of Pediatrics, children with gay parents have no unusual developmental problems and are clear about their own sexual orientation. A 2004 research report by Charlotte J. Patterson, a professor of psychology at the

University of Virginia, noted that no study to date has found that children of lesbian or gay parents are disadvantaged in any significant way relative to children of heterosexual parents. Patterson found that the home environment provided by gay parents is much like those provided by other parents. Both groups of parents tend to offer children emotional support and enable psychosocial growth and well-being.

In 1995, the American Psychological Association compiled a comprehensive review of the research on lesbian and gay parenting. The research on children's development when raised by gay parents focused on development of sexual identity and on social development. The APA review found that children raised by lesbian mothers develop patterns of gender-role behavior that are much like those of other children. The data was limited in this area for children of gay fathers. The research review presents data that support similar findings related to social development. Research suggests that children of gay parents have normal relationships with friends and that their relationships with adults of both sexes are also satisfactory.

Judith Wallerstein, who has studied the effects of divorce on children, found that children with gay parents experience similar emotional and behavior problems when their parents split up as children with heterosexual parents. Other studies confirm those findings. When examining the causes for emotional or behavior problems in children, many researchers find the problems stem from such factors as parents' depression, custody battles, or other conflicts between divorcing or separating parents. The connection between being raised by gay parents and an increase in emotional and behavioral problems in children is not supported by current research.

Fact Or Fiction?

Children raised with gay parents are more likely to become gay adults.

Fact: Research to date shows that children raised by gay and lesbian parents are no more likely to become homosexual than children raised by heterosexuals. In general, the studies suggest that when children of gay parents become young adults, they are more likely to have had or considered same-sex relationships but are no more likely than children of straight parents to identify themselves as lesbian, gay, or bisexual.

A variety of studies reveal that the percentage of children of gay parents who have a homosexual orientation is equivalent to a random sample of the general population. A review of studies assessing 300 children born to gay or lesbian parents in 12 different samples shows no evidence of any disturbances in the development of sexual identity among those studied.

SOCIETAL REACTIONS

Numerous public opinion polls over the past 20 years indicate that attitudes toward gay men, lesbians, and bisexuals have become more positive. Yet compared to other social groups, gay families still experience discrimination in all aspects of daily life. More recently several states have recognized the rights of gay people to employment free of discrimination but there are no federal laws prohibiting discrimination against homosexuals in employment, housing, military service, and public accommodations. Groups representing the rights of gay people such as the American Civil Liberties Union are presenting their case to the federal government about the need to provide the same civil rights protections to gay people that are afforded to racial minorities, women, the disabled, and the elderly. A major step toward achieving this goal was the passing of the 2003 Local Law Enforcement Enhancement Act, formerly known as the Hate Crimes Prevention Act.

Gay parents and their children sometimes experience prejudice and isolation from other family members, neighbors, employers, and society in general. According to *The National Gay and Lesbian Family Study,* published in 2001 by the American Psychological Association, many gay parents are rejected by relatives, coworkers, and even professionals in schools and health-care agencies. Approximately 44 percent of lesbians and 27 percent of gay men reported negative reactions from family members when they shared their decision to have a child. Dr. Lynn Ponton of the National Mental Health Association (NMHA) published a report in 2004 that states that children who are raised by gay parents, are gay themselves, or even perceived as gay by their peers experience prejudice, teasing, and bullying. Her goal is to educate adults and children about what it means to be gay, as well as the harm antigay prejudice can do to the self-esteem and mental health of young people.

TEENS SPEAK

My Parents Are Gay

I found out my parents were gay when I was seven. Up until then, I just thought families had two dads, two moms, or one of each. I just didn't give it that much thought. But when I came home from school and asked my dad what "gay" meant, he sat me down and told me. At first, I thought maybe it was bad to have gay parents. Kids teased me and my dads always asked me if I was okay about that. With so much attention being paid to it, I started to think maybe something was wrong with it. Now that I am a teenager, I know that lots of people are really uncomfortable with this subject and even mean and judgmental. But I still don't really see why people are having so much trouble understanding that when two people love each other, they just want to be a family. Why people judge other people is just something I don't think I will ever understand. My parents are my parents; I love them just as much as anyone else loves their parents.

LEGAL AND FINANCIAL IMPLICATIONS

In almost every state, gay people cannot legally marry one another. In some, they cannot adopt children or become foster parents. Those who already have children may face restrictions related to custody of their children or visitation rights. Because a homosexual relationship is not recognized as a marriage by the federal government or most state governments, gay parents often draw up legal documents to protect a partner's right to inherit property, participate in medical decision making, and assume guardianship of the children.

Without legal protections, gay parents and their children may find themselves unable to claim such benefits as life insurance, Social Security, or an inheritance if a parent dies.

More than one in 10 gay couples in the 2000 Census included a person over the age of 65. Slightly more than 60 percent of these couples have lived together for five years or more. According to the Gay and Lesbian Community center of Cincinnati, if a partner dies, these gay couples will not receive Social Security, a pension, or other survivor benefits. The center also reports that gay couples continue to be penalized financially and legally for lack of a recognized marital status. Gay and lesbian groups have yet to be guaranteed federal protection of their civil rights. This includes their financial and legal rights as well, say members of the Gay and Lesbian Community Center of Cincinnati.

CULTURAL AND RELIGIOUS ISSUES

Even as research and public opinion polls show an overall rise in acceptance of gay men and women, many Americans are opposed to homosexual behaviors. Numerous studies have been conducted by Gregory M. Herek, a professor of psychology at the University of California at Davis, on changing attitudes toward gay people. While the overall attitude toward gay people has become more favorable, when it comes to religion and homosexuality, attitudes remain unfavorable. According to a report by the Pew Forum on Religion and Public Life, religious beliefs are cited as the major reason for these attitudes. The survey, conducted in 2004 found that 55 percent of Americans believe it is a sin to engage in homosexual behavior. The percentage rises to 76 percent among those who claim to have a strong religious commitment. The report suggests that religious beliefs may also be a factor in the recent rise in opposition to gay marriage and parenting.

In the summer of 2003, the Roman Catholic Church, with an estimated 62 million members, issued a formal statement on its position on gay relationships. Church leaders stated that gay men and lesbians were welcome in the church, provided they remain **celibate**—abstain from sexual intercourse. The leaders also condemned discrimination against gays and supported an increase in research funding for the treatment and prevention of HIV/AIDS. Yet, they also clearly stated their opposition to gay marriage and rejected the adoption of children by gay and lesbian parents.

According to Public Agenda, a nonpartisan opinion research organization, even with religious opposition, attitudes about gay relationships are changing even in faith-based communities. With the numbers of gay couples parenting on the rise, social and religious debate over gay marriage and parenting will surely continue. And while some people feel or believe that children in families with gay parents are disadvantaged in some way, this view is not supported by current research.

Q & A

Question: What do parents feel are the advantages and disadvantages their children may face growing up with gay parents?

Answer: In a national study of gay and lesbian parents conducted in 2000 by developmental psychologists Suzanne Johnson and Elizabeth O'Connor, 415 gay and lesbian parents were asked about family life. The study revealed that as many as 82 percent of gay mothers and 85 percent of gay fathers worried about potential bullying and teasing of their children because their parents are gay. Only 17 percent of the mothers and 8 percent of the fathers thought that their children would suffer by not having a role model for the "missing" gender in their parent relationship. Gay parents felt that their children benefited by being more accepting of others and would rely less on stereotypes about gender roles to form opinions about other people.

Source: Johnson, Suzanne M., and Elizabeth O'Connor. *The National Gay and Lesbian Family Study.* Washington, DC: American Psychological Association, 2001.

See also: Family, The New; Religion and the Family

FURTHER READING
Carrington, Christopher. *No Place Like Home.* Chicago: University of Chicago Press, 2000.
Coontz, Stephanie. *The Way We Never Were: American Families and the Nostalgia Trap.* New York: Basic Books, 2000.
Drucker, Jane, and Harold Schulweis. *Lesbian and Gay Families Speak Out: Understanding the Joys and Challenges of Diverse Family Life.* Boulder, CO: Perseus Publishing, 2001.
Garner, Abigail. *Families Like Mine: Children of Gay Parents Tell It Like It Is.* New York: HarperCollins, 2004.
Johnson, Suzanne M., and Elizabeth O'Connor. *The Gay Baby Boom: The Psychology of Gay Parenthood.* New York: New York University Press, 2002.

■ MARRIAGE AND FAMILY, CHANGES IN

Both men and women today are marrying later in life than at any other time in the past 100 years. Changing beliefs about appropriate family roles have led to greater sharing of household and economic responsibilities. These changes in marriage and family have occurred largely in response to economic and cultural pressures.

DOMESTIC PARTNERS

According to the census of 2000, 5.5 million unmarried couples were cohabiting–that is, living together. In 1960, the census reported that fewer than 500,000 unmarried couples were living together. About 60 percent of those couples were between 25 and 44 years of age and 36 percent had children under the age of 15. According to the U.S. Census Bureau, many couples live together before marrying. In 2000, more than half of heterosexual couples who planned to marry cohabited before they were wed. In 1965, that figure was 10 percent. Despite fierce opposition to cohabitation by religious and conservative groups, an increasing number of unmarried couples are living together, either as a prelude to marriage or because of a lifestyle choice.

People cohabit for many reasons. It may be a utilitarian arrangement in which partners live together to share costs and household tasks. They may or may not have an intimate relationship with their housemate. Other couples see cohabitation as a trial marriage, a chance to test their compatibility and decide if they want to marry. Couples who are planning to marry may move in together during the engagement period, often because they see no reason to live apart while preparing for a wedding.

Some cohabiting couples who are intimately involved engage in sex only with each other. They have a **monogamous** relationship. These couples may view cohabitation as a substitute for marriage and do not intend to marry for practical or philosophical reasons. For instance, marriage may mean the loss of financial benefits such as financial support from a former spouse (**alimony**) or a former employer (**pension payments**). One or both of the partners may be separated but not divorced from a previous marriage or have been unhappily married in the past and not wish to marry again. In most states, cohabitation is the only option available to same-sex couples. However, most cohabiting couples are heterosexual.

Fact Or Fiction?

Families are becoming a thing of the past.

Fact: Although the divorce rate remains high, and the percentage of unmarried couples who live together has climbed in recent years, there is no evidence that Americans are giving up on marriage or families. Most people who cohabitate eventually marry, and most people who divorce remarry within a few years of their divorce. While this trend helps to create blended families and other complex family structures, it does not seem to indicate that marriage as an institution is about to dissolve. Americans still want to marry. But they also want the freedom to leave marriages that are not happy. Instead of spending a lifetime in an unhappy marriage, Americans are ending unfulfilling marital partnerships and searching for better marriages and happier family lives.

The rapid increase in the number of cohabiting couples in the United States has prompted some employers and some local governments to recognize these couples as **domestic partners**. While definitions of domestic partnership vary widely, it is usually defined as a stable, intimate relationship between two people who are financially interdependent. Employers may offer domestic partners the same benefit plans, including health insurance, provided to married employees. Some city and state governments also recognize domestic partnerships. Legal status as domestic partners may or may not result in tangible benefits, such as shared health insurance plans.

Within one and one-half years of moving in together, half of cohabiting couples either marry or break up. Domestic partnerships may be less stable than marriages, according to a 2000 study released by the Centers for Disease Control and Prevention (CDC). CDC researchers found that the probability of a cohabitation breaking up within five years is 49 percent compared to the 20 percent chance of a first marriage ending in divorce within five years. After 10 years, the chance that a first marriage will end is 33 percent compared with 62 percent for cohabitation. In general, unmarried couples who live together report poorer relationships than their married counterparts. CDC researchers speculate that the poorer quality reported by cohabiting couples could be due to less commitment to a lasting partnership.

However, the unions of domestic partners who plan to marry do not appear to be significantly different from those who wait until marriage to live together. While some studies have suggested a link between cohabitation before marriage and an increased risk of divorce, a 2003 study by Jay Teachman, a sociologist at Western Washington University, challenges this theory. Teachman asked women who participated in the 1995 National Survey of Family Growth whether they had engaged in premarital sex and cohabitation before marriage. He found no link between divorce and premarital sex, and divorce and cohabitation for women who eventually married their domestic partner. His research suggests that women who are committed to a single relationship do not increase their risk of divorce.

DELAYED MARRIAGE

Both men and women in the United States are waiting longer to marry. In 1890, the median age at first marriage was 26 years for men and 22 years for women. For most of the early 20th century, the age at which people wed decreased steadily, reaching a low of 22.5 years for men and 20.1 years for women in the mid-1950s. By 1959, nearly half of all women were under the age of 19 when they married.

Historian Steven Mintz, a professor at the University of Houston, attributes the decline in age at first marriage during the early 1900s to economic and social factors. As more people left farms to work in cities and towns, a new idea about marriage developed: the **companionate family**, one in which the family is seen as the primary source of emotional satisfaction and personal happiness. These two influences combined to lead many couples to marry as a way to escape the social isolation of the city, seeking intimacy and fulfillment from marriage and early childbearing.

Age at first marriage increased slightly during the 1930s—a period of much poverty and unemployment across the nation. Marriages were postponed as people shared their home with needy relatives and focused on day-to-day survival. When the United States entered World War II in 1941, the economy improved rapidly and the marriage rate increased dramatically. As more and more young men went off to war, the age of first-time brides and grooms dropped. After the war ended in 1945, the economy continued to grow and the age at which couples tied the knot continued to fall.

Since the mid-1950s, however, the median age at first marriage has been rising, with the biggest increases occurring since 1980. In 2003, the median age at first marriage was 27.1 years for men and 25.3

DID YOU KNOW?

Median Age at First Marriage, 1890–2002

Median Age at First Marriage of the Population 15 Years and Over by Sex: Selected Years, 1890 to 2002.

Year	Males	Females
1890	26.1	22.0
1900	25.9	21.9
1910	25.1	21.6
1920	24.6	21.2
1930	24.3	21.3
1940	24.3	21.5
1950	22.8	20.3
1960	22.8	20.3
1970	23.2	20.8
1980	24.7	22.0
1990	26.1	23.9
1993	26.5	24.5
1994	26.7	24.5
1995	26.9	24.5
1996	27.1	24.8
1997	26.8	25.0
1998	26.7	25.0
1999	26.9	25.1
2000	26.8	25.1
2001	26.9	25.1
2002	26.9	25.3

Source: U.S. Census Bureau, 2002.

years for women. In 2002, 54 percent of men had not married by the time they reached their 30th birthdays, while 40 percent of women remained single at 30 years of age.

As F. Philip Rice, professor emeritus at the University of Maine–Orono, observes in *Intimate Relationships, Marriages, and Families,* people may be delaying marriage for several reasons, including increased opportunities for nonmarital sexual intercourse, increased acceptance of cohabitation, and less societal disapproval of single people. Rice suggests that many young adults are waiting to complete college and find their first job before marrying. In addition, women are now encouraged to develop identities outside of marriage and pursue careers and economic self-sufficiency both in and out of marriage.

However, most people do eventually marry. In 2003, according to Census Bureau data, only 12.7 percent of men and 9.5 percent of women had never married by the time they were 45 years old. The trend toward delayed marriage is significant because age at first marriage is the strongest predictor of marital success. Those who marry later are more likely to have a lasting marriage.

MARRIAGE AMONG WORKING COUPLES

In most marriages today, both spouses engage in paid work outside of the home. In the **dual-earner** family, both spouses are part of the labor force. According to the Census Bureau, in 1960, only 18 percent of women who had a child less than one year of age worked outside the home. By 2000, 55 percent of women with a child less than one year of age were in the labor force.

The dual-career family is a subset of the dual-earner family. While in most marriages today, both partners work outside the home, dual-career families are far less common. Both partners in these families are committed to both their professional and family lives. They constantly juggle roles and responsibilities. Pursuit of a career requires commitment and continuous professional development. For most professionals, having a career means full-time employment with little time away from the job and significant responsibilities on the job. The greater time commitment means they have less time to give to their mate and children.

Finding and paying for adequate child care is a challenge for many dual-earner families. In 2004, these parents paid on average more than $7,000 annually for child care, according to a study by Runzheimer

International, a consulting firm. The cost of care in a caregiver's home, averaged $9,100 per year, while the annual cost of a live-in nanny was $27,664. Although government-subsidized child-care programs offer services on a sliding scale basis, dual-earner couples may earn too much to qualify. In addition, many child-care facilities offer services only during standard working hours, which can pose problems for some working couples, especially those on night or evening shifts. Schedule limitations may also affect parents whose jobs require travel, those who work extra hours to complete projects, and those who are required to attend weekend seminars and continuing education courses.

Both dual-earner and dual-career couples balance the combined demands of marriage, child rearing, career, home, and friendships. Despite these challenges, there are tangible benefits to living in a two-income family. Most dual-earner couples enjoy higher incomes and a higher standard of living. In a study published in 2001 in the *Journal of Marriage and the Family*, sociologists Stacey J. Rogers and Danelle D. DeBoer found that as the income of women rises, so does their overall level of marital satisfaction and well-being.

In a 2003 study, also published in the *Journal of Marriage and the Family*, Rogers and her colleague Dee C. May found that job satisfaction and marital happiness were closely related. Rogers and May looked at data from 12 years of interviews with 2,034 married couples. As partners became happier in their marriages, they also became more satisfied with their jobs; when marital happiness decreased, so did job satisfaction at work. Marital happiness had a greater influence on job satisfaction than job satisfaction did on marital happiness. Both men and women were affected about equally. Rogers and May concluded that findings were consistent with previous research that showed the centrality of marital relationships in people's lives.

Q & A

Question: What can I do to reduce the chance that I will divorce?

Answer: Wait to marry, go to college, and delay having your first child until you've been married for at least seven months. According to data from the U.S. Census Bureau, almost half of all women who marry before the age of 18 divorce within 10 years, while less than a quarter of those who wait until they are 25 or older to marry divorce within the same time period. A second important predictor of divorce is education level. White men who have completed five or more years of college, and white women who have completed four years of college are the least likely to divorce. The timing of the birth of the first child in a family is another important predictor of divorce. Women who give birth within seven months of their marriage are twice as likely to divorce as those who wait to have their first child.

Many women who work report greater satisfaction with their lives overall, especially if they enjoy their job and their spouse is willing to help with household tasks and child care. In a study published in 2002 by the *Journal of Marriage and the Family*, a team of researchers led by sociologist Mary Maguire Klute found that the type of job a person holds influences marital equality, which in turn is an important predictor of overall happiness. Klute examined the relationship between the experiences of husbands and wives at work and their attitudes about and behaviors in marriage. She found that people who worked in jobs that required self-direction—for instance, making independent decisions, thinking for oneself, and setting one's own standards for behavior—were more likely to adopt more equal, or **egalitarian** arrangements in their marriages. These couples divided household tasks and child care more equally than did couples whose jobs required conformity—for instance, being neat, on time, and otherwise complying with standards set by authority figures. More egalitarian attitudes and behaviors in marriage, in turn, contributed to greater marital happiness.

MARRIAGE AMONG SAME-SEX COUPLES

In November 2003, the Supreme Judicial Court of Massachusetts ruled that the state could not refuse to allow gay and lesbian couples to marry. In response to an appeal, the court confirmed its decision that barring gays and lesbians from marriage was a violation of the state's constitution. The United States Supreme Court upheld the decision on May 17, 2004, and many same-sex couples rushed to the altar.

Despite the decision in Massachusetts, many gay and lesbian couples continue to experience discrimination. Thirty-eight states and the U.S. Congress have passed laws that explicitly prohibit gay and lesbian couples from marrying and/or refuse to honor gay marriages legal in another state. Although civil unions are allowed in Vermont and California has a domestic partnership system similar to Vermont's civil unions, the rights conferred by these unions are limited. In 1999, the Vermont Supreme Court ordered the state's legislature to extend to same-sex couples the same rights, protections, benefits, and obligations that heterosexual couples are afforded through marriage. Some other states have registration procedures for same-sex couples that grant them limited benefits. However, even the most extensive protections for gay and lesbian couples fall short of those afforded by legal marriages.

Marriage confers about 1,400 benefits, usually composed of about 400 state benefits and 1,000 federal benefits. These benefits include rights such as joint parenting, joint adoption, status of next-of-kin for hospital visits and medical decisions, dissolution and divorce protections for community property and child support, and benefits such as annuities, pension plans, Social Security, and Medicare.

The last half of the 20th century saw profound shifts in the structure and function of marriage and family life in the United States. Many unmarried couples are living together in domestic partnerships, often as a prelude to marriage. Men and women are waiting to marry until they are in their mid-to-late 20s. Several factors may contribute to delays in marriage, including increased opportunities for nonmarital sexual intercourse, increased acceptance of cohabitation, and less societal disapproval of single people. Among married couples, the two-income family has become increasingly common. Two-income couples often face challenges in managing their time and caring for children.

As more women enter the workforce, gender roles are being transformed within families. Women are sharing economic responsibilities, while men are taking on more household tasks and child care responsibilities. Same-sex couples are allowed to marry in Massachusetts and form civil unions or domestic partnerships in Vermont and California. However, gays and lesbians in most states are still fighting for the right to marry.

See also: Adoption; Day Care; Divorce and Families; Families, Blended; Families, Racially Mixed; Family, The New; Family, The Traditional; Gay Parents; Media and the Family; Single-Parent Families; Stepparents; Teenage Parents

FURTHER READING

Coontz, Stephanie. *The Way We Really Are: Ending the War over America's Changing Families.* New York: Basic Books, 1998.

Henslin, James M. *Marriage and Family in a Changing Society.* 4th ed. New York: Free Press, 1992.

Scott, Mary Ann, and Barbara Marliene Schwartz. *Marriages and Families: Diversity and Change.* 4th ed. New York: Prentice Hall, 2002.

■ MEDIA AND THE FAMILY

The mass media includes radio, television, films, the Internet, books, newspapers, and magazines.

IMPACT ON CHILDREN

Messages sent to children in any form can be positive or harmful. According to the American Academy of Pediatrics (AAP), the average amount of time children spent deciphering media messages in 2001 was more than 21 hours per week. Many experts believe the number is low, mainly because people are exposed to media messages not only through active viewing but also through passive exposure. Greg Taillon, author of *Remote Control Wars: The Battle for the Hearts and Minds of Our Youth,* claims the number of hours is probably more than 38 hours per week—almost four times the amount of time children spend on schoolwork.

After a thorough review of the research, the AAP argues that exposure to media has both benefits and risks. The benefits include increased access to information. For example, learning has been revolutionized as a result of access to the Internet. Social relationships both within the family and with friends often center on the shared experience of viewing popular programs or news events. Families today have greater understanding of global events and other cultures because of their access to news from around the world.

While experts recognize the educational and social benefits of exposure to media, they express greater concern over the risks of too much exposure. The research compiled by the AAP lists several downsides to increased exposure to media. More than a thousand studies show an increased risk of aggressive behavior in certain children and adolescents as a result of exposure to violent media messages. The AAP research review also found a connection between the time spent viewing TV programs, playing video games, or working on the computer and childhood obesity. In fact, a 2003 study published in the journal *Pediatrics* reported that the more children watch television, the more likely they are to eat junk food. In the report's conclusion, researchers cited advertising as the reason for an increased desire for junk food. Victor C. Strasburger, a physician and expert on media exposure and emotional and behavioral concerns, has expressed concerns about the negative effects of exposure to sexualized content and the irresponsible use of alcohol, tobacco, and drugs teens are exposed to in the media.

FAMILY PROGRAMS ON TV

The nonprofit organization TV-Turnoff Network tries to raise awareness of the impact of television on family life. The group points out that American children watch an average of three hours of television each day. Although the research suggests that watching television as a family is better for children than watching alone, 80 percent of the time children watch alone and unsupervised.

TV-Turnoff Network recommends that parents decrease the amount of time their children spend watching television. That recommendation is supported by the American Academy of Pediatrics. The group recommends no television viewing for children under the age of two and no more than two hours per day of "high-quality" television programming for older children.

The Media Awareness Network points out that some television shows can benefit family life. Television programs that are educational and expose families to information about other cultures may help both children and their parents see the world from other points of view. News programs and documentaries may help students deepen or expand their understanding of subjects that they are studying in school. Watching television as a family, experts agree, allows parents to teach children to better understand the media messages they see and hear.

Q & A

Question: Can parents really do anything to minimize their children's exposure to negative media messages?

Answer: Yes, as Victor Strasburger reports in *Children, Adolescents and Media*, experts say parents can do a lot to minimize the negative impact media messages have on children related to body image, substance use, sexuality, and violence. Limiting exposure to media messages, discussing media messages, and supervising the use of technology are important ways parents can influence exposure to media messages of all kinds.

ROLE MODELS AND FAMILIES

Media sources provide **role models** for children. Role models are people who are considered worthy of imitation. Role models can provide children with positive examples. However, some children choose individuals who set poor examples by abusing alcohol or drugs as their role models.

Many researchers are concerned that the media exposes children to poor role models. The Media Awareness Network, is particularly troubled by the effects of role models in the fashion industry and the sexualized content often found in advertisements. Although the organization's research finds more positive role models for both boys and girls in the media than ever before, it remains concerned about the effects of negative role models on children's behavior. An organization called Children Now found in its 1997 study that positive role models were found in television programs and advertising aimed at teens. These positive examples showed teens with the ability to make good decisions as well as teens able to problem solve well. The same study revealed however, that media messages still provide images of beauty that are unrealistic and unattainable, especially for girls.

Fact Or Fiction?

Children prefer to play video games and watch television over reading books for pleasure.

Fact: While many children enjoy video games, the computer, and television, in *Zero to Six: Electronic Media in the Lives of Infants, Toddlers, and Preschoolers* Vicky Rideout presents studies that show reading is still an enjoyable pastime for children. In a study done in 2003, 79 percent of children six and under read or were read to most days. The average time spent reading was slightly less than an hour a day. This year alone, publishers reported millions of dollars in sales of children's books to parents. While these sales figures are higher than in previous years, organizations such as TV-Turnoff Network continue to worry that time spent watching or interacting with computer games and video games do have children reading less.

MEDIA LITERACY

The Center for Media Literacy is a nonprofit educational organization whose aim it is to educate people about the influence of media on families. The group's definition of media literacy or media education is widely used: "Media literacy is a 21st century approach to education. It provides a framework to access, analyze, evaluate and create messages in a variety of forms—from print to video to the Internet. Media literacy builds an understanding of the role of media in society as well as essential skills of inquiry and self-expression necessary for citizens of a democracy." Experts including the American Academy of Pediatrics (AAP) agree that the negative effects of media on children can be minimized and the positive effects maximized when parents engage in media education with children.

The Centers for Disease Control and Prevention, the Substance Abuse and Mental Health Services Administration (SAMHSA), the AAP, the National Education Association (NEA) Health Information Network, and the U.S. Department of Health and Human Services (HHS) all have studies showing that media education or media literacy may result in young people becoming less vulnerable to the negative aspects of media exposure. In the AAP review of research, experts state, "A media-educated person will be able to limit use of media; make positive media choices; select creative alternatives to media consumption; develop critical thinking and viewing skills; and understand the political, social, economic, and emotional implications of all forms of media."

See also: Family Rules

FURTHER READING
Healey, Jane M. *Endangered Minds.* New York: Simon and Schuster, 1999.

Perse, Elizabeth M. *Media and Society.* New York: Lea Books, 2001.

Rideout, Vicky. *Zero to Six: Electronic Media in the Lives of Infants, Toddlers, and Preschoolers.* Menlo Park, CA: Kaiser Family Foundation, 2003.

Steyer, James P. *The Other Parent: The Inside Story of the Media's Effect on Our Children.* New York: Atria, 2003.

Strasburger, Victor C. *Children, Adolescents and Media.* New York: Sage Publications, 2002.

Winn, Marie. *The Plug-In Drug: Television, Computers and Family Life.* New York: Penguin, 2002.

■ PETS IN THE FAMILY

Pets are tame animals kept by a family as companions. Many families all over the world keep pets such as dogs, cats, birds, and fish. Some even own more exotic pets like monkeys, raccoons, alligators, and pythons. Some families regard such farm animals as horses, rabbits, and llamas as family pets as well.

Fact Or Fiction?

The domestic dogs that we keep as pets developed from the wolf.

Fact: Although pet dogs did develop from wolves, dogs have changed as a result of thousands of years of involvement with humans. In the beginning, humans may have raised wolf cubs as guards. Through generations of human selection and random breeding, those wolves became domesticated, or tamed. North American wolves were ancestors to some dog breeds, such as the Alaskan Malamute, while Asian and European wolves were the stock for other breeds. DNA testing has traced these links.

For many Americans, it's impossible to picture a home without a dog or cat. Pets are great companions. A 2004 survey by Stephen Sundlof in *FDA Consumer* found that Americans care for about 77 million pet cats and 65 million dogs. Two issues surrounding the decision to acquire a pet include allergies and the responsibility of taking care of the animal.

CHILDREN'S IMMUNE RESPONSE AND PETS

When a human comes into contact with an irritant, such as cat saliva or fur, the immune system in the body responds to it. The individual's reaction to the irritant is known as an **immune response** or immune reaction. If contact with a cat or dog results in watery eyes, a stuffy nose, asthma, or a skin rash, a person is said to have an allergic reaction to the animal.

Recent studies in 2002 in the *Journal of the American Medical Association* and the *Lancet* suggest that pets do not cause allergies, except in very specific instances. In a study conducted at three American medical colleges, scientists followed 474 children from birth to age seven. Researchers concluded that exposing a child to two or more dogs or cats in his or her first year may reduce the risk of allergy. However, another study found that children born to mothers with asthma were more likely to develop wheezing around a cat. But for children whose mothers do not have asthma, exposure to a cat in early childhood reduced the risk of asthma and allergies.

A study in the *Journal of Allergy and Clinical Immunology* followed 285 infants from birth to one year. Each infant had at least one parent with an allergy or asthma. The researchers found eczema in 12 percent of infants with dogs and 43 percent of infants without a pet. Early exposure to a dog appeared to increase interleukin-10 levels in the children. Interleukin-10 has been shown to help prevent allergies. Some studies indicate that not only children, but also adults can benefit from having pets. According to Sundlof's article, pets help people lower their blood pressure.

TEACHING RESPONSIBILITY

Pets provide an opportunity to teach children responsibility. Children need to be shown just how dependent animals are on them for food, water, and exercise. People are not born knowing how to treat and care for pets, however. Children under 10 are rarely able to care for a cat or dog on their own. They may not realize how often a bird needs to eat to stay alive, that a turtle needs meat along with vegetable matter to survive, or that cats must have a bowl of water to drink.

Q & A

Question: What is the ASPCA?

Answer: The American Society for the Prevention of Cruelty to Animals (ASPCA) tries to prevent cruelty to animals by offering national programs in humane education, through public awareness and government advocacy, and by offering shelter and medical services for and placement of unclaimed animals. The New York City headquarters includes a full-service animal hospital, behavior center, adoption facility, and humane law enforcement department.

Since 1866, the ASPCA has been committed to alleviating pain, fear, and suffering in all animals. It is the oldest humane organization in the United States and was founded by Henry Bergh, a philanthropist and diplomat who recognized the inhumane treatment suffered by many animals throughout the nation. The ASPCA is a privately funded, not-for-profit corporation.

A parent who understands how to care for pets can provide a good role model for his or her children. Parents and children can work together to keep their pet healthy.

If children become lax in caring for a pet, they should be reminded of their responsibility to their pets. If reminding does not help, parents may have to take over the responsibility or find a new home for the animal. An article in 2000 on pets and children by the American Academy of Child and Adolescent Psychiatry stresses that pets should not suffer from lack of food or care because a child does not shoulder his or her responsibility.

Mother Earth News warns against animal abuse. Intentional and repeated abuse of animals by older children should be viewed as a serious matter. A child who abuses is not just going through a phase. Studies show that children who deliberately abuse animals will often later abuse other children, property, and adults.

TEENS SPEAK

My Dog Is Precious to Me

I always have my dog Copper. I'm not lonely when I'm with him. He goes running with me. I practice homework with him because he listens. He understands words in Spanish now. I'm shy, but when he's with me, I can talk easily to other people.

Everyone in my family likes Copper. In the morning, he licks my sister awake. He's fun to watch and he herds us around. As soon as he hears the keys to the van jingle, he runs out and circles the van until we're all inside and then he jumps into his seat in the center of the middle seat.

Sometimes Copper is bad. He lets the rabbit out of the cage to watch it run. He is also hilarious. When we drive by the cows on the university campus farm, Copper closes his eyes, lifts his nose, and breathes in the smell of the animals. He's that way when we pass the zoo, too. He really likes that smell.

All of us (mom, dad, and four kids) care about our dog. When he escapes, we worry and run around the neighborhood looking for him. When he's sick, we worry and worry. When I saw the small kids across the street dragging their dogs and flinging them around, I asked my mother to go over and talk to them. And she did. Having Copper makes me worry about all animals. I wish everyone would.

Pet owners are responsible for their pet's behavior. Every year about 4.5 million dog bites occur in the United States, according to the Centers for Disease Control and Prevention (CDC). About 26 percent of children who are bitten require medical attention. Dog bites are more serious among young children. Probably because of their small size, they receive bites mainly on the head and neck. Teens and adults receive bites mainly on their hands and arms. The CDC suggests that a person not pet or make eye contact with an unfamiliar dog and not pet any dog without allowing it to see and sniff you first. Children and adults also need to learn how to approach a dog. When

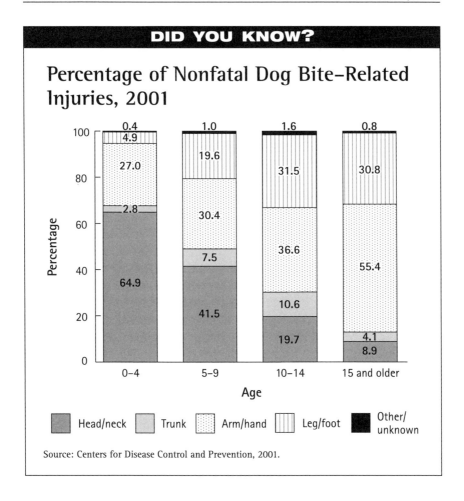

DID YOU KNOW?

Percentage of Nonfatal Dog Bite–Related Injuries, 2001

Source: Centers for Disease Control and Prevention, 2001.

a strange dog comes near, they should remain quiet and calm. If they run or panic, the dog may run after them.

COMPANIONSHIP

Many people report feeling happier caring for a pet. The CDC says that the company of a pet can lower blood pressure and decrease cholesterol and triglyceride levels—possibly because pets, especially dogs, need to be walked daily. Researchers at the Mayo Clinic have also noted that dog owners are more likely to survive a heart attack than non-dog-owners.

Pets provide more than companionship. Dogs and even rabbits visit hospitals and nursing facilities to provide patients and elderly residents with attention. Specially trained dogs assist people with disabilities, helping them handle everyday tasks. Seeing-eye dogs guide those who are blind. Other dogs hear for their human companions. Still others help by picking up items from the ground or alerting their companion to a possible seizure.

The Salt Lake City Public Library uses dogs as reading companions. Once a week, kids from five to nine years old read aloud to Reading Education Assistance Dogs. The director of the program says that children like reading to dogs because dogs do not laugh at mistakes. Children who lack confidence in their reading ability are able to relax by reading aloud to the dogs.

Pets can provide companionship and support for their owners. The only drawbacks are allergies and the need for owners to assume responsibility for their pets.

See also: Death in the Family; Family Rules

FURTHER READING
Gerstenfeld, Sheldon. *ASPCA: A Complete Guide to Dogs.* San Francisco: Chronicle Books, 1999.
Herriot, James. *All Creatures Great and Small.* New York: St. Martin's Press, 1972.
Humane Society of the United States. *Complete Guide to Cat Care.* New York: St. Martin's Press, 2002.
Puotinen, C. J. *Encyclopedia of Natural Pet Care,* Rev. ed. Los Angeles: Keats Publishing, 1998.

■ RELIGION AND THE FAMILY

Religion is a formal expression of or institution based on a belief in a divine or higher power that controls human destiny. In 2000, Harris Interactive, a national polling service, found that 94 percent of Americans claim that they believe in God. According to the Institute for Youth Development, religious faith is also strong among young people. Their studies show that 94 percent of teens say they believe in God and nearly nine in 10 teens consider their religious beliefs important to them.

The Heritage Foundation cites considerable research that demonstrates that regular religious practice is both good for the individual and for society. For example, a 1995 study published in the *Journal of Social Issues* found religious practices strongly linked with positive indicators of adolescent mental health. Another study cited by the Heritage Foundation reported that church attendance was strongly connected to indicators of family stability: "It is a powerful answer to many of our most significant social problems, some of which have reached catastrophic proportions. The practice of religion is good for individuals, families, states, and the nation. It improves health, learning, economic well-being, self-control, self-esteem, and empathy."

REARING CHILDREN IN FAITH

In many families, religion is an important part of family life. Their faith helps parents manage both work and family and is a vital resource in teaching their children about faith and morality. Religion can also strengthen family relationships. Penny Edgell, director of the Religion and Family Project at the University of Minnesota, found in her 1999 study that despite ongoing social change, religion and families still go hand and hand.

Raising children with faith or in a faith community is important to many families. In other families, religion may be a source of tension. Debates over religion within the family have been going on for generations and continue today. Whether a person focuses on organized religion or a sense of spirituality and faith, beliefs are individual and personal.

In 2003, the Barna Research Group, a marketing research firm serving nonprofit organizations and various media and financial corporations, found that 85 percent of parents believe that they are responsible for teaching their children about spirituality and faith. Religious education is defined as a tool used to transmit knowledge and values pertaining to a particular faith. Exposure to the stories, beliefs, theologies, and practices of a family's religion will give children the tools they need to make up their own minds about life's big questions.

The National Study of Youth and Religion (NSYR) is an ongoing project whose purpose is to research the influence of religion and spirituality on the lives of adolescents in the United States. Their findings suggest that religiously involved families are more likely to have stronger relationships than families that are not religiously active.

According to Mark Baker, clinical director of the LaVie Counseling Center, children benefit from learning that there is something greater than themselves in the spectrum of life. David J. Wolpe, author of *Teaching Your Children about God*, says that parents who model their faith and talk early and often about God in everyday life have children that gain a sense of comfort and learn to know God. In a 1998 study, conducted by the Barna Research Group, 47 percent of teens say that their parents have the greatest influence on their spiritual development.

Parents interested in teaching religion, faith, or spirituality should begin by sharing their own beliefs. Conversations are meaningful when parents talk openly and honestly about faith and the mysteries of life. Every family is different when it comes to spiritual beliefs, so how parents proceed with religious teaching is personal. Laying a strong foundation for ongoing communication is an important step in this process of introducing religion.

Q & A

Question: Should parents teach their children their own beliefs or wait until their children are old enough to make their own decision about religion?

Answer: According to Martha Fay, author of *Do Children Need Religion? How Parents Today Are Thinking about the Big Questions*, children need to be taught about religion more today than ever before because of our fast-paced and constantly changing society. While many parents oversee the spiritual direction of their children in churches and synagogues, others struggle on their own. Parents are looking for a way to teach religion that gives children the best of what religion has to offer but does not build resentment. She goes on to observe that parents want "to give their children what they need but not what will trap or limit them."

INTERFAITH FAMILIES

While statistics are elusive on the exact number of interfaith families in the United States, many faith communities believe that the number is rising, particularly among young adults. James Davidson, a professor of sociology at Purdue University, shared statistics from his 2000 report. Davidson claims that between 29 and 40 percent of Catholics marry non-Catholics. Egon Mayer, director of research for the Jewish Outreach Institute, cites a 1990 national study that suggests 50 percent of Jews marry non-Jews.

According to Interfaith Family, an online community, interfaith families should speak openly about how to mix and mesh traditions such as weddings, ceremonies, and holiday celebrations as well as how to raise children. For many interfaith families, the religious goal is to honor the distinctiveness of each religious tradition and not to try and create a new blend.

Interfaith marriages pose challenges for families, religious establishments, faith communities, and society at large. Often, families feel lonely and isolated from faith communities and sometimes from extended families, too.

Fact Or Fiction?

Growing up in an interfaith family is too confusing to children.

Fact: When parents take an active role in teaching children about their family's faith, children need not be confused. Robin Margolis, an interfaith religious educator, says that the best way to make growing up in an interfaith family a positive experience is to give children information about both religions. She recommends that instead of blending religious beliefs, expose children to the rich traditions of both. Later, she says it is important for parents to respect their adult children's choice regarding religion.

In a 2001 article entitled "Raising Children in Two-religion Families," Gayle Peterson, a family therapist, says many interfaith families ascribe to dual or integrated celebrations. According to Peterson, interfaith families may consciously choose what part religion will play in family life. She says that because of the need for interfaith families to integrate or choose religious teachings that fit with individual beliefs and values, many families create a more personal and conscious faith life.

See also: Death in the Family; Family Traditions; Gay Parents

FURTHER READING
Gruzen, Lee F. *Raising Your Jewish/Christian Child: How Interfaith Parents Can Give Children the Best of Both of Their Heritages.* New York: Newmarket Press, 2001.
Schaper, Donna E. *Raising Interfaith Children: Spiritual Orphans or Spiritual Heirs.* New York: Crossroad Publishing, 1999.
Yust, Karen M. *Real Children, Real Faith.* New York: Jossey-Bass, 2004.

■ SINGLE-PARENT FAMILIES

A single-parent family is composed of a parent and one or more children. The parent may have never been married or have been widowed or divorced. Single-parent families face a number of financial, psychological, and societal challenges.

FINANCIAL ISSUES

According to the Census Bureau, 27 percent of all children in the United States are living in single-parent households. The nation is home to more than 11.9 million single parents. Of single-parent households, 84 percent are headed by a female, while males head about 16 percent. These households include a disproportionate number of African Americans. Sixty-four percent of African-American children under the age of 18 live with one parent or neither parent. In comparison, about 26 percent of white children under the age of 18 live with a single parent or neither parent.

Single parents face a host of challenges in raising their children. They must constantly balance the demands of their job, child care, and their own needs. All too often, they face financial difficulties. While both women and men who become single as a result of divorce or the death of a spouse often experience a drastic decrease in income, this decrease is often more significant for women. Census data reveals that in 2001, the average income of single-mother families was $28,142, while single-father families had an annual average income of $40,715. By comparison, two-parent families earned an average of $60,471 a year. In addition, the incomes of divorced women who receive full child support from their ex-partners are on average 25 percent lower than those of divorced men who receive child support payments.

Fact Or Fiction?

Marriage would solve single mothers' poverty problems.

Fact: Researchers and policy makers agree that married women are less likely to be poor—in 2002, families with single mothers and their children made up half of all families in poverty—but they disagree about solutions to the problem. Programs that promote marriage for poor women are often touted as a way to help single women and their children leave welfare rolls. However researchers at the Institute for Women's Policy Research (IWPR) have found that single mothers are poorer for three primary reasons: they are likely to be paid less than men for the same work, to work at lower-paying jobs, and to work fewer hours than men because they assume more responsibilities for childcare. IWPR researchers maintain that equal pay for women and men, more education, and child-care subsidies are the keys to helping single mothers move out of poverty.

Single parents are more likely to be poor than married couples. The association between single parenthood and poverty is demonstrated strikingly in the District of Columbia, where two out of every three children do not live with married parents. Washington, D.C., also has one of the highest percentages of children living in poverty in the nation. Census Bureau data show that in 2002, 33 percent of children in Washington, D.C., lived below the federal poverty level of $14,494 for a family of three.

The Census Bureau reports that in 2002, 9.2 percent of all families in the nation lived in poverty. About half of those families—3.6 million—were headed by a single female parent. Of all female-headed households, 26.5 percent were in poverty. Children in these families were five times as likely to be living in poverty as those who lived with two parents. Among children living in mother-only family groups, the poverty rate ranged from 50 percent for Native American and Alaska Native children to 28 percent for white children. Families headed by a single male parent were less likely to be poor but still more likely to be in poverty than households headed by two adults.

Of households headed by a single male, 564,000 were in poverty, representing 12.1 percent of all single-father families.

One reason that many single-parent families have less income than two-parent families may be that single parents are unable to work as many hours as married couples. Census Bureau data shows that between 1993 and 2001, the percentage of custodial parents employed in a full-time year-round job grew from 45.6 percent to 55.3 percent. In 2001, about 28 percent of custodial parents worked part-time or for part of the year. Custodial mothers were more likely than fathers to work part-time, although their full-time year-round employment increased from 40.9 percent to 52.3 percent during those eight years. In contrast, 71.7 percent of custodial fathers were employed in full-time, year-round jobs in 2001.

Single mothers of all ethnic backgrounds and education levels face a formidable wage gap. In 2004, according to the Bureau of Labor Statistics, women who were employed full-time earned 76 cents for every dollar that men earned in similar jobs. Researchers from the Institute for Women's Policy Research (IWPR) predict that women will not earn the same pay for performing the same work, or **economic parity**, until 2050.

The discrepancy in wages is slightly greater for single parents. According to IWPR, working single mothers earn 71 percent of the hourly wages of working single fathers—even when both groups have similar levels of education. In analyzing census data, IWPR researchers found that single fathers tended to work in industrial, manufacturing, construction, and managerial jobs. In contrast, women tended to work in service jobs in restaurants, department stores, and hospitals. The difference in jobs and wages leads to what researchers call "sex segregation" in the labor market. That segregation translates into a $5,000-a-year gap between low-income men and women.

IWPR researchers suggest that the need for child care, transportation, and special job skills may also affect a single parent's ability to find and keep a job that pays enough to maintain a household. Single parents who lack job skills and/or experience may need to enroll in a training program or attend college. They may also need to develop emotional and other support systems that will help them become effective heads of households and wage earners. Inadequate child care is often a barrier to a woman's full-time employment. To make ends meet, many single parents rely on a combination of wages, government assistance programs, and contributions from family and friends.

PSYCHOLOGICAL IMPACT

Like any other family, a single-parent family can provide a healthy environment for its members. Children thrive in a warm, supportive home, regardless of whether it is headed by one or two parents. Studies also suggest that children adjust better when they have a good relationship with a single parent than when they live with two parents who are in constant conflict. Parents who are inaccessible, rejecting, or hostile can be more damaging to children than absent parents.

However, many single-parent families face particular emotional and psychological challenges. In "The Diversity, Strength, and Challenges of Single-Parent Households," a 2003 review of recent research concerning single-parent families, psychologist Carol Anderson points to a large body of research on the most common challenges for single parents and their children. Those challenges include the need to "go it alone," cope with the loss of a relationship, and endure financial hardship—all of which leave single parents more vulnerable to psychological problems such as depression.

According to Anderson, several studies suggest that teens in single-parent families are more likely to drop out of high school and become a parent. As adults, they are more likely to be unemployed and rely on public assistance. However, as Anderson observes, many of these studies do not take into account other factors—including poverty (both before and after a parental divorce), moving to a new (and usually poorer and less safe) neighborhood, family size, ethnicity, and the single parent's educational level—all of which can affect a child's adjustment and well-being.

In 1994, sociologists Sara McLanahan and Gary Sandefur published the results of a study designed to examine the factors that may be responsible for children of single parents faring less well than those in two-parent families. Their analysis, published in *Growing Up with a Single Parent: What Hurts, What Helps*, showed that even after adjusting for differences in race, parent's education, family size, and neighborhood, children in single-parent families had more social, behavioral, and emotional problems than those living with two biological parents. The research showed little difference between single-parent families created by divorce and those that were the result of out-of-wedlock births.

McLanahan and Sandefur did find one important variable: family income. Their analysis showed that the loss in income that occurred when the custodial parent became a single parent—whether by divorce, death, or nonmarital birth—was the single most important factor for the decline in well-being of children in one-parent families. About half of the decline in children in single-parent families was due to a lower income.

Other studies have demonstrated that children in single-parent families are less likely to do well in school. McLanahan and Sandefur, for instance, found that children of single parents were 50 percent more likely to drop out of school than children in two-parent families. However, a study published in the *Journal of Educational Research* in 2004 suggests that children's performance in school seems to be more strongly affected by a parent's involvement, education, and abilities than his or her marital status.

Researchers led by Henry Ricciuti, professor of human development at Cornell University, assessed the school performances and behavior of 1,500 children of single mothers from white, black, and Hispanic families. The children were interviewed when they were six and seven years old and again when they were 12 and 13. In both sets of interviews, researchers found that living with a single mother did not affect a child's readiness for school or contribute to social or behavioral problems.

Researchers at Cornell also found that children's educational performance and behavior was most strongly affected by the mother's education and ability level. Less influential but still important were family income and the quality of the home environment. Those links were consistent across ethnic and racial groups. The researchers concluded that when single mothers are educated, have adequate income, expect positive achievement from their children, and have a network of social resources, single parenthood does not increase a child's risk of poor educational performance or behavior problems. However, the children of single mothers who lack those resources may indeed be at risk of poor academic performance, substance abuse, and delinquency.

In comparison to married parents, single parents have little relief from the responsibilities of parenting. In two-parent families, spouses typically rely on each other for social and emotional support. Spouses help each other with childcare, transportation, and negotiating conflicting or competing demands. But most single parents, as Anderson observes, cope with child care, household responsibilities, work, and social life without the help of a partner.

TEENS SPEAK

I Live with a Single Dad

I've lived with my dad since my parents divorced about 10 years ago. I was six years old when they split up, and I remember feeling sad and confused for a long time afterwards. I didn't understand why my mom left, but I did know that they fought a lot before the divorce. My mom moved to an apartment and my dad and I stayed in our old house. I saw her on weekends and during holidays for the first year after they divorced. Then the consulting firm my mom works for transferred her to their office in France. My dad and I stayed in Phoenix, where he's a partner in a law firm. Dad and I get along pretty well. He's a great cook, and he's taught me how to cook Thai, Mexican, and a few other cuisines. We often have fun making a mess in the kitchen; sometimes we even clean it up. Both of us are lousy housekeepers, which is just as well. He has to travel out of town occasionally, so I sometimes stay with my friend Julia and her mom. But most of the time, he's around. He takes me to soccer practices and flute lessons, and he shows up at every one of my flute recitals. He does the best job he can at being both "mom" and "dad."

Sometimes though, I wish my mom were still around. Some things are hard to talk to my dad about. The hardest thing is explaining to my friends that I live with my dad and not my mom. About half of my friends' parents are divorced, and most of them live with their moms. Some of them also have stepfathers.

I spend a month each summer overseas with my mom and Jacques, the man she married about a year ago. Jacques has a daughter about my age, so my visits to France are fun and filled with lots of interesting things to do,

and my mom will always be my mom. But my home is in Arizona with my dad.

Not surprisingly, considerable data show that single parents are more likely to experience loneliness. Sociologists suggest that there are two types of loneliness. People who experience **social isolation** feel lonely because they lack a social network of friends and acquaintances. Those who experience **emotional isolation** are lonely because they lack a single intense relationship.

Divorced, separated, and widowed people are more likely to experience both types of loneliness. In a 1991 study published in *Psychological Reports*, psychologists Randy Page and Galen Cole found that among adults who said they were lonely, 20 percent were divorced, 30 percent were separated, and 20 percent were widowed. Only 14.5 percent of the never-married said they felt lonely. Of married people, 4.6 percent reported feelings of loneliness. In an international survey published in the journal *Sociology* in 1998, Steven Stack, a sociologist at Wayne State University in Detroit, assessed the relationship between marital status and loneliness. Stack found similar patterns in 17 industrialized nations: the married were least lonely, and the divorced, separated, or widowed were the most lonely.

The drop in income that often affects single parent households also increases the chance of loneliness. A 1991 study published in *Psychological Reports* showed that people in families with incomes of less than $10,000 were almost five times more likely to report loneliness than those in families with incomes of $75,000 or more.

SOCIETAL VIEWS

With more than half of all marriages ending in divorce and an increasing number of unmarried women choosing to have children, the shame or disgrace once attached to single-parent families is lessening. More than 60 percent of children will live in a single-parent home before they reach the age of 18.

The changes in attitudes regarding single parents are reflected most strongly in the increasing number of unmarried women who choose to have children. Between 1940 and 1990, births to unmarried mothers in the United States increased from less than 4 percent to 28 percent. Between 1990 and 2002, the percentage of births to unmarried mothers rose from 28 to 34 percent, according to data from the National Center for Health Statistics. The most notable increases were among educated white women in professional positions. Among never-married, college-educated women, the birthrate doubled; among never-married women who work in a professional or managerial capacity, the birthrate tripled.

Many single mothers express concern about their marital status and how it affects their ability to cope as a mother. However, for some of these women, the desire to have a child outweighs the social, emotional, and financial challenges of single parenting.

GOVERNMENT ASSISTANCE

For many parents, the transition to single parenting means a loss of income, increased responsibilities, and a lack of job opportunities. Many single parents turn to the government for assistance for basic needs, childcare, and health insurance. Government assistance programs can be divided into two general categories: those in which benefits are based on income level and need, and those in which benefits are based on work history, such as unemployment insurance or social security. Single parents can access these programs by contacting the local office of their state's human services or labor and employment departments.

Income level and need are used to determine whether a family qualifies for the following programs:

- Temporary Aid to Needy Families (TANF). In 1996, Congress passed the Personal Responsibility and Work Opportunity Reconciliation Act (PRWORA). Better known as welfare reform, the act was designed to reduce dependence on government benefits and increase paid employment and marriage. PRWORA replaced Aid for Families with Dependent Children (AFDC) program with TANF. Under AFDC, low-income single mothers were entitled to receive monthly payments as long as they had a child in their care. Under TANF, a person can receive cash assistance for no more than five years during his or her lifetime. Cash benefits vary depending on the state in which the person lives, but 99 percent of TANF recipients received a monthly payment of $351 or less in 2003. People who receive TANF benefits are also required to work, volunteer, or attend a vocational training program for at least 30 hours per week.

- Food stamps. Some single-parent families are eligible for food stamps, a program run by the U.S. Department of Agriculture (USDA). Families receive monthly assistance in buying food. The amount they receive is based on income and family size. Families do not receive cash. Instead they receive paper coupons or an electronic benefits transfer (EBT) card. Those who use an EBT card have an account established in their family's name. Every month, the government deposits money into that account to use when paying for groceries.

- Housing assistance. Housing assistance is available to low-income families through the Department of Housing and Urban Development (HUD). Eligibility is determined by the family's income and the median family income in the area in which they live. HUD defines low-income families as those whose income is less than 80 percent of the median income in the area. HUD offers several programs to these families, ranging from housing facilities and assistance in paying rent to home-buying and home renovations.

- Child care. Low-income single-parent families may also be eligible for assistance with child-care. Eligible families can take advantage of subsidized childcare services, usually through a certificate or a contract with a childcare provider. The provider must meet basic health and safety requirements. Children three to five years old can enroll in Head Start, a national program that provides day care, education, and developmental services for low-income children and social services to their families. Each Head Start program is run by a community-based nonprofit organization or a school system. Intellectual, social, and emotional growth is promoted through a variety of learning experiences.

■ Health insurance. Low-income families may qualify for Medicaid and the state-run Children's Health Insurance Program (CHIP). Medicaid is a program run by both federal and state governments that provides health care to low-income people. Qualification requirements for Medicaid programs vary, but families must be below the federal poverty level, which is updated yearly and varies according to family size. In 2004, a three-person family who earned $15,670 or less was eligible and so was a family of four earning $18,850. Children in families with slightly higher incomes may be covered under CHIP, which is designed to ensure that children at all income levels have access to health care. While the income limits in CHIP vary by state, in most states, they are set at about 200 percent of the poverty level.

Q & A

Question: Should I drop out of high school and go to work to help my single mom make ends meet?

Answer: Dropping out of high school to go to work may provide a short-term fix to your family's financial problems, but in the long run, it's not likely to help you and your family permanently move out of poverty. In fact, dropping out makes it more likely that you will find yourself struggling to make ends meet as you grow older. You are more likely to be able to help your mom and siblings in a substantial way if you finish high school and seek financial assistance to go to college. In the meantime, you and your family can investigate other options to make ends meet, including part-time work and government assistance programs designed for families like yours.

FAMILY SUPPORT

Many single parents depend on their extended families for emotional, physical, and financial support. About half of all low-income single mothers live with other adults, including their own parents, siblings, boyfriends, or roommates. Women who work full time are most likely

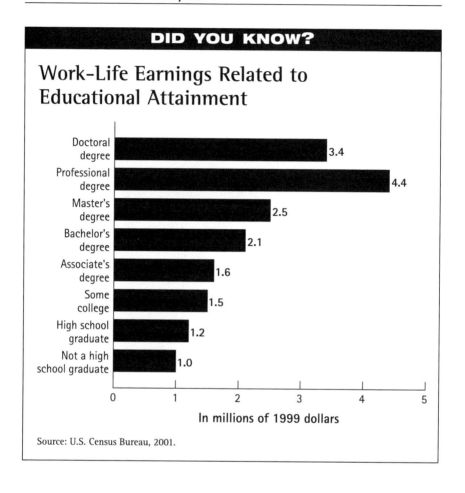

DID YOU KNOW?

Work-Life Earnings Related to Educational Attainment

Doctoral degree — 3.4
Professional degree — 4.4
Master's degree — 2.5
Bachelor's degree — 2.1
Associate's degree — 1.6
Some college — 1.5
High school graduate — 1.2
Not a high school graduate — 1.0

In millions of 1999 dollars

Source: U.S. Census Bureau, 2001.

to live with other adults of their own generation, while younger women are more likely to live with parents or grandparents.

In 2002, according to the Census Bureau, 5.6 million children were living with a grandparent. Of those, 2.3 million lived with their single mother and her parent or parents, while 373,000 lived with their single father and his parent or parents. African-American children were the most likely to live in their grandparent's household. Nine percent of African-American children lived with a parent and grandparent, while 6 percent of Latino, 4 percent of white, and 3 percent of Asian-American children lived in three-generation households.

Single parents may be able to parent more effectively if they have the support of their extended families. In a study published in

2002 in the journal *Demography*, Thomas DeLeire and Ariel Kalil of the School of Public Policy Studies at the University of Chicago reported that teens may benefit from living in three-generation households. DeLeire and Kalil examined data from 11,213 teens who participated in the National Educational Longitudinal Survey. First, they determined what type of family the teen lived in when he or she was in eighth grade: married-parent, single-parent, extended family, and other possible structures (including two unmarried biological parents). Then they examined how well the teens were doing during their senior year in high school or two years after high school. The researchers looked for such indicators of well-being as substance abuse, sexual activity, high school graduation, and college attendance.

When they compared the teens' behaviors with the structures of their families, DeLeire and Kalil found that teens who lived in single-parent families were generally less likely to graduate from high school or attend college, more likely to smoke or drink, and more likely to begin sexual activity at an early age. However, teens who lived with a single parent and a grandparent showed developmental outcomes that were as good—and often better—than teens who lived with two married parents. DeLeire and Kalil concluded that the presence of a grandparent may be especially beneficial to low-income teens.

OVERCOMING THE STIGMA

Until the last quarter of the 20th century, children born to unmarried mothers were considered "illegitimate," and divorce was seen as a failure. But as divorce and births to unmarried mothers have become more common, single-parent families have come to be seen as one of many alternative family structures.

There are more than 11.9 million single-parent families in the United States; the great majority are headed by a female parent. Single parents face a host of challenges in raising their children alone. Yet most single parents provide their children not only with food, clothing, and shelter, but also with a supportive environment.

Many single parents rely on extended families and friends for emotional and social support; some turn to government assistance programs for help. The image of the welfare mom who sits at home and collects dollars is a myth. The truth is that most single parents work both within and outside the home.

See also: Day Care; Death in the Family; Divorce and Families; Family, The New; Family, The Traditional; Marriage and Family, Changes in; Teenage Parents

FURTHER READING
Edin, Kathryn. *Making Ends Meet: How Single Mothers Survive Welfare and Low-Wage Work.* New York: Russell Sage Foundation, 1997.
McLanahan, Sara, and Gary Sandefur. *Growing Up with a Single Parent: What Hurts, What Helps.* Cambridge, MA: Harvard University Press, 1994.
Schultz, Margaret A. *Teens with Single Parents: Why Me?* New York: Enslow Publishers, 1997.
Wagonseller, Bill R. *Coping in a Single-Parent Home.* New York: Rosen Publishing Group, 1997.

■ STEPPARENTS

Stepparents are the spouses of one's parents by a subsequent marriage. The relationship between teens and stepparents is often turbulent. Some of the major challenges faced by stepparents are gaining respect, providing appropriate discipline and guidance, and negotiating their relationship with their new partner's ex-spouse.

GAINING RESPECT

Stepchildren are often reluctant participants in families created by a parent's remarriage. Children face several key tasks after a parent remarries. Children must adjust to the fact of their biological parent's remarriage, deal with possible changes in their own relationship with the biological parent, and form a relationship with a new stepparent, according to E. Mavis Hetherington, a leading researcher in stepfamily dynamics and professor of psychology at the University of California. Children may be disappointed or angry that a parent has remarried, and may resent the entry of another adult into the family.

Dealing with a new stepparent may be most difficult for teens, according to Hetherington. In a 1992 study published in *Monographs of the Society for Research in Child Development*, Hetherington and colleagues found that teens may feel that by accepting the new stepparent they are being disloyal to the noncustodial biological parent. These feelings may lead them to reject stepparents' efforts to extend friendship. In addition, Hetherington observes, teens are in the midst of their own transition from childhood to adulthood and dealing with the accompanying physical, social, emotional, intellectual, and behavioral changes. They are preparing to leave home and begin their own lives, becoming more independent and making decisions on their own. They are learning how to develop mature friendships and intimate relationships while maintaining close relationships with their parents and siblings. In stepfamilies, teens face the added task of negotiating a relationship with a person who is not quite a parent yet plays a fatherly or motherly role in their lives.

The vaguely defined role of the stepparent may add to the difficulties often experienced by stepparents and stepchildren. As sociologist Anne C. Jones notes in a study published by *Social Work* in April 2003, myths—unrealistic beliefs—about the "lesser" status of stepfamilies can cause problems in those families. Fairy tales and folklore abound with images of wicked stepmothers—images that may be difficult for even the most compassionate and caring stepmother to overcome. Jones notes that children in the United States grow up surrounded by fictional portraits of stepparents as abusive and dangerous. Neither are idealized stories about stepfamilies, such as television's *Brady Bunch,* helpful. According to Jones, these "one big happy family" stories create unrealistically high expectations that are likely to lead to frustration and disappointment.

Fact Or Fiction?

Stepmothers are cruel to their stepchildren.

Fact: Stepmothers often do experience conflict with stepchildren, but not because they're the slave-driving, stepchild-hating stepmothers of Cinderella or Snow White nor the self-absorbed and disinterested stepmothers portrayed in television shows. Stepmothers simply tend to be more involved than stepfathers in their stepchildren's everyday lives. Many stepmothers quickly take on responsibilities, such as taking children to school and other activities and providing emotional support and discipline. The greater amount of time spent together creates more chances for conflict. However, it also provides an opportunity for a special bond to develop between stepmothers and stepchildren.

Many stepparents unrealistically expect their stepchildren to immediately offer them love, affection, and respect. Both stepfathers and stepmothers, hoping for a successful marriage, may try to gain immediate favor with their stepchildren. Yet, as Hetherington found in a 1999 study, *Coping with Divorce, Single Parenting, and Remarriage: A Risk and Resiliency Perspective*, stepchildren–especially stepdaughters–may meet stepparents' efforts with resistance and aversion. In turn, stepparents may withdraw, feel less close, and offer less warmth and guidance than biological parents in non-stepfamilies.

Q & A

Question: Should I love my stepmother?

Answer: When a parent remarries, many teens feel confused, conflicted about loyalties, angry, and even sad. Even if you don't feel negatively toward your new stepparent, you may not feel excited and happy about the changes she brings. You do not need to feel love toward your new stepmother right away. You may eventually develop a close, loving bond with her—or you may not. For now, be patient, treat her respectfully, and try to get to know her. Ask her if she would be willing to spend some time alone with you so you can talk about some of your feelings. If tempers keep flaring and you can't get along, your family may want to talk to a therapist.

Gender may affect interactions with teen stepchildren, as well as the teen's well-being. In 2003, the *Journal of Divorce and Remarriage* published a study on teens' self-esteem and their relationships with their biological parents and stepparents. Study author Ellen C. Berg, a professor of sociology at California State University, found that teens scored highest on measures of self-esteem when they felt closer to their biological mothers or stepmothers. The effect of closeness to stepfathers was not as great, leading Berg to suggest that feelings of closeness to the female parent with whom the teen lives may have the most impact on teens' self-esteem.

Biological parents often want their children to get along with their stepparents, which may lead to confusion about the true nature of the relationship between teens and stepparents. According to a study published in 2004 by the *Journal of Divorce and Remarriage*, biological parents and teens often perceive teens' relationships with their stepparents differently. The study, conducted by a research team led by Susan Silverberg Koerner of the University of Arizona, compared biological mothers' and teens' perceptions of the teens' relationship with the mothers' new partners. Of the 83 mother-daughter pairs, 47 had different perceptions of the teen-stepparent (or partner) relationship.

Mothers and daughters differed in their perceptions of three major areas: the quality of the relationship between the teen and the mother's new partner, the impact of the new partner on the family's life, and the impact of having a partner on the relationship between the mother and the teen. For instance, the mother often perceived the teen's relationship with the stepfather as "good" or "fine," while the teen felt uncomfortable or irritated by the mother's partner. In another common scenario, the mother acknowledged that problems had occurred early in the relationship but felt that things had been resolved, while the teen described the present relationship with the partner as "poor" or disliked the partner. In yet another variation, the mother focused on negative experiences between the teen and her partner while the teen described the partner (or his or her relationship with the partner) as "fine" or "good."

The researchers concluded that the differing perceptions of mothers and teens had a variety of causes. The mothers and teen may not have been communicating well, and they could have been holding back information or feelings from each other in an attempt to protect their relationship. Finally, the mothers and teens may have different investments in the relationship with the stepfathers. Mothers may hope that all will go smoothly, while teens may feel disloyal to their biological fathers if they easily accept the mother's new partner.

DISCIPLINE

As a responsible adult, the stepparent is accountable for the well-being, guidance, and protection of children. Yet conflicts over child discipline top the list of relationship problems for many remarried couples.

In 1971, psychologist Diana Baumrind described three parenting styles—authoritative, permissive, and authoritarian. According to Baumrind, parents who use an authoritative style are firm in their decisions, clear in their guidelines, keep track of their children's activities, and have relatively high expectations for their children. Authoritative parents also offer their children warmth and affection, reason with their children, and encourage children to reach agreements through verbal exchanges. Permissive parents tend to respond to children's needs; they are less apt to punish and expect less of their children. Authoritarian parents tend to be highly demanding, expect unquestioning obedience, make decisions without explanations, and offer less warmth.

Psychologists and sociologists still use these categories to describe types of parenting, although more recent research, such as a study of parenting styles published by *Child Development* in 1992, suggests that parents often use a combination of different styles. The 1992 study, which was conducted by researchers from the Department of Psychology at Temple University, was one of many that supported Baumrind's finding that children tend to fare best when parents use an authoritative style. The Temple University researcher found that authoritative parenting leads to better school performance and school engagement among teens. According to Baumrind, adults who were reared in authoritative households tend to have a lively, happy disposition, feel self-confident about their ability to master tasks, regulate their emotions well, have well-developed social skills, and are less rigid about gender-typed traits.

A study published by the journal *Communication Quarterly* suggests that the effects of parenting styles may be more complex between stepparents and stepchildren. Tamara Golish of the University of Nebraska interviewed 115 teens and young adults who lived in stepfamilies. She asked them about the parenting styles used by their stepparents. Golish found that more authoritarian stepparenting tended to increase the tendency of stepchildren to avoid talking about important topics with stepfamily members. When stepparents were more permissive or more authoritative, children were more open about their feelings and less likely to avoid difficult topics. Teens who perceived their stepparents parenting style as authoritarian were generally less satisfied with their relationship with their stepparent. When stepparents showed low or high degrees of permissiveness, teens were also less satisfied; in contrast, teens felt moderately satisfied with moderately permissive stepparents. Teens were more accepting of stepparents who were authoritative.

TO ADOPT OR NOT TO ADOPT?

Stepparents often provide stepchildren with tangible support such as food, clothing, and housing, and many form deep emotional bonds with stepchildren. But a stepparent is not legally required to support a spouse's children nor does the stepparent have parental rights. Marrying a child's custodial parent does not give an adult legal rights to the child. The stepparent has no legal ties to the child if the marriage ends, or the biological parent dies or becomes incapacitated. For this reason, many remarried couples choose to have the stepparent legally adopt his or her spouse's biological children.

Adoption of a stepchild signifies a practical commitment on the part of the stepparent. The stepparent takes on parental responsibilities to nurture, provide for, and protect the child and releases the noncustodial parent of parental responsibilities. Stepparent adoption also signifies an emotional commitment to the marriage and the new family. For these and other reasons, stepparent adoption is the most common type of adoption in the United States.

In most cases, the noncustodial parent must consent to the adoption. In consenting, the noncustodial parent gives up all parental rights and is relieved of parental responsibilities, including child support. Parental rights include the right to visit and make decisions about medical treatment or education. If the noncustodial parent refuses to consent to the adoption, the adoption cannot take place except in specific circumstances. Some states allow parental rights to be terminated if the noncustodial parent is absent or has not exercised parental rights such as visiting or communicating with the child. In most states, termination of parental rights is allowed when a parent has willfully failed to support the child or has **abandoned** the child for a certain length of time, usually a year. Abandonment usually means that the absent parent hasn't communicated with or financially supported the child. In 47 states, older children must also consent to their own adoption. In most states, children age 12 or older must consent to their own adoption. In Puerto Rico, a child age 10 or older must consent.

Stepchild adoption can have great emotional and financial impact on the family, especially if the noncustodial parent is alive, in frequent contact with the child, and paying child support. Children may feel that they must divide their attention and loyalty between their adoptive stepfather and biological father. After the adoption, the noncustodial parent no longer has the legal right to spend time with the child, known as **visitation rights**. On the other hand, adoption may signify stability and security to children, who may feel uncertain about their parent's remarriage. In general, the less contact children have with their noncustodial parent, the more likely it is that stepparent adoption will be to the benefit of the family. The family's economic circumstances may also dictate whether adoption is a good choice. If the noncustodial parent is paying child support on a regular basis, the loss of that income should be taken into account when considering stepparent adoption.

DEALING WITH THE OTHER PARENT

Dealing with a new spouse's former partner may be one of the most difficult aspects of a stepparent's life. Stepparents can easily become caught in a web of angry feelings between their new spouse, stepchildren, and the noncustodial parent. When ex-spouses do not get along well, the relationship between stepparents and stepchildren may be strained.

On the other hand, when stepparents are able to build positive relationships with their spouse's ex-partner, children may benefit, as suggested in a study published by the *Journal of Marriage and the Family* in February 2004. The study was authored by William Marsiglio, a sociologist at the University of Florida. Marsiglio examined the actions and attitudes that allowed stepfathers to develop fatherlike relationships with their stepchildren and to "claim" those children as their own. He interviewed 36 stepfathers at length for the study. He found that stepfathers tended to use either cooperative or competitive approaches in response to biological fathers' involvement. Stepfathers who used a cooperative approach claimed their stepchildren as their own while acknowledging that the biological father was an important person, and another father figure, in the child's life. Stepfathers who used a competitive approach saw the biological father as a competitor who did not have anything to do with their desire and ability to claim their stepchildren as their own. When stepfathers used a cooperative approach, stepfamilies were better able to see themselves as a cohesive group.

Likewise, a study published in 2001 by the *Journal of Marriage and the Family* suggests that children benefit when they have warm relationships with both biological and stepfathers. The study, "When Children Have Two Fathers: Effects of Relationships with Stepfathers and Non-custodial Fathers on Adolescent Outcomes," was authored by University of Nebraska sociologists Lynne White and Joan G. Gilbreth. White and Gilbreth surveyed 189 children, as well as their mothers and stepfathers, about the effects of children's relationships with biological and stepfathers on their well-being. White and Gilbreth found that children who felt strong and affectionate bonds with their stepfather and biological mother had fewer behavior problems. More children who lived in stepfamilies said they had good relationships with their biological, noncustodial fathers than did children who lived in single-parent families. According to White and Gilbreth, their results support the idea that children benefit when stepfathers are perceived as a second father—as opposed to a substitute father.

These and other studies suggest that stepfamily members may benefit when families are able to establish a **parenting coalition** in which the divorced and remarried biological parents and the stepparents cooperate in rearing their biological children and stepchildren. Children have contact with both of their parents and with their stepparents. In this type of cooperative arrangement, the children's needs, as well as the needs of the adults, can be met more easily. The sharing of parenting responsibilities reduces the burden on parents and ensures that children are not used as messengers to carry parents' anger back and forth. Children are better able to perceive the stepparent as another important adult in their lives, not as a person who is interfering with their relationship with their parent. Parenting coalitions minimize power struggles between households and recognize stepparents as important people in an ever-changing family.

Stepfamilies face several tasks, including the establishment of relationships between stepchildren and stepparents. Stepparents who expect stepchildren to love and respect them immediately are likely to be disappointed. Discipline is a common problem between stepparents and stepchildren. Stepparents who use an authoritative parenting style are most likely to gain the respect of their stepchildren. Stepparent adoption can have both positive and negative effects on the stepfamily. While adoption can represent a commitment to the spouse's children and ensure they are cared for if a biological parent dies, it may also mean loss of child support payments and lessen children's contact with the noncustodial biological parent. Children may benefit when their biological and stepparents see themselves as sharing, rather than competing, in their parental roles.

See also: Adoption; Arguments and the Family; Divorce and Families; Families, Blended; Families, Divided; Family, The New; Marriage and Family, Changes in

FURTHER READING
O'Connor, Anne. *The Truth about Stepfamilies: Real American Families Speak Out about What Works and What Doesn't When It Comes to Creating a Family Together.* New York: Avalon Publishing Group, 2003.
Shomberg, Elaine Fantle. *Blending Families: A Guide for Parents, Step-Families, Step-Grandparents and Everyone Building a Successful New Family.* New York: Berkeley Publishing Group, 1999.

■ TEENAGE PARENTS

Teenage parents are those under the age of 20. Parenthood is a life-changing event for a person of any age, but for teen parents, the responsibilities of rearing a child may interfere with their own growth into adulthood. How many teens in the United States are parents, and what challenges do they and their children face?

FACTS AND FIGURES IN AMERICA

The teenage birthrate in the United States has decreased steadily since 1991, from 62 births per 1,000 teenage girls to 43 in 2002, a 30 percent drop. Yet the teen pregnancy and birthrate in the United States is still one of the highest in the industrialized world. The rate is twice as high as in the United Kingdom or Canada and nine times as high as in the Netherlands or Japan. In 2002, according to the National Center for Health Statistics, there were 549,000 live births among women under the age of 20, representing 10.8 percent of all births in the United States. The majority of teen births occur to women age 18 to 19, but younger teens have a significant number of children. In 2001, almost 8,000 teenagers under 14 years old gave birth. Most teen pregnancies—more than four out of five—are unplanned. About 25 percent of teen mothers will give birth to another child within two years of their first.

The great majority—79 percent—of teen parents are single. Data from the National Center for Health Statistics show that in 1960, only 15 percent of teens who gave birth were unmarried. In 2002, 80 percent of teen mothers were unmarried. Teens accounted for 34 percent of all births to unmarried women in 2002, a decrease from 50 percent in 1970. This figure does not represent an increase in teen marriages

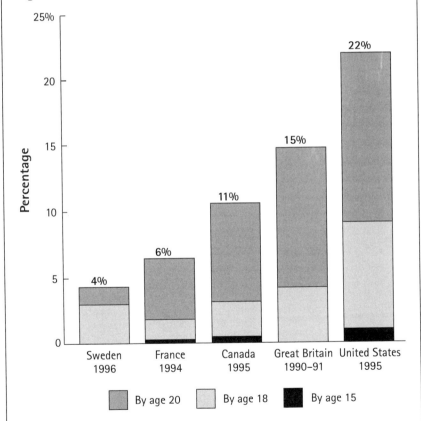

DID YOU KNOW?

Teen Parents in the United States and Other Developed Countries

Percentage of 20–24-year-old women who gave birth by ages 15, 18, or 20

Source: Darroch, Jacqueline E., Susheela Singh, and Jennifer J. Frost. "Differences in Teenage Pregnancy Rates among Five Developed Countries: The Role of Sexual Activity and Contraceptive Use." *Family Planning Perspectives*, 2001.

but an increase in the number of older unmarried women who are choosing to become mothers.

Teen fathers are likely to be older than teen mothers, sometimes significantly. According to the Alan Guttmacher Institute (AGI), a nonprofit research organization focused on sexual and reproductive health issues, about 20 percent of infants born to unmarried minors are fathered by men five or more years older than the mother. Nor are teen mothers likely to marry. Less than 8 percent of unmarried teen mothers marry the baby's father within one year of giving birth.

According to the AGI, approximately 14 percent of teens who become pregnant miscarry, and 30 percent end their pregnancies through abortion. Latina teens are most likely, and African-American teens least likely, to have a pregnancy that ends in a live birth. Among teens who give birth, more than 96 percent keep their babies; less than 4 percent make an adoption plan for their infants.

An analysis of public policy issues surrounding teen parenthood was published in 2003 as part of the collection *All Our Families: New Policies for a New Century*. Author Jane Mauldon, a public policy researcher at the University of California–Berkeley, describes poverty and teen parenthood as "twinned experiences." Mauldon cites statistics from the AGI that show teens from low-income families are nine times more likely to give birth to a child than are teens from higher-income families. While 38 percent of teens live in low-income families, they account for 83 percent of teen births. This may be because low-income teens are more likely to start having sex at a young age, less likely to use contraception, and less likely to have abortions, according to Mauldon.

Mauldon suggests that poverty is both a cause and result of teen pregnancy. She suggests that for teenage women living in low-income families and communities, motherhood may offer a sort of "pseudo-adulthood" that allows the teen to assume meaningful responsibilities—such as caring for a child—and status. At the same time, she can remain dependent on her family and, often, the government, so she is not completely cut off from her support systems. Teens who have not succeeded in other parts of their lives, such as school, may believe that motherhood provides a chance to show that they have mastered important skills. Mauldon also points out that many teenage mothers are emotionally needy, often because they have experienced abuse, neglect, or molestation. AGI research shows that almost one-fourth of teen women who become sexually active before age 17 report experiences of involuntary sex.

Overall, about 28 percent of women who became parents during their teens are poor while in their 20s and early 30s. In 1993, the *Journal of Research on Adolescence* published a study of teen motherhood and later poverty. The researchers were led by Kristin Anderson Moore, president and senior scholar at Child Trends, a nonpartisan research organization that studies children and families. Anderson and her colleagues found that more than 60 percent of African-American teenage mothers, half of Latinas, and one-fourth of whites are still in poverty when they are in their late 20s. In comparison, 7 percent of women who have their first child after adolescence are poor during young adulthood. Teen parents are also more likely to depend on welfare than teens who do not have children to care for. In 2002, the National Campaign to Prevent Teen Pregnancy reported that almost half of all teen mothers—and three-fourths of unmarried teen mothers—begin receiving welfare within five years of the birth of their first child. However, most teen parents come from low-income backgrounds, making it likely that they would have been poor even if they had not had children during adolescence.

One reason for the enduring poverty of teen parents may be that teen parents are less likely to complete high school According to the AGI, less than 40 percent of mothers who have a child before age 18 ever complete high school, and fewer teen fathers complete high school than those who wait to become parents until they are 21 years old. Their low educational levels make it unlikely that they will ever qualify for a job that pays well.

However, research also suggests that there may be an even stronger effect in the other direction: Teens who fail in school are more likely to become teen parents. In 1990, *American Sociological Review* published a study on the relationship between first births among teens and high school completion. Researchers from the University of California at Los Angeles analyzed a nationally representative sample of 5,305 teenage women. Twelve percent of the teenagers in the study had dropped out of school before giving birth, and almost all of these had dropped out before becoming pregnant. Only 5 percent were still enrolled in school when they gave birth. Among those who were still in school when they gave birth, 61 percent graduated or earned a

GED. Among those who dropped out before giving birth, only 29 percent eventually graduated or earned a GED.

CHALLENGES FOR TEEN PARENTS

While the demands of parenting are great at any age, teen parents often face additional challenges. Teens are at a critical stage in the development of their identities. How will they move out of their family home and create a home of their own? What occupation will they choose? What values will they live their lives by? Early parenthood can interfere with these developmental tasks. The teen parent has little time for dating, friendships, schooling, and career choices. Most teen parents have not yet completed their education, have little money, and lack job skills. They often must take on part-time work to pay for the expenses of having a child.

TEENS SPEAK

I'm a Teenage Mom

My mother was the one who first recognized that I was pregnant. I think I already knew, but I denied it until the day my mother said to me, "Marcia, I think you're pregnant." She took me to see her obstetrician, a physician who specializes in delivering babies. The doctor ran more tests and confirmed that I was almost four months pregnant.

That's when reality hit me: I was 15 years old, about to have a baby, and alone. My baby's father didn't want anything to do with me. He had been lead quarterback on the football team at my high school, the guy everybody wanted to date. When he wanted to have sex, I said yes because I thought it meant he loved me. But he broke up with me about a week after I had sex with him.

My labor was horrible. It lasted almost 30 hours, and it was the most painful experience I have ever had. The doctor said it was difficult because my pelvis was so small. When it was all over, I had a little girl. I named her Sara.

Sara is six months old now. She often wakes up in the middle of the night crying, and I can't figure out what she wants. It's not like having a doll, or even a dog. I can't leave her alone. I'm usually exhausted: I can't remember the last time I slept more than four hours. I rarely go out with my friends anymore, partly because I'm too tired by Friday night, and partly because my parents won't watch her on weekends. As far as dating anyone, forget it. Everyone at my school knows that I'm a mom, and no guys want to take on that responsibility. Besides, what teenage guy wants to go on a date with a baby stroller?

Before I got pregnant, I planned to become a veterinarian. But that's not going to happen now, at least not until Sara is almost grown. Still, I'm determined to finish school and get a decent job so I can move out of my parents' house someday. I may even be able to go to college, but it will be a lot harder than if I didn't have to care for a child. I wish I'd waited until I was older to become a mom.

Several studies have examined the connection between teen parenthood and psychological problems such as an overwhelming feeling of sadness and grief, known as **depression**. In a 1998 issue of the *International Review of Psychiatry* researchers from the University of Iowa reviewed 59 studies of women's experiences of depression shortly after giving birth, known as **postpartum depression**. They found that depression occurs in almost half (48 percent) of teen mothers, compared to 13 percent of adult mothers.

In 2002, the journal *Adolescence* published a study that examined the feelings of teens who experienced postpartum depression. The study was authored by Donna Clemmens in the School of Nursing at the University of Connecticut. Clemmens interviewed 20 mothers who were between the ages of 16 and 18. All of the mothers had reported feeling depressed after the birth of their babies.

The teens in Clemmens study described the experience of teen motherhood as "being hit by a nor'easter storm." All of the mothers said they felt changed, different, and that they had been hit suddenly with the realization that they were, indeed, mothers. This sense of the suddenness of being a mother was described as being "very depressing." Most felt torn between two realities: being an adolescent and being a mother, and some felt overwhelmed by the demands of motherhood, school, and being a teen. All of the mothers said they felt abandoned and rejected by their babies' fathers and their friends. Some felt "blinded" and lost by what had happened to them, as if everything was falling down on them. However, many felt that they had emerged stronger from the experience and wanted to warn other teens about the reality of teen motherhood.

Teen parenthood often affects the teen's own parents, especially if the teen continues to live at home. In 2000, the *Journal of Family Psychology* published a study of depression in African-American and white teen mothers and their mothers. Heidi Schweingruber, professor of psychology at Rice University, and Ariel Kalil, a public policy scholar at the University of Chicago, interviewed 56 low-income teenage mothers and their mothers, 30 of whom were African American and 26 of whom were white. Many of the teen mothers in the study showed symptoms of moderate to severe depression. African-American grandmothers (mothers of the teens) also experienced high levels of depression—significantly higher than those of white grandmothers.

Teenage mothers and their families bear the brunt of teen parenthood, but teen fathers are also affected. Teen fathers who choose to honor their parenthood because of a sense of responsibility or because of affection and commitment to the mother or child may find their lives drastically altered. They may decide to marry the teen mother, which often means changing their plans for completing their education, choosing an occupation, and pursuing other life goals. The father may be met with resentment and anger from the family of the teen mother. In addition, at a time when his financial resources are few and uncertain, the teen father may be called upon to provide financial assistance to the teen mother and his child, known as **child support**.

Q & A

Question: I'm a teen dad. My son's mother and I are no longer dating, but I want to be a part of my son's life. How can I?

Answer: If you haven't done so already, establish that you are the father of the child, called paternity. You can do this at a hospital or at the county birth records office. If you don't establish your paternity, you will have no legal right to visitation or custody of the child. Next, create a child support agreement with the mother of your child. How much can you reasonably pay? Quitting school to work full-time is a bad idea. Instead, consider staying in school and getting a part-time job. Finally, visit, write, call, or e-mail your son as often as you can. Your son needs your emotional support—attention, care, affection, and love—as well as his mother's.

Teenage marriages are rare and generally unstable. Census Bureau data show that in 2002, only 2.4 percent of teens age 15 to 19 had ever been married, compared to 11 percent in 1975. In September 2004, the nonprofit research institution Child Trends published a report titled "The Relationship Between Teenage Motherhood and Marriage" on its Web site. Child Trends researchers found that patterns of marriage and birth among teens have shifted over time, from a general trend of marriage before pregnancy, to marriage as a result of pregnancy, to not marrying at all.

Fact Or Fiction?

If teen parents married, they and their children would have fewer problems.

Fact: There are three compelling reasons why marriage does not provide long-term stability to teen parents. First, teens who marry are more likely to divorce than are young adults. Second, married teen mothers are actually *less* likely to finish high school than those who remain unmarried, making it less likely that they will be able to find a job that pays well. Third, most teen fathers (and young adult partners of teen mothers) have low educational levels, little work experience, and few job skills. Thus, although early marriage may provide a short-term solution to poverty and the challenges of single-parenting, for most teen parents, early marriage may really be a route into long-term underemployment and fewer life options.

The researchers performed analyses of data from Fragile Families, a nationally representative sample of births in metropolitan areas in the United States. At the time of the child's birth, about one-third of unmarried teen mothers said they were "certain" they would marry the child's father and an additional 23 percent said the chances were "good" that they would marry. One year later, only 8 percent had married. Teens who do marry are not likely to stay married. One-third of marriages that occur before the woman is 18 end in divorce within five years. Almost half will end in 10 years.

STAYING IN SCHOOL

Less than 40 percent of teenage mothers graduate from high school, and far fewer go on to college. Most drop out because of the demands of parenting, the need to work, and a lack of time. While peers are going to football games and experimenting with relationships, teen mothers are changing diapers and warming baby bottles when they're not working to make ends meet. Even the most popular of teens often find that their popularity wanes. Teen fathers often find themselves working to help support their children, whether or not they are involved in parenting.

Many states have programs designed to help teen parents stay in school. For instance, in Idaho, teen fathers older than 16 but younger than 18 years are required to pay only $50 per month in child support. After the teen turns 18 years old or graduates from high school, child support payments increase. The goal of the Idaho program is to allow the teen father to complete high school so that he will be better able to support his child. Many high schools offer programs for teen mothers that include on-site day care services, early childhood education, and other support services. Such programs recognize that teens face special challenges in both pregnancy and parenthood.

A few schools, such as Milwaukee's Lady Pitts School Age Parent Center, focus exclusively on helping pregnant and parenting teens navigate both school and parenthood. All of the 165 students at Lady Pitts are pregnant or parenting teens. Other programs are designed to help pregnant teens to gain the job and parenting skills they need. Most have three goals: to help teen parents complete high school, improve their job skills and employability, and to promote the health and development of teens' children. For instance, California's "Cal-Learn" program, which serves parenting teens who receive welfare, combines guidance with financial incentives. Each teen parent is assigned a "case manager" who helps her to organize school, child care, health care, and other needs. Teens receive an extra $100 for every report card that shows they're making satisfactory progress in school. If they drop out, or if they receive a report card showing unsatisfactory progress, $100 is deducted from their welfare check. Upon graduation, they receive a $500 bonus. University of California,

Berkeley investigators evaluated the program in 2000. The program increased graduation rates among teens who had dropped out of school but returned to earn their GEDs. By their 20th birthday, nearly half (47 percent) of the teens in the program had graduated or earned their GED, in comparison to 33 percent of those not enrolled in the program.

Programs to help teen fathers are also becoming more common. In 2000, *Adolescence* published a study on the effects of a parenting program on young African-American fathers. Study author Carl Mazza, a sociologist at the City University of New York, followed 60 African-American fathers who were enrolled in parenting classes. All of the fathers attended weekly parenting classes that focused on learning how to meet their infants' needs. Half the fathers also met regularly with a social worker who assisted them with their own needs. At the end of six months, the group that attended parenting classes and met with the social worker had made significant gains in employment, had plans for future careers, felt positive about their relationships with their children, used birth control more frequently, had developed ten-year plans for their lives, and had more close friends. Fathers who only attended parenting classes did not make similar gains in these areas. For instance, almost all (97 percent) of the fathers in the social worker group were employed, in comparison to 31 percent of the group that only received parenting classes. Likewise, 87 percent of the group that received help from a social worker had specific career plans while less than half of the group that only attended parenting classes had made vocational plans. Mazza concluded that programs that focus only on teaching parenting skills to young fathers are ineffective and suggests that one-on-one intervention with a social worker may help teen fathers to become responsible adults and effective parents.

HOW DO KIDS FARE?

The children of teen parents are at risk in many areas of their lives, and this risk may begin during the teen's pregnancy. Studies such as one published in 1993 by the *Journal of Adolescent Health* suggest that one reason children of teen parents have more problems may have more to do with poverty and lack of prenatal care. According to the AGI, teens are less likely than adult mothers to receive medical care during pregnancy, known as **prenatal** care. Pregnant teens are also more likely to experiment with drugs, alcohol, tobacco, use caffeine, and eat a nutritionally poor diet during pregnancy. All of these behaviors increase the risk of damage to the **fetus**—the unborn baby from the eighth week after fertilization to birth.

Teenage mothers are at greater risk of giving birth to low birth weight babies—infants weighing less than 2,500 grams, or 5.5 pounds, at birth—than are women age 24 to 35. Data from the National Center for Health Statistics show that nearly one out of 10 babies born to 15- to 19-year olds, and more than one out of eight born to African-American teens in that age group, are low birth weight. Low birth weight is associated with childhood health problems, frequent hospitalization, and other complications. It is not clear whether this is due to the age of the mother or to lack of prenatal care, lack of knowledge about pregnancy, or other factors associated with the low-income status of many teen parents.

Women who smoke are twice as likely to have a low birth weight baby than those who do not, according to a study published by the Future of Children in 1995. Researchers found the women most likely to smoke during pregnancy are those who live at or near poverty levels, have less than a high school education, and are young. Education level also affects the probability of having a low birth weight baby. In 1989, 24 percent of low birth weight babies were born to mothers who had not completed high school.

But race and socioeconomic class may only partly affect the chance of a teen mother giving birth to a low birth weight infant. In 1995, the *New England Journal of Medicine* published a study of teen mothers in Utah. Findings showed that among 134,000 white, mostly middle-income women and teenagers who had their first babies between 1970 and 1990, 13–19-year-olds gave birth to low birth weight babies more frequently than women over 20 years of age. This was true even when the women were married, well-educated, and had adequate prenatal care.

Studies have consistently shown that children of teen parents may not acquire language, learning, and thinking abilities as quickly as those of adult mothers. In 1979, the National Institute of Child Health issued a report that showed infants of teen mothers performed less well than infants of adult mothers on tests of child development at eight months of age, at four years, and at seven years. In 1981, a study of national data published in the book *Teenage Parents and Their Offspring* showed that the percentage of children of teen mothers who were mildly retarded was higher than that in the general population. In 1992, *Development and Psychopathology* published a study of teen mothers and their children who showed symptoms of depression. In 1996, the journal *First Language* published a study of infants' language use. At one year of age, infants of teen mothers were less able to use words and communicate verbally than were infants of adult mothers.

Several studies have shown that teen mothers' depression may lead to problems for their children. Findings from several studies of national data conducted during the 1980s and 1990s indicate that infants and children of depressed mothers are more likely to have problems, including sleep disorders, accidents, growth failure, and psychologically based health problems. For instance, in 1996, the *American Journal of Orthopsychiatry* published a study of the relationship between teen mothers' depressive symptoms and their children's development. Researchers from Oklahoma State University found that the children of depressed mothers were more likely to have difficulty dealing with the comings and goings of their mothers, a measure of emotional health called attachment. The researchers concluded that the mother's depression affects her ability to interact with her child and interferes with the attentiveness and nurturance needed by her infant to develop securely.

In 2000, the journal *Adolescence* published a study of depressed teen mothers and their children. A research team led by Kristen S. Sommer of the University of Notre Dame conducted the study. Sommer and her colleagues studied 121 adolescent mothers and their children to find out what specific characteristics of teen mothers cause delayed development in their children. Only 28 percent of the children of the depressed teen mothers scored within normal ranges in all three areas of development that the researchers tested for: intellectual and learning ability, social and emotional functioning, and ability to adapt to change. The teen mothers' parenting IQ and amount of social support were the most important influences on children's intellectual development. Social and emotional problems were most common in the children of teen mothers who withdrew from their children and families and had little social support. The teen mothers' style of parenting best-predicted children's abilities to adapt.

Other studies support Sommer's finding that emotional and physical support of the teen's family can be a key factor in the child's development. For instance, in 1994, *Child Development* published a study of the children of economically disadvantaged teenage mothers in New York City. A team of researchers from Yale University conducted the study. At 28 to 36 months of age, 13 percent of the children had behavior problems severe enough to need clinical treatment. These children were most likely to be African-American boys whose mothers had shown symptoms of depression or had experienced stressful events during the first year after giving birth. Children had fewer problems when their teen mothers received emotional support from friends or family. They fared best when teen mothers were living with their own grandmothers, suggesting that the teens' grandmothers may have been more supportive than their own mothers.

Although the behavioral and emotional problems of children of teen parents may stem partly from their parents' inadequate parenting skills, many teen parents can improve those skills. In 2003, the journal *Ambulatory Pediatrics* published a study of the effects of a group learning program on teen mothers' parenting skills and attitudes. Researchers from Harvard Medical school developed a program aimed at increasing parenting skills and improving attitudes of teen mothers. Teens attended classes as a group. All adolescent mothers in the study were offered enrollment in a 12-week parenting curriculum and were compared with those who did not attend the parenting classes. Ninety-one young mothers attended parenting classes; 54 did not. Teen mothers who attended parenting classes showed improvement in parenting skills and their ability to deal with life hassles. The researchers concluded that group-based interventions on parenting and life skills of young mothers may improve the social, emotional, and intellectual functioning of children born to teen parents.

Although the teenage birthrate in the United States dropped by 30 percent between 1991 and 2002, the teen pregnancy and birthrate in the United States is still one of the highest in the industrialized world. The great majority of teen parents are single and come from low-income families. While 38 percent of teens live in low-income families, they account for 83 percent of teen births. Because teens are at a critical stage in the development of their own identities, the demands of parenting may be overwhelming for them. Less than 40 percent of teenage mothers graduate from high school, and far fewer go on to college. Teen mothers who drop out of school before becoming pregnant are least likely to finish school. Almost half of teen mothers experience depression after the birth of their babies, which may contribute to the behavioral, emotional, and intellectual problems often seen in children of teen mothers. Children of teen parents may have fewer developmental problems when teen parents develop their parenting skills and enlist the support of family members.

Having a child during teenage years can be a handicap; much depends on how the teen parents chose to cope with the situation. Many teen mothers and fathers finish school, attend college, gain work experience, and go on to have satisfying careers and family lives. Support programs that offer training in self-esteem, relationships, health care, birth control, parenting, life skills, decision making, and goal setting have been shown to be effective in helping teen parents negotiate the demands of early parenthood.

See also: Adoption; Arguments and the Family; Day Care; Family, The New; Single-Parent Families; Teens in Trouble

FURTHER READING

Coles, Robert. *The Youngest Parents: Teenage Pregnancy as It Shapes Lives.* New York: W.W. Norton, 2000.

East, Patricia. *Adolescent Pregnancy (Research Monographs in Adolescence).* Mahwah, NJ: Lawrence Erlbaum Associates, 1996.

Harvey, John H., and Mark A. Fine. *Children of Divorce.* Mahwah, NJ: Lawrence Erlbaum Associates, 2004.

Hughes, Tracy. *Everything You Need to Know about Teen Pregnancy.* New York: Rosen Publishing Group, 1999.

Simpson, Carolyn. *Coping with Teenage Motherhood.* New York: Rosen Publishing Group, 1997.

■ TEENS IN TROUBLE

Adolescence is a period of transition from childhood to adulthood. It is a time of physical, emotional, and behavioral changes. Understandably, many teens (and their parents) wonder whether their feelings, attitudes, and behaviors are "normal." Are they cause for concern?

The American Academy of Child and Adolescent Psychiatry (AACAP) maintains that most teens find it difficult to deal with peer pressure, dating, their own emerging sexuality, issues of independence, and anxiety over schoolwork. Many are also dealing with violence at home or in their community, the availability of alcohol and illegal drugs, and depression.

When adolescents face such serious issues, family life is likely to be affected. Experts at the AACAP note that parents and professionals sometimes fail to identify the emotional and behavioral problems affecting teens. Yet if left untreated, these problems can lead to more serious problems. Early identification of adolescents who need special attention is important.

PHYSICAL HEALTH

Most adolescents are physically healthy. Yet large numbers of teens struggle with health issues related to unplanned pregnancy, sexually transmitted diseases, and violence.

The National Campaign to Prevent Teen Pregnancy notes that the United States has higher rates of teen pregnancy and births than other western countries. About 34 percent of young women become pregnant at least once before they reach the age of 20. The 2003 U.S. Teenage Pregnancy Statistics with Comparative Statistics for Women reports nearly 1 million teen pregnancies each year. Eight in 10 of these pregnancies are unplanned pregnancies, with 79 percent occurring to unmarried teens.

In a research study about the influence of families on teen pregnancy, the National Campaign to Prevent Teen Pregnancy found that 45 percent of teens say that parents have had a strong influence on their decision not to have sex prior to marriage. Other studies seem to confirm those findings.

In a study conducted by the Division of General Pediatrics and Adolescent Health at the University of Minnesota, researchers found that adolescents who had strong emotional relationships with their parents were less likely to become sexually active at an early age. In another study conducted by the National Campaign to Prevent Teen Pregnancy, researchers found that teenage girls cite religious or moral values as the reasons they have chosen not to have sexual intercourse before marriage. Other reasons included a desire to avoid pregnancy, fear of contracting a sexually transmitted disease, and not having met the right person.

Sexually transmitted diseases (STDs) are acquired through intimate sexual contact with someone who is already infected with the disease. Every year, more than 13 million people become infected with STDs. According to the Alan Guttmacher Institute, a nonprofit research center focusing on sexual and reproductive health, one in four sexually active teens becomes infected with an STD every year. Common STDs are chlamydia, gonorrhea, genital warts, and herpes. According to the National Campaign to Prevent Teen Pregnancy, teens with strong ties to their parents and a stable family life are less likely to become sexually active early, therefore decreasing exposure to STDs.

Violence is yet another major health problem for teens. In a 2000 report titled the *National Crime Victimization Survey*, the U.S. Department of Justice defines domestic violence as violent crimes committed by current or former spouses, boyfriends, or girlfriends. The most likely victims are young women between the ages of 16 and 24. Many people think that violence within a relationship occurs only between married persons. Yet experts define domestic violence to include any violence—including physical, verbal, and emotional abuse—between people who are dating, regardless of their sexual orientation. Abusive behavior is any act aimed at hurting or controlling another person. A violent relationship is about power and control and means more than being hit by a person who says they love or care about the victim.

The Centers for Disease Control and Prevention (CDC) has had difficulty determining how prevalent dating or domestic violence is among teens. The problem, they say, is that different studies and surveys ask about the issue in different ways and therefore get different results. Some studies only ask about physical abuse, while others include questions about psychological and emotional abuse and sexual violence. Current estimates of dating violence among middle school and high school students range from 28 percent to 96 percent.

When teens are abused (whether the abuse comes from within the family or from a relationship outside the family), the effects are similar. Those effects include eating and sleeping disturbances, poor school performance, and difficulties with relationships at home or at school. Some teens may become depressed and even suicidal.

Q & A

Question: If teens witness violence within the family, are they at higher risk to become victims of dating violence?

Answer: Psychologists Jeffrey Edleson and Sandra A. Graham-Bermann explore this topic at length in the American Psychological

Association report "Domestic Violence in the Lives of Children." They found that teens living with domestic violence have difficulty forming trusting, lasting relationships and may be more likely to find themselves in violent dating or marital relationships.

Experts theorize that because teens are formulating their own ideas about relationships by watching the relationships of their parents, they may not have the best models on which to base a healthy relationship.

EMOTIONAL HEALTH

Teens often experience stress at school or at home, worry about their family's financial problems, or deal with a wide variety of fears related to growing up. For some teenagers, their parents' divorce, the formation of a new family with stepparents and step-siblings, or moving to a new community can be very emotional and can intensify typical issues of adolescence.

Teens need adult guidance to understand the emotional and physical changes they are experiencing. For some, managing these complex feelings is overwhelming. The American Association for Child and Adolescent Psychiatry claims that approximately five percent of children and adolescents experience depression. Recent surveys indicate that as many as one in five teens may suffer from clinical depression. **Depression** is more than just feeling down or blue about something that went wrong during the day. There are two types of depression. The first is called major depression, dysthymia, or reactive depression. It is the inability to interact with friends and family and even hope that things will get better with time. The second type is called bipolar disorder or manic depression. Those who are diagnosed with this condition don't feel happy one minute and sad the next. Instead they have times when they become so overexcited that they may become reckless and times they feel so sad that they may become suicidal. The highs are very high and the lows are very low.

Depression can be difficult to diagnose in teens because of the many myths about moody adolescents. Even teens do not always understand the significance or depth of their own depressed feelings. The National Mental Health Association claims that some teens feel so depressed that they consider ending their lives. Suicide is the third leading cause of death among adolescents. Each year, almost 5,000 teens, ages 15 to 24, kill themselves. The suicide rate for this age group has nearly tripled since 1960.

According to the American Academy of Child and Adolescent Psychiatry, depression and suicidal feelings are treatable emotional conditions. Early recognition and diagnosis along with appropriate treatment are the keys to success.

SUBSTANCE ABUSE

Some teens abuse alcohol and other drugs for a variety of reasons, including curiosity, because it feels good, to manage stress, and to fit in. The research is vague on which teens are likely to experiment but stop before they become addicted and which will develop serious substance abuse issues. The National Institute on Drug Abuse found that even though the percentage of young adolescents using any drug is decreasing, some drug abuse, such as the use of club drugs, like Ecstasy, and steroids are on the rise.

Teenagers at risk for developing substance abuse issues are those with a family history of substance abuse, those who are depressed, those with low self-esteem, and those who do not feel they fit in.

Teenagers abuse a variety of drugs, both legal and illegal. Legally available drugs include alcohol, prescribed medications, inhalants, and cough, cold, sleep, and diet medications. Illegal drugs commonly abused are marijuana, cocaine, crack, speed, LSD, PCP, opiates, heroin, and Ecstasy.

The reasons that some adolescents develop serious drug problems are many. Among the factors that place adolescents at increased risk are a lack of parental supervision, poor communication between parents and teens, unclear rules for behavior both in and outside the home, and conflict within the family.

Two studies conducted by the National Institute for Drug Abuse found that parents and friends can have a positive influence on behavior related to alcohol and drug abuse. One study showed that positive family and peer influences may remain strong even into young adulthood and can be found across socioeconomic, ethnic, and gender lines. Both studies reported that positive family and clear and consistent rules reduce the risk of smoking cigarettes and marijuana and other drug use, while negative family influences tend to increase the risk of use. The same was found with positive and negative peer relationships.

Experts at the National Clearinghouse for Alcohol and Drug Information claim that a telling sign that a teen has a serious problem with drugs is when the use of drugs becomes more important than any other activity including those that were previously important to the teen. Friendship groups may change and relationships with family members can become more distant or conflicted.

Fact Or Fiction?

If I say no to alcohol, I won't fit in.

Fact: The National Institute on Alcohol Abuse and Alcoholism says that teens often overestimate the numbers of other teens who drink. While resisting the pressure to drink is a real issue for teens, it is easier to refuse than you might think. Experts suggest practicing excuses and how to say "no, thanks." They recommend spending time with friends who do not drink. They also urge teens to stay active and enjoy physical activities, as most drinking occurs when teens are just "hanging out." And finally, they warn against going to parties and other social situations unprepared. A teen has a greater chance of resisting peer pressure and the temptation to drink if he or she has a plan to handle the pressure.

Early recognition and treatment of any of the issues affecting teens and family life are important for both parents and teens. Families should seek help to get the information and resources they need to take appropriate action to restore physical and emotional health.

FURTHER READING

Cobain, Bev. *When Nothing Matters Anymore: A Survival Guide for Depressed Teens.* Minneapolis: Free Spirit Press, 1998.

Immell, Myra. *Teen Pregnancy.* Farmington Hills, MI: Greenhaven Press, 2000.

McAllister Groves, Betsy. *Children Who See Too Much: Lessons from the Child Witness to Violence Project.* Boston: Beacon Press, 2003.

Monti, Peter M., ed. *Adolescents, Alcohol and Substance Abuse: Reaching Teens Through Brief Interventions.* New York: Guilford Press, 2004.

■ VIOLENCE AND THE FAMILY

Actions, attitudes, or words that harm or threaten other members of a family. The violence may be directed at a child, partner, parent, spouse, or sibling. It can occur between family members of the same or different generations. Family violence is a widespread problem in the United States, often resulting in emotional and physical harm, and sometimes death.

PHYSICAL AND SEXUAL VIOLENCE

Violence in a family can be physical, sexual, or psychological. It can be directed from an adult to a child, an adult to another adult, or from a sibling to another sibling. **Child abuse** involves physical injury of a child by the adult who is supposed to be the child's caretaker. **Sexual abuse** occurs whenever there is any form of sexual contact between an adult and a child. When violence occurs between adult partners, it is called **intimate partner violence.**

The consequences of abuse are serious and long-lasting. Children who experience violence often suffer life-long psychological consequences, including depression, poor self-esteem, substance abuse, and other mental and emotional problems. During early childhood and adolescence, their development may be slowed or halted. Preschoolers may be anxious, experience nightmares, and display inappropriate sexual behavior. School-age children may be fearful, aggressive, or hyperactive. They may have problems at school, suffer nightmares, experience mental illness, and seem to go backwards in their development in a condition called regressive behavior. Adolescents may become depressed, withdrawn, and suicidal. They may injure themselves, engage in illegal activities, run away from home, and abuse illicit drugs and alcohol.

Fact Or Fiction?

Women don't commit violent acts against their partners.

Fact: Women are less likely to commit violent acts against their partners than men are, but an increasing number of women are resorting to violence in their disputes with their partners. Still, men and women tend to assault each other in different ways. In the National Violence Against Women Survey, 22.1 percent of women, compared to 7.4 percent of men, said an intimate partner had assaulted them at some point in the relationship. Other data from the survey suggest that women are less likely than men to commit severe assaults, such as beating their partner, threatening him with a gun or knife, or using a gun or knife. However, between 1972 and 1992, the number of minor assaults—such as slapping, pushing, grabbing, or shoving—that women engaged in against their husbands increased.

Intimate partner violence and child abuse often go hand in hand. Men who are physically violent toward their partners are also likely to be sexually violent and direct that violence toward their children. Adults who experienced or witnessed violence in their families as children are more likely to commit acts of violence toward their partners and children or to become victims of violence.

MEASURING VIOLENCE IN THE FAMILY

In 2002, according to estimates from the National Clearinghouse on Child Abuse and Neglect, an estimated 896,000 children were victims of child abuse and neglect. Of those, more than 60 percent suffered neglect, 18.6 percent were victims of physical abuse, almost 10 percent were sexually abused, and seven percent were emotionally maltreated. Many children were victims of more than one type of maltreatment.

About 48 percent of child abuse cases reported in 2002 were male and 52 percent were female. Female children are more likely to be victims of sexual abuse, while males are more likely to be emotionally abused and experience serious physical injuries. More than half of all victims of abuse and neglect are white, 26.1 percent are African American, and 11 percent are Latino. Native Americans and Asian Americans account for less than three percent of reported cases of child maltreatment.

Children who are four years old and younger are the most likely to die as a result of child abuse and neglect. Forty-one percent of children who died as a result of maltreatment in 2002 were younger than a year, while 76 percent were under four years of age. Of those, the majority were boys. In 2002, 553 boys and 387 girls died as a result of maltreatment. About 56 percent of fatalities were male children and 44 percent were female.

TEENS SPEAK

About a Year Ago, My Father Broke My Arm

I had returned home after seeing a movie with my friends. He had been sitting at home, drinking, while I was at the movie. The minute I opened the door, he started yelling at me about how inconsiderate I was to stay out that late and how much concern I had caused my mother. I ignored him—after all, I had told my mother where I was going and she had said it was okay.

He yelled louder, and I kept ignoring him. I was smearing peanut butter on a piece of bread when I heard him come up behind me. He shoved me into the kitchen counter, so hard that it knocked my breath away. I heard the bones in my forearm snap when I hit the counter.

I knew better. I had learned a long time ago that it is best to disappear when he is on one of his drinking sprees. Anybody who is in the way—my mother, the dog, the cat, or me—is a potential target. Once he even got so angry that he smashed the fish bowl. We had all learned to disappear.

My mother took me to the emergency room. When the nurse asked what happened, I told her that I fell. I couldn't tell her that my father had slammed me into the counter. My mother didn't say anything to the nurse in the emergency room either. I knew why: She had been there before herself, with a broken nose, cracked ribs, and more that she had never told me about.

The next day at school I told my friends I had fallen off my bike. But my math teacher, Mrs. Harding, asked me to stay after school so she could have a word with me. She asked me how I had hurt my arm. When I started to tell the "falling down" story she asked, "How did you get that bruise on your cheek? It sure looks to me like someone hit you. Would you like to talk about it?" That's when I started crying.

I didn't know where to go for help. I talked with Mrs. Harding for a long time that night. She asked me about my family, my dad, and how he treated me. She was the first person who ever used the word *abuse* to me. I had never thought of myself as being abused before. Dad's angry drunken sprees had always been a part of life.

When I got home that night, Dad was furious because I was late and he was waiting for dinner. He slapped me across the face. I could hear Mom crying in the back room. That's when I knew I had to get out of there. I called the number of the domestic violence shelter that Mrs. Harding had given me.

I stayed at the shelter for a week. I moved in with my best friend Bess and her family after that. I started working after school at a fast-food restaurant down the street, and my mother sends me money when she can. In her last letter she said she was saving up so she could get away. I worry about my mom—but I know that she needs to make her own decision to leave. I hope she will. It was the hardest, but best, decision I ever made.

Statistics from the National Child Abuse and Neglect Data System show that 1,400 children died as a direct or indirect result of abuse and neglect in 2002. However, many experts believe child fatalities due to abuse and neglect are greater than these statistics suggest. Because states define key words such as *child homicide, abuse,* and *neglect* differently, the number and types of child fatalities linked to maltreatment vary. In addition, child abuse and neglect may be involved in some deaths that are attributed to accidents, sudden infant death syndrome (SIDS), or other causes.

A study published in *Pediatrics* in 2002, "Under-ascertainment of Child Maltreatment Fatalities by Death Certificates," confirms that these estimates are low. A team of researchers led by Tessa Crume of the Colorado Department of Public Health and Environment compared data on child maltreatment fatalities with information on the death certificates of children who died in Colorado between January 1990 and January 1998. Crume and her colleagues estimate that more than half of children's deaths resulting from abuse or neglect were not recorded.

Almost 60 percent of those who maltreat the children they are supposed to be caring for are women, and in 40 percent of cases, the mother acts alone. About 40 percent of women and 30 percent of men who maltreat children are younger than 30. A female parent acting alone was most commonly responsible for neglect—46.9 percent of cases—and physical abuse—32.1 percent of cases. A male parent acting alone was responsible for sexual abuse in 21.5 percent of reported cases.

Q & A

Question: My father sexually abused me, then told me that he would hurt my mom if I told anyone. What do I do?

Answer: It's common for abusers to try to manipulate their victims into keeping quiet, either by convincing them that the abuse is their own fault or threatening to hurt them or someone they love if they tell. But keeping the abuse a secret doesn't protect anyone. It only allows the abuse to continue. Talk to someone you can trust: a friend's parent, teacher, counselor, doctor, or other adult.

Violence toward children is often linked to violence toward adult intimate partners. According to the Centers for Disease Control and Prevention (CDC), each year a current or former partner or date physically or sexually assaults an estimated 1.5 million women and 835,000 men in the United States. The costs of health care for these incidents is more than $5.8 billion a year. Nearly $4.1 billion is spent on medical and mental health-care services. Although both women and men can be victims of intimate partner violence, estimates from the National Violence Against Women Survey show that one out of four women in the United States has reported a physical assault or rape by an intimate partner, in comparison with one out of 14 men. Women are also more likely than men to be murdered by an intimate partner, with women ages 20 to 29 being at the greatest risk. Ethnicity and race also make a difference. About one out of every three African-American women and one out of every four white women experience intimate partner violence.

Researchers believe that maltreatment of children—including child abuse, sexual abuse, and neglect—and intimate partner violence is far more prevalent than these statistics show. Violence in families often goes unreported, partly because of shame or confusion surrounding such events. Even when incidents are reported, data collection methods may be flawed.

Violence in a family can be physical, sexual, and psychological. Intimate partner violence and child abuse often go hand in hand. Children who are exposed to family violence may experience depression, poor self-esteem, substance abuse, and other mental and emotional problems. When they become adults, they are more likely to commit acts of violence toward their partners and children or to become victims of violence.

While violence does not occur in every family, it is widespread: Nearly 1 million children are victims of maltreatment every year and an estimated 1.5 million women and 835,000 men are physically or sexually assaulted by a current or former partner or date. Research suggests that both child maltreatment and intimate partner violence are underreported.

See also: Arguments and the Family; Death in the Family; Families, Divided; Teens in Trouble

FURTHER READING

Pagelow, Mildred. *Family Violence.* New York: Praeger, 1984.

Sadler, A. E. *Family Violence.* San Diego, CA: Greenhaven Press, 1996.

HOTLINES AND HELP SITES

Center for Adoption Research
URL: http://www.centerforadoptionresearch.org
Mission: The Center for Adoption Research is dedicated to developing practical responses to the real world challenges presented by adoption and foster care.
Programs: The center was established in 1996 to study issues related to foster care and adoption. It provides independent research, analysis, and evaluation of adoption and foster care policy and practice. The center is developing professional training programs and resources in disciplines, including medicine, education, social work, policy, and law.

Centers for Medicare & Medicaid Services (CMS)
URL: http://www.cms.hhs.gov
Affiliation: The Centers for Medicaid & Medicare Services (CMS) is a federal agency within the U.S. Department of Health and Human Services.
Programs: The CMS administers the Medicare program and works in partnership with states to administer Medicaid, the Children's Health Insurance Program (CHIP), and Health Insurance Portability and Accountability Act (HIPAA) standards. Through Medicare, Medicaid, and CHIP, about one in four Americans receive health-care coverage. Nearly 40 million people are covered by Medicare, about 33 million are eligible for Medicaid, and CHIP helps states expand health coverage to as many as 5 million uninsured children.

Children of Lesbians and Gays Everywhere (COLAGE)

URL: http://www.colage.org

Phone: (415) 861-5437

Mission: Children of Lesbians and Gays Everywhere (COLAGE) engages, connects, and empowers people to make the world a better place for children of lesbian, gay, bisexual, and transgender parents and families. COLAGE is the only national and international organization in the world specifically supporting young people with gay, lesbian, bisexual, and transgender parents.

Families and Work Institute

URL: http://www.familiesandwork.org

Mission: Families and Work Institute is a nonprofit center for research that provides data to inform decision making on the changing workforce, changing family, and changing community.

Programs: The institute offers some of the most comprehensive research on the U.S. workforce.

Name: Family Caregiver Alliance (FCA)

URL: http://www.caregiver.org

Mission: Founded in 1977, Family Caregiver Alliance (FCA) was the first community-based nonprofit organization in the country to address the needs of families and friends providing long-term care at home.

Programs: FCA now offers programs at national, state, and local levels to support and sustain caregivers. It provides information, education, services, research, and advocacy to support and sustain the important work of families nationwide caring for loved ones with chronic, disabling health conditions.

The Future of Children

URL: http://www.futureofchildren.org

Affiliation: The Future of Children is a publication of the Woodrow Wilson School of Public and International Affairs at Princeton University and the Brookings Institution.

Mission: The Future of Children seeks to promote effective policies and programs for children by providing policy makers, service providers, and the media with timely, objective information based on the best available research.

National Adoption Information Clearinghouse (NAIC)

URL: http://naic.acf.hhs.gov

Phone: (888) 251-0075

Affiliation: The National Adoption Information Clearinghouse (NAIC) is a service of the Children's Bureau, Administration for Children and Families, U.S. Department of Health and Human Services.

Mission: The NAIC was established by Congress in 1987 to provide free information on all aspects of adoption.

Programs: The NAIC Web site provides comprehensive information on domestic and intercountry adoption.

National Campaign to Prevent Teen Pregnancy

URL: http://www.teenpregnancy.org

Phone: (202) 478-8500

Affiliation: The National Campaign to Prevent Teen Pregnancy, founded in February 1996, is a nonprofit, nonpartisan initiative supported almost entirely by private donations.

Mission: The mission of the National Campaign to Prevent Teen Pregnancy is to improve the well-being of children, youths, and families by reducing teen pregnancy. The campaign's goal is to reduce the teen pregnancy rate by one-third between 1996 and 2005.

National Clearinghouse on Child Abuse and Neglect Information

URL: http://nccanch.acf.hhs.gov

Affiliation: The National Clearinghouse on Child Abuse and Neglect Information is a service of the Children's Bureau, Administration for Children and Families, U.S. Department of Health and Human Services.

Mission: The service was established in 1974 by the Child Abuse Prevention and Treatment Act to collect, organize, and disseminate information on all aspects of child maltreatment.

National Domestic Violence Hotline

URL: http://www.ndvh.org

Phone: (800) 799-7233 or (800) 787-3224 (TTY)

Programs: The National Domestic Violence Hotline provides victims of domestic violence with a toll-free hotline 24 hours a day, 365 days a year. With a database of more than 4,000 shelters and service providers across the United States, Puerto Rico, Alaska, Hawaii, and the U.S. Virgin Islands, the hotline provides callers with information that they might otherwise have found difficult or impossible to obtain. Bilingual staff and a language line are available for every non-English-speaking caller. Deaf abused women can also find help at the hotline by calling the TTY line.

National Institute on Media and the Family (NIMF)
URL: http://www.mediafamily.org
Phone: (888) 672-KIDS (5437)
Mission: The National Institute on Media and the Family (NIMF) maximizes the benefits and minimizes the harm of media on children and families through research, education, and advocacy. Founded by psychologist David Walsh, Ph.D., in 1996, the Institute is a nonprofit, national resource center for research, information, and education about the impact of the media on children and families. The vision of the NIMF is to build healthy families and communities through the wise use of media.

National Network for Child Care (NNCC)
URL: http://www.nncc.org
Affiliation: National Network for Child Care (NNCC) is supported by the Cooperative State Research, Education and Extension Service, U.S. Department of Agriculture, and CYFERNet–the Cooperative Extension System's Children, Youth, and Family Network.
Mission: The NNCC's goal is to share knowledge about children and child care from the vast resources of the land grant universities with parents, professionals, practitioners, and the general public.
Programs: The NNCC unites the expertise of many of the nation's leading universities through the outreach system of cooperative extension. The NNCC Web site offers more than 1,000 publications and resources related to child care, an e-mail listserv, and support and assistance from experts in child care and child development. A newsletter is published four times a year.

Office of Family Assistance (OFA)
URL: http://www.acf.dhhs.gov/programs/ofa
Affiliation: The Office of Family Assistance (OFA) is located in the U.S. Department of Health and Human Services, Administration for Children and Families.

Programs: The OFA oversees the Temporary Assistance for Needy Families (TANF) program that was created by the Welfare Reform Law of 1996. TANF became effective July 1, 1997, and replaced what was then commonly known as welfare: Aid to Families with Dependent Children (AFDC) and the Job Opportunities and Basic Skills Training (JOBS) programs. TANF provides assistance and work opportunities to needy families by granting states the federal funds and wide flexibility to develop and implement their own welfare programs.

Option Line
URL: http://pregnancycenters.org
Phone: (800) 395-HELP (4357)
Programs: Option Line consultants refer each caller to a pregnancy resource center in her area for answers to questions about abortion, pregnancy tests, STDs, adoption, parenting, medical referrals, housing, and many other issues. The toll-free number is available 24 hours a day, seven days a week. Callers from across the country can reach a trained, caring person and then be connected to a pregnancy resource center near them for one-on-one help.

Parents, Families, and Friends of Lesbians and Gays (PFLAG)
URL: http://www.pflag.org
Phone: (202) 467-8180
Affiliation: Parents, Families, and Friends of Lesbians and Gays (PFLAG) is a national nonprofit organization with more than 250,000 members and supporters and over 500 affiliates in the United States. This vast grassroots network is cultivated, resourced, and serviced by the PFLAG national office, located in Washington, D.C., the national board of directors, and 14 regional directors.
Mission: To promote the health and well-being of gay, lesbian, bisexual, and transgender persons, their families, and their friends through: support, to cope with an adverse society; education, to enlighten an ill-informed public; and advocacy, to end discrimination and to secure equal civil rights.
Programs: PFLAG provides opportunity for dialogue about sexual orientation and gender identity and acts to create a society that is healthy and respectful of human diversity.

Parents Without Partners

URL: http://www.parentswithoutpartners.org

Phone: (800) 637-7974

Mission: Parents Without Partners provides single parents and their children with an opportunity for enhancing personal growth, self-confidence, and sensitivity toward others by offering an environment for support, friendship, and the exchange of parenting techniques.

Single and Custodial Fathers Network, Inc.

URL: http://www.scfn.org

Phone: (412) 853-9903

Programs: The Single and Custodial Fathers Network, Inc. is an international, member-supported, nonprofit organization with members throughout the world. The network provides education, research, and supportive services to single and custodial fathers. Membership includes both single and custodial fathers and is open to anyone interested in supporting fathers in their roles as parents.

Teen Advice Online

URL: http://www.teenadviceonline.org

Programs: Teen Advice Online is the largest online archive of questions and answers asked by teens. Maintained by a team of volunteers 13 and older, the site provides a forum for teens to ask and volunteer advice.

TeenGrowth.com

URL: http://www.teengrowth.com

Programs: TeenGrowth focuses exclusively on the educational health issues of adolescents. The site provides a secure environment where teens can ask questions and find reliable and useful information about subjects such as emotions, peer pressure, drugs, alcohol, puberty, sex, fitness, and stress. The Medical Advisory Board, comprising well-known and respected physicians in the pediatric community, oversees all content on the site, thereby guaranteeing its medical accuracy.

U.S. Department of Housing and Urban Development (HUD)

URL: http://www.hud.gov

Phone: (202) 708-1112

Affiliation: HUD is a federal agency.

Mission: HUD's mission is to increase homeownership, support community development, and increase access to affordable housing free from discrimination. To fulfill this mission, HUD will embrace high standards of ethics, management and accountability and forge new partnerships—particularly with faith-based and community organizations—that leverage resources and improve HUD's ability to be effective on the community level.

GLOSSARY

abandonment   the refusal of a parent to physically, emotionally, or financially support his or her child

Activities of Daily Living (ADL)   the scale used to measure a person's ability to perform physical tasks

adoptive parents   adults who assume parental rights and responsibilities for a child not related by birth

alimony   payment to or from a former spouse as part of a separation or divorce agreement

Alzheimer's disease   a progressive, degenerative brain disorder

artificial insemination   a process by which pregnancy is achieved without sexual intercourse

assets   the monetary resources of an individual, family, or business

bereavement   sadness about the loss of a loved one

birth families   biological parents and siblings

bisexual   being sexually attracted to both men and women

celibate   abstaining from sexual intercourse

child abuse   physical or emotional injury of a child

child support   money paid by a parent to help support children not living with him or her

cohabitation   the practice of living together without marriage

common-pot method and the **two-pot method**   common economic patterns used by blended families to benefit and raise the children according to their needs

community property states   states in which all property obtained during the marriage—other than a gift or inheritance—belongs equally to both spouses

companionate family   a family which is seen as the primary source of emotional satisfaction and personal happiness

compromise   a mutually acceptable solution that is not exactly what either party to a dispute wanted but is fair and can meet each person's minimum needs

custody   legal responsibility for the care and protection of a child

debt   an amount owed to another

depression   overwhelming feeling of sadness and grief

domestic partners   a stable, intimate relationship between two people who are financially interdependent

dual earner   a family in which both spouses are part of the labor force

economic parity   earning the same pay for performing the same work

effective preferences   the actions people take when they focus on broad concerns, such as the long-term consequences of their actions and the implications for others

egalitarian   characterized by an arrangement of equality in a marriage

emancipate   to legally release a child from the control of a parent or guardian

estrangement   alienation of family members from each other due to unresolved conflict

ethnicity   the cultural heritage of a particular group

exit   an actively destructive response in a family in which the offended person leaves, threatens to end the relationship, or engages in abusive acts such as yelling or hitting

fertility rate   the average number of children a woman has in her lifetime

fetus   the unborn baby from the eighth week after fertilization to birth

foster parents   persons licensed to care for a child by the government or a social service agency

given preferences   the actions people take when they focus on short-term, self-centered, immediate reactions to an event

guardianship   a legal proceeding by which a court appoints an individual to assume the care of a person who is unable to care for himself or herself

heterosexual   being attracted to people of the opposite sex

homosexual   being attracted to people of the same sex

immune response   the reaction of a person's body to an irritant

income tax   a tax on earnings payable to city, state, and/or federal governments

intercountry adoptions   international adoptions

interracial marriage   a marriage in which the husband and wife are of different races

intimate partner violence   violence between adult partners in a relationship

integrative agreements   creative ways worked out to resolve problems and restore peace

joint custody   custody arrangements in which parents share physical and legal custody

legal custody   custody arrangements that determine who will make decisions about how a child is raised

logrolling   making concessions on one issue if the other person will make concessions on another, while still maintaining commitment to one's central goals

long-term care   health services provided to people with chronic conditions, physical disabilities, and/or cognitive impairment

mediator   a person who usually has a background in law or the behavioral sciences and specializes in helping couples resolve the issues that arise in a divorce

Medicaid   a federal-state program that provides health-care assistance to low-income people

Medicare   a federal health insurance program for people 65 and over and certain disabled people under 65

monogamous   description of couples who engage in sex only with each other

next-of-kin   a person's closest living relative either by blood or by marriage

obstetrician   a physician who specializes in delivering babies

parenting coalition an arrangement in which the divorced and remarried biological parents and the stepparents cooperate in rearing their biological children and stepchildren

parenting coordinator a person who works within the structure of a couple's divorce decree to help parents settle disagreement about children

paternity identification of the father of a child

pension payments income received upon retirement

perpetrator a person who commits an offensive action

physical custody custody arrangements that define where the child will live

physical dependence the physical craving for and the compulsive use of a substance despite harmful psychological, physical, or social consequences

power of attorney a legal document that authorizes another person to act on one's behalf

prenuptial agreement a legal agreement arranged prior to marriage stating who owns property acquired before marriage and, during the marriage, and how property will be divided in the event of divorce

prenatal care medical care during pregnancy

profit sharing a plan in which employers share their profits with employees at the employer's discretion

reconstituted families another term for blended families

role models people who are considered worthy of imitation

separation a couple's decision to live apart by mutual agreement or under a court order

sexual abuse   any form of sexual contact between an adult and a child

sexually transmitted disease (STD)   communicable disease transmitted by sexual intercourse or genital contact

sexual orientation   a person's romantic, emotional, or sexual attraction to a person of the opposite sex and/or one's own sex

sibling   a brother or sister

sibling rivalry   competition between brothers and sisters for their parents' attention, approval, and affection

social isolation   loneliness due to a lack of a social network of friends and acquaintances

sole custody   custody arrangements that legally establish care by one parent

staff ratio   the number of children in a day care situation related to the number of staff to care for them

stepfamilies   families formed by parents' subsequent marriages

transracial adoption   the adoption of a child of one race by parents of another

transsexual   showing a strong desire to live one's life as a member of the opposite sex

visitation rights   the legal right to spend time with one's child

wills   legal documents expressing a person's wishes regarding the disposal of his or her property after death

INDEX

Page numbers in **boldface** indicate extensive coverage of a topic. Page numbers in *italic* indicate graphs or sidebars.

A

AACAP. *See* American Academy of Child and Adolescent Psychiatry (AACAP)
AAP. *See* American Academy of Pediatrics (AAP)
AARP. *See* American Association of Retired Persons (AARP)
ACS. *See* American Community Survey (ACS)
Activities of Daily Living (ADL) 51
"Adjustment in Conflicted Marriage and Divorce" (Kelly) 46
Adolescence 167, 171, 173
adoption 4–5, **13–23**. *See also* divorce and families; families, blended; families, racially mixed; family, the new; gay parents; marriage and family, changes in; stepparents
    fact vs. fiction 19–20
    family dynamics and 20–23
    foster care and 15–16
    gay parents 18–19, 84–86
    international 16
    Minnesota/Texas Adoption Research Project 19–20, 22
    questions and answers 20–21
    rates in United States and abroad 13–16
    readings 23
    siblings and 21
    special needs children 15
    stepparents, adoption of stepchild 159–160
    transracial 16–18, 23, 80
Adoption and Foster Care Analysis and Reporting System (AFCARS) 15–16
Adoption and Safe Families Act (ASFA) 15, 22–23
Adoption by Lesbians and Gays: A National Survey of Adoption Agency Policies, Practices, and Attitudes 18–19
adult day care 54–55
AFCARS. *See* Adoption and Foster Care Analysis and Reporting System (AFCARS)
AFL-CIO. *See* American Federation of Labor-Congress of Industrial Organizations (AFL-CIO)
AGI. *See* Alan Guttmacher Institute (AGI)
Aid for Families with Dependent Children (AFDC) 149
Alan Guttmacher Institute (AGI) 164, 177–178
Allen, Sarah 97
All Our Families: New Policies for a New Century (Mauldon) 164
Alstein, Howard 17
alternative families 84–85
Alzheimer's disease 56–57
Amato, Paul
    "Parental Divorce and the Wellbeing of Children" 46
Ambulatory Pediatrics 174
American Academy of Child and Adolescent Psychiatry (AACAP) 175–176, 179
American Academy of Pediatrics (AAP) 35, 115
    gay parents, adoption by 18, 86
    media and the family 129–130, 132
American Association for Child and Adolescent Psychiatry 178

American Association of Retired Persons
(AARP) 53
American Automotive Association (AAA) 104
American Civil Liberties Union 117
American Community Survey (ACS) 51
American Federation of Labor-Congress of
Industrial Organizations (AFL-CIO) 95
American Journal of Orthopsychiatry 173
American Psychological Association (APA)
"Domestic Violence in the Lives of
Children" 177–178
families, blended 65, 69, 71
family traditions 102
gay parents 116, 117
National Gay and Lesbian Family Study,
The 117
American Public Health Association 35
American Society for the Prevention of
Cruelty to Animals (ASPCA) 135
American Sociological Review 165
Americans with Disabilities Act 33
American University 17
Anderson, Carol 145
APA. See American Psychological
Association (APA)
Aquilino, W. S. 62
arguments and the family 24–29. See also
divorce and families; families, divided;
teens in trouble; violence and the family
causes of 28
fact vs. fiction 27
questions and answers 28–29
readings 29
siblings, quarrels among 24–27
teens speak 24–25
Arizona, University of 157
artificial insemination 4
ASFA. See Adoption and Safe Families Act
(ASFA)
ASPCA. See American Society for the
Prevention of Cruelty to Animals (ASPCA)
assets, marriage and 112
assisted living centers 54
authority in family 98–99

B
Baker, Mark 140
Barber, Brian K. 27
Barna Research Group 139
Barnett, Rosalind 95–96
Baruch, Grace 95–96
Baumrind, Donna 157–158
Baylor College of Medicine 65
"Becoming a Family Member: Family
Conflict and the Development of Social
Understanding in the Second Year"
(Dunn) 25

Bengtson, Vern 102
Berg, Ellen C. 156
Bergh, Henry 135
blended families 3
Booth, Alan
"Parental Divorce and the Wellbeing of
Children" 46
Borden, Lee 108
Bray, James 65
Brazelton, T. Berry
Irreducible Needs of Children, The 34
British Columbia, University of 22
Brookings Institution 79
Brooks, Jane B.
Process of Parenting, The 98,100
Brown University 33
Bryner, Charles
"Children of Divorce" 49
Buhrmester, Duane 26
Bureau of Labor Statistics
history of family life in America 2
traditional family 88
Bush, George W. 84

C
California, same-sex couples 128
California, University of at Berkeley 164,
170–171
California, University of at Davis 119
California, University of at Los Angeles 27, 165
California, University of at San Francisco 46
California State University 156
Cal-Learn program 170
Capital Region Race Relations Association 81
Carlson, Rebecca S. 35
CDC. See Centers for Disease Control and
Prevention (CDC)
Census Bureau. See U.S. Census Bureau
Center for Adoption Research 187
Center for American Progress 110
Center for Media Literacy 132
Center for Medicare & Medicaid Services
(CMS) 187
Center for the Childcare Workforce 36
Center for the Study of Biracial Children
80–82
Center for Twin and Family Research 20–21
Centers for Disease Control and Prevention
(CDC)
cohabitation 122
media and the family 132
pets in the family 136, 137
teens in trouble 177
violence and the family 185
"Changes in Wives' Income: Effects on
Marital Happiness" (Rogers and DeBoer) 94
Cheboud, Elias 81

Chicago, University of 153, 168
Child Development 158, 173–174
Child-Parent Centers 33
Children, Adolescents and Media
  (Strasburger) 131
Children Now 131
"Children of Divorce" (Bryner) 49
Children of Lesbians and Gays Everywhere
  (COLAGE) 188
Children's Aid Society of New York 31
Children's Defense Fund 31, 33, 34, 37
Children's Health Insurance Program (CHIP)
  151
child support 113
Child Trends 169
City University of New York 171
civility 77–78
Clemmens, Donna 167–168
Clinton, Bill 80
Coady, Susan 103, 105
cohabitation 88, 121–123
  legal documents *108*
  statistics 4
Cole, Galen 148
college degree of householder, percentage of
  children under 18 *13*
Colorado Department of Public Health and
  Environment 184–185
Communication Quarterly 158
companionship, pets and 137–138
Compassionate Friends, The (TFC) 38
compromise 73–74
Connecticut, University of 167
consistency 101
Coontz, Stephanie
  *Way We Never Were: American Families
  and the Nostalgia Trap, The* 90
*Coping with Divorce: A Risk and Resiliency
  Perspective* (Hetherington) 68, 156
Cornell University 146
credit cards, marriage and 112–113
Crume, Tessa
  "Under-ascertainment of Child
  Maltreatment Fatalities" 184–185
cultural issues
  gay parents 119–120
  traditional family 93–94

D

Darling, Nancy
  "Parenting Style and Its Correlates" 99
Davidson, James 140–141
Davis, Laura
  I Thought We'd Never Speak Again 77
day care **29–38.** *See also* financial
  management, marital; single-parent families
  adult day care 54–55

advantages for children 32–33
alternatives 30
availability 35, 37
curriculum development 37
expensive nature of 30–32
fact vs. fiction 34
financial assistance 31–32
funding 37
future of 37
health problems 36
issues and concerns 35–36
number of hours per week, children in
  day care *32*
questions and answers 33
readings 37–38
safety 35–36
separation issues 34
staffing difficulties 36
types of 30
death in the family **38–42.** *See also* family
  traditions; religion and the family
  adult response to grief 38–39
  bereavement 38–40
  children's response to grief 39–40
  comforting children 40
  fact vs. fiction 41
  questions and answers 41–42
  readings 42
  religion, role in grieving 41–42
"Death in the Family: Helping Children
  Cope" 39
DeBoer, Danielle D.
  "Changes in Wives' Income: Effects on
  Marital Happiness" 94
debt, marriage and 112–113
Dedmon, Angela 26
delayed marriage 123–125
DeLeire, Thomas 153
Demography 153
Denver, University of 26
Department of Veterans Affairs 59
depression 178
  postpartum depression 167
Development and Psychopathology 173
discipline, stepparents 157–158
"Diversity, Strength, and Challenges of
  Single-Parent Households, The" 145
divorce and families **42–51.** *See also*
  arguments and the family; families,
  blended; families, divided; family, the new;
  family, the traditional; marriage and
  family, changes in; single-parent families;
  stepparents; violence and the family
  amicable divorce, children and 48–50
  custody 44, 50–51
  difficult divorce, children and 45–47
  elderly family members 62

divorce and families *(continued)*
  fact vs. fiction 45
  mediators 44, 48
  questions and answers 62, 126–127
  readings 51
  separation issues 42–43
  split families 43–44
  teens speak 47–48
divorce rate 2, 3, 88
Do Children Need Religion? How Parents Today Are Thinking about the Big Questions (Fay) 140
dog bite–related injuries, 2001 *137*
Doherty, George W.
  Extended Familes 83
Doherty, William 103
"Dollars, Dependency, and Divorce: Four Perspectives on the Role of Wives' Income" (Rogers) 93
domestic partners. *See* cohabitation
"Domestic Violence in the Lives of Children" (Edleson and Graham-Bermann) 177–178
Donenberg, Geri R. 85–86
Dougy Center 39–40
Downing, Chris 81
dual-career family 125–126
Dunn, Judith Frances
  "Becoming a Family Member: Family Conflict and the Development of Social Understanding in the Second Year" 25
"Dynamics of Parental Remarriage, The" 68

E

Early Child Care Research Center 36
earnings gap 95
"Economic Behavior of Stepfamilies, The" (Fishman) 68–69
Edgell, Penny 139
Edleson, Jeffrey
  "Domestic Violence in the Lives of Children" 177–178
educational attainment
  householder, percentage of children under 18 *13*
  work life earnings and *152*
elderly family members 51–63. *See also* day care; death in the family; family, the new; family, the traditional; financial management, marital; marriage and family, changes in; religion and the family
  adult day care 54–55
  Alzheimer's disease 56–57
  assisted living centers 54
  costs and incomes 57–59
  disabilities 51–53
  divorce 62
  expenses 57–59

fact vs. fiction 52–53
life expectancy by ethnicity and gender *52*
living with family members 59–62
nursing homes 52–53
questions and answers 62
readings 62–63
teens speak 60–61
Epkins, Catherine C. 26
ethnic differences
  elderly family members 58
  life expectancy *52*
  single-parent families 144
  teenage parents 164–165
  violence and the family 182
Evan B. Donalds Adoption Agency 18–19
Evergreen State College 90
extended families 83–84
Extended Families (Doherty) 83

F

fact vs. fiction
  adoption 19–20
  arguments and the family 27
  day care 34
  death in the family 41
  divorce and families 45
  elderly family members 52–53
  families, blended 64–65
  families, divided 74–75
  family, the new 85–86
  family, the traditional 91–92
  family rules 99–100
  family traditions 103–104
  financial management, marital 113
  gay parents 116–117
  "latchkey children" 91–92
  marriage and family, changes in 122
  media and the family 131–132
  pets in the family 133–134
  religion and the family 141
  single-parent families 143
  spanking 99–100
  stepparents 155
  substance abuse 180
  teenage parents 169–170
  teens in trouble 180
  violence and the family 181–182
fairness 100
families, blended 63–72, 88. *See also* arguments and the family; divorce and families; families, divided; families, racially mixed; family, the new; family, the traditional; financial management, marital; marriage and family, changes in; single-parent families; stepparents
  fact vs. fiction 64–65
  finances 68–69

home, giving up 69
playing favorites, perception of
  65–66
questions and answers 66
readings 72
relocation 70–73
remarriages 63–65
school, changing 70
state, relocating to 70–73
stepchildren, getting along 66–68
teens speak 66–67
families, divided 82–78
  alternatives 74–75
  civility 77–78
  compromise 73–74
  fact vs. fiction 74–75
  fairness 75–77
  questions and answers 77
  reasons for division 72–73
families, racially mixed 78–82, 86. *See also*
  adoption; family, the new
  acceptance by society 79–81
  fitting in 81
  identification and 81
  impact on teens 81–82
  questions and answers 81
  readings 82
  teens speak 80
Families and Work Institute 188
family, the new 2–5, 83–87. *See also*
  families, racially mixed; gay parents;
  religion and the family
  alternative families 84–85
  culturally mixed families 86
  extended families 83
  fact vs. fiction 85–86
  gay parents, adoption 84–86
  questions and answers 84–85
  racially mixed families 86
  readings 86–87
  teens speak 83–84
family, the traditional 87–98. *See also* day
  care; divorce and families; families,
  blended; families, racially mixed; family,
  the new; family traditions; marriage and
  family, changes in; single-parent families
  cultural pressures 93–94
  existence of 89–91
  fact vs. fiction 91–92
  financial adjustments 92–93
  gender roles 88–89
  household division of labor 95–97
  overview 87–89
  questions and answers 96–97
  readings 98
  sharing responsibilities 95–96
  single-bread-winner families 92–94

  staying at home 94–95
  teens speak 89–90
Family Caregiver Alliance (FCA) 57, 58, 188
family life in America 1–9. *See also*
  arguments and the family; divorce and
  families; families, divided; gay parents;
  marriage and family, changes in; single-
  parent families; stepparents; teenage parents;
  teens in trouble; violence and the family
  history of 1–2
  new family 2–5
  self-test 5–8
Family Pride Coalition
  Issues and News 85
family rules 98–101. *See also* family, the
  traditional; media and the family; pets in
  the family; teens in trouble
  authority 98–99
  consistency 101
  fact vs. fiction 99–100
  fairness 100
  questions and answers 100–101
  readings 101
family traditions 102–107. *See also* death in
  the family; family rules; religion and the
  family
  describing 103
  fact vs. fiction 103–104
  holidays 104
  new traditions, celebrating 105–106
  old traditions, honoring 105
  questions and answers 106
  readings 107
  relatives, including in 106–107
  "rites of passage" 106
  teens speak 102–103
Fay, Martha
  *Do Children Need Religion? How Parents
  Today Are Thinking about the Big
  Questions* 140
FDA Consumer 133–134
feminism, traditional family and 96–97
fertility rate 3
Filstrup, Jane
  *Monday through Friday: Day Care
  Alternatives* 30
finances. *See also* financial management,
  marital
  elderly family members 57–59
  families, blended 68–69
  family, the traditional 92–93
  single-parent families 142–145
financial management, marital 107–114.
  See also day care; death in the family; gay
  parents
  assets 112
  child support 113

financial management, marital *(continued)*
 credit cards 112–113
 debt and 112–113
 fact vs. fiction 113
 health insurance 114
 insurance benefits 109
 name changes 112
 next-of-kin privileges 111
 pensions 109–110
 power of attorney 107, 113
 prenuptial agreement 107, 108
 property 110
 questions and answers 111
 readings 114
 record keeping 111
 Social security benefits 109
 tax benefits 109
 wills 108
 workers' compensation 110
First Language 173
Fishman, Barbara
 "Economic Behavior of Stepfamilies, The"
  68–69
Florida Department of Children and Families
 35
Florida, University of 160
food stamps 150
For Better or for Worse: Divorce Reconsidered
 (Hetherington and Kelly) 50
For Richer Not Poorer: The Money Book for
 Couples (Hayden) 112–113
foster care, adoption and 15–16
Fragile Families 169
Frey, William 79
Fuligni, A. J. 27
Furman, Wyndol 26
Future of Children, The 172, 188

G
gay parents 114–120. *See also* family, the
 new; religion and the family; same-sex
 couples
 adoption 4, 18–19, 84–85
 children in gay partnerships 115–116
 cultural issues 119–120
 fact vs. fiction 116–117
 financial implications 118–119
 legal implications 118–119
 questions and answers 120
 readings 120
 religious issues 119–120
 societal reactions 117
 teens speak 118
gender differences
 life expectancy 52
gender roles 88–89, 94, 97
Gilbreth, Joan G. 161

Gillespie, Peggy 79
Golish, Tamara 158
Graham-Bermann, Sandra A.
 "Domestic Violence in the Lives of
  Children" 177–178
Greene, Alan 40
Greenspan, Stanley
 Irreducible Needs of Children, The 34
 Growing Up with a Single Parent: What
  Hurts, What Helps (McLanahan and
  Sandefur) 145–146

H
Harris Interactive 138
Harris Interactive/Modern Woodmen of
 America 104
Harvard Medical School 174
Hate Crimes Prevention Act 117
Hawkins, Alan 97
Hayden, Ruth
 For Richer Not Poorer: The Money Book
  for Couples 112–113
Head Start Program 32–33, 150
health insurance
 marriage and 114
 single-parent families 151
Heard, Holly E. 48, 49
help sites 187–193
Herek, Gregory M. 119
Heritage Foundation 139
Hetherington, E. Mavis
 Coping with Divorce: A Risk and
  Resiliency Perspective 68, 156
 For Better or for Worse: Divorce
  Reconsidered 50
HHS. *See* U.S. Department of Health and
 Human Services
history of family life in America 1–2
HIV/AIDS prevention 119
holidays, family traditions 104
hotlines and help sites 187–193
housing assistance 150
Howard M. Metzenbaum Multiethnic
 Placement Act of 1994 (MEPA) 16
HUD. *See* U.S. Department of Housing and
 Urban Development (HUD)
"Human Cost of Waiting for Child Care, The"
 31

I
Illinois, University of at Chicago 85–86
Illinois, University of at Urbana-Champaign
 26
"Impact of Day Care on Child Development,
 The" (Palacio-Quintin) 33
Indian Child Welfare Act (1978) 16
Institute for Women's Policy (IWPR) 95, 144

Institute for Youth Development 138
insurance benefits of marriage 109
Interethnic Adoption Provisions Laws 16
interfaith families 140–141
International Review of Psychiatry 167
interpersonal conflict, defined 72
*Intimate Relationships, Marriages, and
Families* (Rice) 125
Irreducible Needs of Children, The (Brazelton
and Greenspan) 34
Issues and News 85
I Thought We'd Never Speak Again (Davis) 77

J

Jewish Outreach Institute 141
Johnson, Lyndon B. 104
Johnson, Suzanne 115, 120
Jones, Anne C. 155
Journal of Adolescent Health 171
Journal of Allergy and Clinical Immunology
134
Journal of Divorce and Remarriage
156–157
Journal of Educational Research 146
Journal of Family Psychology 65, 168
Journal of Homosexuality 115
Journal of Marriage and the Family
  divorce, adjustment of children to 70
  domestic labor and marital satisfaction 96
  dual-earner couples 126, 127
  gatekeeping behavior 97
  stepparents 160–161
  women's income 89, 93
Journal of Research on Adolescence 165
Journal of Social Issues 139
Journal of the American Medical Association
134

K

Kalil, Ariel 153, 168
Kelley, Matt 81
Kelly, Joan B.
  "Adjustments in Conflicted Marriage and
  Divorce" 46
Kelly, John 50
King, Valarie 48, 49
King's College (United Kingdom) 25
Klute, Mary Maguire 127
Koerner, Susan Silverberg 157
Kramer, Laurie 26–27
Kübler-Ross, Elisabeth 49

L

labor market 95
"Labor Market and Socioeconomic Effects
  on Marital Stability" (Tzeng and Mare)
  63–65

Lady Pitts School Age Parent Center 170
Lancet 134
"latchkey children" 91–92
LaVie Counseling 140
Lavoie, Rick 100
Leach, Penelope 100
Lieberman, Susan A. 106
life expectancy by ethnicity and gender
  52
Local Law Enforcement Enhancement Act
  (2003) 117
long-term care health insurance 59
Loving v. Virginia 80

M

Maine-Orono, University of 125
Mare, Robert
  "Labor Market and Socioeconomic Effects
  on Marital Stability" 63–65
Marin Child Care Council 35
marriage and family, changes in **121–129.**
  see also adoption; day care; divorce and
  families; families, blended; families,
  racially mixed; family, the new; family, the
  traditional; gay parents; media and the
  family; single-parent families; stepparents;
  teenage parents
  delayed marriage 123–125
  domestic partners 121–123
  fact vs. fiction 122
  median age at first marriage, 1890-2002
    124
  questions and answers 126–127
  readings 129
  same-sex couples 127–128
  working couples, marriage among
    125–126
Marsiglio, William 160
Maryland, University of 17
Massachusetts, same-sex couples 127–128
Mauldon, Jane
  *All Our Families: New Policies for a New
  Century* 164
Maven Foundation 82
May, Dee C. 126
Mayer, Egon 141
Mayo Clinic 106, 137
Mazza, Carl 171
McLanahan, Sara
  *Growing Up With a Single Parent: What
  Hurts, What Helps* 145–146
"Meals on Wheels" 60
media and the family **129–133.** *See also*
  family rules
  fact vs. fiction 131–132
  family programs on TV 130
  impact on children 129–130

media and the family *(continued)*
  media literacy 132
  questions and answers 130–131
  readings 132–133
  role models and families 131
Media Awareness Network 130, 131
median age at first marriage 3
  1890-2002 *124*
Medicaid 59, 151
Medicare 58, 59
MEPA. *See* Howard M. Metzenbaum
  Multiethnic Placement Act of 1994 (MEPA)
Mesrkhani, Violet 38
MetLife Market Survey of Nursing Home and
  Home Care Costs 57–58
Minnesota, University of 103
  Center for Twin and Family Research
    20–21
  Division of General Pediatrics and
    Adolescent Health 177
  Religion and Family Project 139
Minnesota/Texas Adoption Research Project
  19–20, 22
Mintz, Steven 123
Modern Woman, The 93–94
*Monday through Friday: Day Care
  Alternatives* (Filstrup) 30
*Monographs of the Society for Research in
  Child Development* 154
Mother Earth News 135

N
NABSW. *See* National Association of Black
  Social Workers (NABSW)
NADSA. *See* National Adult Day Services
  Association (NADSA)
NAIC. *See* National Adoption Information
  Clearing House (NAIC)
Nakazawa, Donna 79
name changes, marriage and 112
Nassau Community College 17
National Adoption Information Clearing
  House (NAIC) 4, 15, 22, 189
National Adult Day Services Association
  (NADSA) 54–55, 58
National Association for the Education of
  Young Children 35
National Association of At-home Mothers
  93
National Association of Black Social Workers
  (NABSW) 17
National Campaign to Prevent Teen
  Pregnancy 165, 177–178, 189
National Center for Health Statistics (NCHS)
  divorce rate 2
  fertility rate 2
  single-parent families 149

teenage parents 162–163
traditional family 88
unmarried mothers 4
National Child Abuse and Neglect Data
  System 184
National Clearinghouse for Alcohol and Drug
  Information 179–180
National Clearinghouse on Child Abuse and
  Neglect 182, 189
National Council for Adoption (NCFA) 14,
  15
National Crime Victimization Survey 177
National Domestic Violence Hotline 189–190
National Economic Development and Law
  Center (NEDLC) 31
National Educational Longitudinal Survey
  153
National Gay and Lesbian Family Study, The
  117
National Health and Safety Performance
  Standards 35
National Health Interview Survey (NHIS) 16
National Institute for Drug Abuse 179
National Institute of Child Health and
  Human Development (NICHD) 32–34, 36,
  172
National Institute on Media and the Family
  (NIMF) 190
National Mental Health Association (NMHA)
  117, 178
National Network for Child Care (NNCC)
  190
National Nursing Home Survey 53
National Opinion Research Center 88
National Study of Youth and Religion (NSYR)
  139–140
National Survey of Family Growth 123
National Violence Against Women Survey
  182
NCFA. *See* National Council for Adoption
  (NCFA)
NCHS. *See* National Center for Health
  Statistics (NCHS)
Nebraska, University of 158
NEDLC. *See* National Economic Development
  and Law Center (NEDLC)
Neuropsychiatric Institute 38, 40
Newell, Lloyd 103
New England Journal of Medicine 172
next-of-kin privileges 111
NICHD. *See* National Institute of Child Health
  and Human Development (NICHD)
NMHA. *See* National Mental Health
  Association (NMHA)
North Carolina, University of at Chapel Hill
  75
Notre Dame, University of 173

NSYR. *See* National Study of Youth and Religion (NSYR)

O

O'Connor, Elizabeth 115, 120
Office for Young Children 33
Office of Family Assistance (OFA) 190–191
Ohio State University 103, 105
Oklahoma State University 173
Oppenheimer, Valerie 89
Option Line 191
Oregon Alliance of Children's Programs 82
"Outcomes of Transracial Adoption" (Silverman) 18

P

Page, Marianne E. 44
Page, Randy 148
Palacio-Quintin, Ercilia
  "Impact of Day Care on Child Development, The" 33
"Parental Divorce and the Wellbeing of Children" (Amato and Booth) 46
"Parenting Style and Its Correlates" (Darling) 99
Parents, Families, and Friends of Lesbians and Gays (PFLAG) 191
Parents Without Partners 192
Patterson, Charlotte J. 115–116
Pediatrics 130, 184
Pennsylvania State University
  Population Research Center 46
pensions 109–110
Personal Responsibility and Work Opportunity Reconciliation Act (PRWORA) 149
Pertman, Adam 80
Peterson, Gayle
  "Raising Children in Two-Religion Families" 141
pets in the family 133–138. *See also* death in the family; family rules
  companionship 137–138
  dog bite-related injuries, 2001 *137*
  fact vs. fiction 133–134
  immune response of children and 134
  questions and answers 135
  readings 138
  responsibility, teaching 134–137
  teens speak 136
Pew Forum on Religion and Public Life 119
Phoenix, University of 80
Ponton, Lynn 117
Population Research Center 46
postpartum depression 167
power of attorney 107, 113
prenuptial agreement 107, 108

Process of Parenting, the (Brooks) 98, 100
property, marriage and 110
Psychological Reports 148
Public Agenda 119–120
Purdue University 141

Q

questions and answers
  adoption 20–21
  arguments and the family 28–29
  day care 33
  death in the family 41–42
  divorce 62, 126–127
  elderly family members 62
  families, blended 66
  families, divided 77
  families, racially mixed 81
  family, the new 84–85
  family, the traditional 96–97
  family rules 100–101
  family traditions 106
  feminism and traditional family 96–97
  financial management, marital 111
  gay parents 120
  marriage and family, changes in 126–127
  media and the family 130–131
  pets in the family 135
  religion and the family 140
  single-parent families 151
  stepparents 66, 156
  teenage parents 168–169
  teens in trouble 177–178
  violence and the family 185

R

race differences
  adoption 15–16
  elderly family members 58
  remarriages 63
  single-parent families 142, 143, 152
  teenage parents 164–165, 168, 174
  violence and the family 182
"Raising Children in Two-religion Families" (Peterson) 141
Rando, T. 39
reblended families 3, 88
record keeping
  financial management, marital 111
"Relationship Between Teenage Motherhood and Marriage, The" 169
religion and the family 138–142. *See also* death in the family; family traditions; gay parents
  fact vs. fiction 141
  gay parents 119–120
  grieving, role of religion 41–42

religion and the family *(continued)*
  interfaith families 140–141
  questions and answers 140
  readings 142
  rearing children in faith 139–140
remarriages 63–65
*Remote Control Wars: The Battle for the
  Hearts and Minds of Our Youth* (Taillon)
  129
Resources for Living 84
responsibilities
  family, the traditional 95–96
  pets in the family and 134–137
Ricciuti, Henry 146
Rice, F. Philip
  *Intimate Relationships, Marriages, and
    Families* 125
Rice University 106, 168
Richardson, J. L. 33
Rideout, Vicky
  *Zero to Six: Electronic Media in the Lives
    of Infants, Toddlers, and Preschoolers*
    131
risk, self-test 5–8
"rites of passage" 106
Rodgers, Kathleen 70
Rogers, Stacy J.
  "Changes in Wives' Income: Effects on
    Marital Happiness" 94
  "Dollars, Dependency, and Divorce: Four
    Perspectives on the Role of Wives'
    Income" 93
role models and families 131
Rose, Hilary 70
Royal College of Psychiatrists 39
Runzheimer International 125–126
Rusbult, Caryl 75
Rush-Presbyterian-St. Luke's Medical Center
  56

S
same-sex couples. *See also* gay parents
  marriage among 127–128
  statistics 4
SAMHSA. *See* Substance Abuse and Mental
  Health Services Administration (SAMHSA)
Sandefur, Gary
  *Growing Up with a Single Parent: What
    Hurts, What Helps* 145–146
Schumacher, Ruth B. 35
Schwartz, Elizabeth 85
Schweingruber, Heidi 168
self-test, risk 5–8
sexually transmitted diseases (STDs)
  177–178
Sibling Interaction and Behavior Study
  (SIBS) 20–21

siblings
  adoption and 21
  quarrels among 24–27
Silverman, Arnold R.
  "Outcomes of Transracial Adoption" 18
Simon, Rita 17
Single and Custodial Fathers Network, Inc.
  192
single-breadwinner families 92–94
single-parent families **142–154**. *See also*
  day care; death in the family; divorce and
  families; family, the new; family, the
  traditional; marriage and family, changes
  in; teenage parents
  educational attainment, work life
    earnings and *152*
  fact vs. fiction 143
  family support 151–153
  financial issues 142–145
  government assistance 149–151
  history of unmarried mothers 91
  percentages of unmarried mothers 4
  psychological impact 145–148
  questions and answers 151
  readings 154
  societal views 148–149
  stigma, overcoming 153
  teens speak 147–148
Smeeding, Timothy 31
Social Security benefits of marriage 109
Social Work 39, 155
Sociology 148
Sommer, Kristen S. 173
Southern California, University of in Los
  Angeles 102
spanking 99–100
special needs children, adoption 15
Stack, Steven 148
Stanford University School of Medicine
  40
"State Efforts for Enforce Safety and Health
  Requirements" 35
State of America's Children, The 31, 37
stepparents **154–162**. *See also* adoption;
  arguments and the family; divorce and
  families; families, blended; families,
  divided; family, the new; marriage and
  family, changes in
  adoption of stepchild 159–160
  discipline 157–158
  fact vs. fiction 155
  other parent, dealing with 160–161
  questions and answers 66
  readings 162
  respect, gaining 154–157
Stevens, Ann Huff 44
Stevens, Daphne 96

Still a Man's Labor Market: The Long-Term
  Earnings Gap 95
Strasburger, Victor C.
  Children, Adolescents and Media 131
Stuber, Margaret 38
substance abuse 179–180
Substance Abuse and Mental Health Services
  Administration (SAMHSA) 132
suicide 178
Sullivan, Richard 22
Sundlof, Stephen 133–134
Syracuse University 31

T

Taillon, Greg
  Remote Control Wars: The Battle for the
  Hearts and Minds of Our Youth 129
tax benefits of marriage 109
Teaching Your Children about God (Wolpe)
  140
Teachman, Jay D. 2, 89, 123
Teen Advice Online 192
teenage parents **162–175**. *See also*
  adoption; arguments and the family; day
  care; family, the new; single-parent
  families; teens in trouble
  birth weight 172
  challenges for 166–168
  children of, impact on 171–175
  fact vs. fiction 169–170
  percentage in U.S. and other developed
    countries **163**
  questions and answers 168–169
  readings 174
  socioeconomic class 172
  statistics, U.S. 162–166, 174
  staying in school 170–171
  teens speak 166–167
Teenage Parents and Their Offspring 172–173
TeenGrowth.com 71, 192
teens in trouble **175–180**
  emotional health 178–179
  fact vs. fiction 180
  physical health 176–177
  questions and answers 177–178
  readings 180
  substance abuse 179–180
  violence within family 177–178
teens speak
  arguments and the family 24–25
  divorce and families 47–48
  elderly family members 60–61
  extended families 83–84
  families, blended 66–67
  families, racially mixed 80
  family, the new 83–84
  family, the traditional 89–90

family traditions 102–103
gay parents 118
siblings, quarrels among 24–25
single-parent families 147–148
teenage parents 166–167
violence and the family 183–184
Temple University 158
Temporary Aid to Needy Families (TANF)
  149–150
Texas, University of 26
TFC. *See* Compassionate Friends, The (TFC)
transracial adoption 16–18, 23
TV-Turnoff Network 132
Tzeng, Jessie
  "Labor Market and Socioeconomic Effects
  on Marital Stability" 63–65

U

"Under-ascertainment of Child Maltreatment
  Fatalities" (Crume) 184–185
unmarried mothers. *See* single-parent
  families
U.S. Census Bureau
  adoption 15, 16
  cohabitation 88
  day care 30, 37
  divorce 44, 126–127
  dual-career family 125
  elderly family members 51, 58
  extended families 83
  family structure 2–3
  gay parents 115, 118
  gay parents, adoption 85
  household division of labor 94
  racially mixed families 79
  remarriage 63, 64
  single-parent families 142–144, 152
  teenage marriage 169
  traditional families 94
U.S. Department of Agriculture (USDA) 150
U.S. Department of Health and Human
  Services
  day care 31–32
  media 132
U.S. Department of Housing and Urban
  Development (HUD) 150, 192–193
Utah State University 96

V

Vermont, same-sex couples 128
Vietnam War 104
violence and the family 177–178, **181–186**.
  See also arguments and the family; death
  in the family; families, divided; teens in
  trouble
  fact vs. fiction 181–182
  measurement of 182–186

violence and the family *(continued)*
  physical violence 181–182
  questions and answers 185
  readings 186
  sexual violence 181–182
  statistics 185
  teens speak 183–184
Virginia, University of 116

W
Wallerstein, Judith 45–46, 116
Wardle, Francis 80–81
Ward, Susan M.
  Why Consistency Is Important 101
Washington College of Law 17
Washington State University 70
Wayne State University 148
Way We Never Were: American Families and the Nostalgia Trap, The (Coontz) 90
Western Washington University 89, 123

"When Children Have Two Fathers: Effects of Relationships with Stepfathers and Noncustodial Fathers on Adolescent Outcomes" 160–161
White, Lynne 161
Why Consistency Is Important (Ward) 101
wills 108
Wolpe, David J.
  Teaching Your Children About God 140
workers' compensation 110
working couples, marriage among 125–126

Y
Yale University 174

Z
Zero to Six: Electronic Media in the Lives of Infants, Toddlers, and Preschoolers (Rideout) 131